KARL GEARY

Juno Loves Legs

Harvill *Secker*

LONDON

3 5 7 9 10 8 6 4

Harvill Secker, an imprint of Vintage, is part of the Penguin Random House group
of companies whose addresses can be found at global.penguinrandomhouse.com

Penguin
Random House
UK

Copyright © Karl Geary 2023

Karl Geary has asserted his right to be identified as the author of this
Work in accordance with the Copyright, Designs and Patents Act 1988

First published by Harvill Secker in 2023

A CIP catalogue record for this book is available from the British Library

penguin.co.uk/vintage

HARDBACK ISBN 9781787303102
TRADE PAPERBACK ISBN 9781787303119

Typeset in 11.5/16 pt Bembo Std by Jouve (UK), Milton Keynes
Printed and bound in Great Britain by Clays Ltd, Elcograf S.p.A.

The authorised representative in the EEA is Penguin Random House Ireland,
Morrison Chambers, 32 Nassau Street, Dublin D02 YH68

Penguin Random House is committed to a sustainable future
for our business, our readers and our planet. This book is made
from Forest Stewardship Council® certified paper.

MIX
Paper from
responsible sources
FSC
www.fsc.org   FSC® C018179

In memory of Angie

ONE

'If the young are not initiated into the village, they will burn it down just to feel its warmth.'

African proverb

1

'Be still,' says Mam and with one hand she folded a piece of cream satin material along the nape of Miss Anderson's neck. With her other hand she pulled the fabric tighter across her waist and, taking a pin from the collection she held in her mouth, pinned it.

Mam's hands were spotless clean but her nails were stained and it made them look dirty even though she scrubbed them with a nail brush and soap and even though we only had cold water, they were clean. Her hand crossed down the arch of Miss Anderson's back. Under the light bulb, the material shimmered. I wanted to touch it. My hands were dirty.

She stood back and her eyes watched around Miss Anderson's figure for that sharp edge where the wedding dress met the world. She told her again, 'Be still,' so the woman stood with her arms draped at her side, unnatural as a moulded figure stuck on a wedding cake. Mam picked up the trail of the dress: she knew the weight of fabric. She dropped it, picked it up, dropped it again.

'Put that kettle on, Juno. Will you have a biscuit, Miss Anderson? Mmm, you'd better not.'

I ran to the kitchen. It was full of things Mam and me, up

before first light, had cleared away so that there would be a space for Miss Anderson to stand. Our tiny two-up two-down house was stuffed to the last crevice. Mam held on to everything, except horoscopes she read in the *Herald*. If she liked one, it was cut out carefully, placed like a keepsake in a biscuit box. 'Rubbish,' she said if she didn't like it, and they got themselves torn out, crumpled, thrown on the fire.

I didn't want to miss anything, so I ran back as the kettle boiled. We didn't get many wedding dresses: mostly it was hems and buttons, skirts let out after Christmas. The tea was made and I brought it through on a tray. Mam, holding the chalk then, on her knees making long vertical lines in an upward stroke. I put the tea down, close to Miss Anderson, but not too close or I'd be murdered. She didn't drink. We always made it and they never drank. They didn't like to touch off anything in our house, you could just tell – as soon as they got inside they swept a look from floor to ceiling and their bodies stiffened. I liked to put my finger in the cup after, when the tea went cold and there was a layer of skin that, once punctured, grabbed hold of my pinkie. Sometimes I thought to spit in it before it was served, but there was no point.

Mam called me over to hold one end of the sheet around Miss Anderson while she undressed. She was old to be married, easily thirty and flushed with the excitement. Mam unzipped her at the back, told her again and again how beautiful she looked. She thought it would help her to get paid. It wouldn't.

'Do you think so, Peggy?' says Miss Anderson.

'Just the most beautiful bride.'

I could see through the white sheet, a bleached Miss Anderson on the other side, a rotten creature hatching from its satin shell. She pushed the dress past her big boobs, as far as her hips, and let out an audible sigh.

6

'Now,' says Miss Anderson. The dress sat coiled on the floor. Stepping out, she says it again, 'Now. I suppose the question is, how long do you think it will take?'

'Well, let me see,' says Mam. She was nervous. 'This is Wednesday. By the time I –'

'My sisters are coming this weekend, they'll be dying to see it, maybe Friday? Yes, Friday, I could come by in the afternoon on the way past.' Mam sucked in and chewed on her lower lip.

'Do you think that would be alright? You'd be doing me a great favour, Peggy.'

Mam carefully picked the dress off the floor, raised it above her head, shook it once. 'Give me over that hanger, Juno . . . Yes, that's fine, Miss Anderson. Friday, around teatime.'

'The afternoon would be better, around three.'

'Three? Right, right, three. Right so.'

When Miss Anderson left, Mam flung the dress, hanger and all, across the room. It seemed to float like a great balloon before breaking across the hard upright of a chair. Mam collapsed down onto the settee. She dipped her head and put her hand across her face. She stayed like that for a long time. Unmoving.

'Do you want a cup of tea, Ma? Ma? Do you want one, Ma?' She stood so quickly it was as if she'd never sat, then she bent to pick the dress up from where it landed and restrung the hanger.

'Get those cups cleared up, and fold that sheet. Put it back in its box . . . get ready for school.'

But I didn't do any of that, I just gawked. She screamed at me then. 'Juno, I'm not going to tell you again. Now.' She stepped quickly around the room, pulling and shoving at everything. 'I'm fed up, the state of this place, mortified, people coming and going, looking at us. I've had it. Friday? I'll have to go up to Mangers for thread. I haven't the few coppers for it, don't mind the bus fare. Juno, move. I'm not going to tell you again.'

I took the rattling cups on the metal tray into the kitchen and washed them. 'Get out to school when you're done, and quick about it. I'm not having them onto me again. And you can tell that layabout I have work to do. I don't want him under my feet all day.'

Dad was upstairs. He was hiding. Mam shooed him away when she had someone coming. Their bedroom door was open and he was sitting in his undershirt on the edge of the unmade bed, lines deep as a dry riverbed criss-crossed the back of his neck. A ciggy smouldered in his hand. Legs crossed, bare feet, he stared idly into the room. I came down the stairs without my bag. Mam lamped me across the ear and sent me back up. I went past him again, but that time I didn't look. Mam shouted up at him; he shouted down at her. They were two mouths and I was their ear.

2

It was already spring, but cold enough that once outside my breath folded in small clouds. The litter of cars in our front garden was dappled with rain. They shone on their breeze-block pedestals, idle, grass grown up in rutted clumps. Missus G was out on her side of the wall, walking her bins. She looked at the cars, and at me, then went back inside unsmiling. Cow.

Sometimes Da was paid for fixing a car before the car was fixed – the promises he made, one hand holding the money in his pocket, the other fingers crossed. That was what you got if you paid Da before a car was fixed. 'Those gifted hands.' I've heard people say it, even Missus G. 'Gifted,' that's what she said. I overheard her and an unwanted feeling for him flared like a lit match, and puff, extinguished. I gave a car a good boot as I passed, hollow as Missus G's lonely steel bin – bang bang bang.

A car moved off somewhere in the estate, its engine revving, but I couldn't see it. It was silent then. I walked to the roundabout where the massive chestnut tree had grown before they laid down the new road. The council had tarmacked around it for reasons nobody understood. It died slowly, choked I suppose. The church road veered downhill and the top of the spire could be seen in the near distance. I looked into all the windows as I passed, just to be nosy, and my books and jotters bounced on my back with every step and the leather strap of my school bag with its thick buckle dug in through my uniform and left a mark.

I cut through the wooded area at the back of the church. In spring, ferns unfurled at night, dropping dew in the morning, and the pathway was choked ever tighter by brambles and nettles. I went past the huge rocks covered with graffiti. Green and brown bottles, broken and unbroken, gathered with cigarette butts, tangled in the undergrowth.

I'd been warned not to go that way. Years earlier, some auld lad had grabbed our Derry off the path and pulled her into the bushes. She was bleeding after and she never said, but I saw how the tea towels Mam brought her came back stained. Mam never told me not to talk about it with anyone, I just knew, and for the longest time at home the fighting stopped and the house was quiet as a library, the air thicker. Mam prayed; her big Bible brimming with mass cards, laminated prayers and other missives, stayed glued to her hand. She says, 'We take nothing from this world, and the sooner we know it, the better.' I wondered if that was true, and if it was, who had told her? It was true that people were always trying to take things away from you, especially if you only had a little. Derry's narrow bed lay next to my mine, and I saw how her eyes glistened open at night, how sleep was a gateway that frightened her.

She was not dead, our Derry. She married, had kids. Two, maybe three. She didn't visit.

3

Sister stood close behind Seán McGuire. Her navy material falling in long shapeless folds, only her face and hands exposed like some prisoner, their pale fingers past the bars of a dark cell. Sister held a wooden ruler like a warning, knocking it against her open hand.

Sister says:

'You are horrible and sinful children.'

We say:

'Yes, Sister.'

Sister says:

'You will be punished and sorry some day. Laugh if you want now.'

Sister says:

'I'll have the last laugh.'

Sister's face was so beautiful a face. I was careful not to look for too long, but when she was angry at us she held her mouth open and showed us her teeth, and her chin doubled against the tight wrapping of her veil. I wanted to take the ruler from her hand and sit her down and push the ruler underneath the fabric, give both sides of her face a good scratch all the way to her covered ears. She must have been driven demented with that close fabric itching and her skin sweating under there all day, and even though her body wasn't her body any more, she must have felt that.

Sister passed my desk and I could see the tips of her fingers were dusted white with chalk. They had left a white line where her fingertips rubbed the fabric around her thighs. A bright upturned smile. Sister, your thighs are smiling.

She called Seán McGuire to the front of the class and told him to stand and face us. He was a blond boy, rail-thin and tall for his age. His name was spoken and he was caught in a state of disbelief, blinking into the classroom. He stood out of his chair and I thought about those animals off the telly, still wet from their mother's tummy, unsure of their own narrow hind legs, unsure they won't buckle at that first step. He walked slowly, one hand at his mouth, biting at the knuckle of his wet thumb.

'Seán here decided not to do his homework. Isn't that right, Seán? You're too good for all that, too good for us.' Seán's face reddened and his eyes looked over the class without seeing at all. Of all the children Sister hated, it was Seán she hated most.

'Hasn't Seán a pretty face?' Sister says. 'The face of a lovely girl, hasn't he?' And she gave a tiny laugh, and the cheer in her voice encouraged the class to laugh, only a small laugh at first, then, feeling it safe, more.

'A little angel face. Will we put Seán on the top of the tree come Christmas?'

The colour deepened in Seán's face

'I tell you what we're going to do with you now, Seán,' Sister says. 'I have the very thing for a pretty boy like you.' She reached into a drawer behind her desk and took up lengths of pink and yellow ribbon, raising them up for the class to see.

'What will it be, yellow or pink?' The children start to howl with the fun of it, their blushed faces and small eyes. They called out the names of the colours. The eejit who sat by me couldn't make his mind up and called both.

Sister remained neutral. She gently took hold of a strand of Seán's hair, parting it from the rest, and carefully tied a pink bow, stepping back then to see its effect. I watched her leave us, just for a flash, to a secret thought. Her own mam maybe, tying a ribbon in her hair? Years before she covered her hair forever, for Jesus.

She stepped around Seán, smiled at the class for effect, and carefully made a yellow bow, just behind his ear, her clean fingers pointed with great care.

Sister says:

'Now, children, isn't Seán a pretty girl?'

We say:

'Yes, Sister.'

She was satisfied then, cheerful. 'Stand up there now, Seán, and we'll have a look at you.' She pulled a chair into the aisle, tapping it once with her hand. 'Up you go, there's a good girl.' There had been a few quick tears before, but they were away then. Gone.

He stood on the chair and was told to turn for the boys and girls. He twirled without resistance. Round and round the garden.

'Does he look like a Seán, or is he more like . . . a Mary?' There was more laughter. Colin Murphy laughed so much that snot poured out his nose and he struggled to find the next breath.

Sister had the ruler again and instructed Seán to jump down off the chair. Seán, thinking she was finished, got down, relieved. His fingers went to his hair and he started to unknot the ribbons. She rapped him hard on the knuckles and without raising her voice she says, 'Did I tell you you could take those out? Did you hear me say "take them out", class?'

We say:

'No, Sister.'

She says:

'No, I did not say so. And where does my authority come from, class?'

We say:

'God, Sister.'

She says:

'That's right, class. Our Holy Father in Heaven.'

Seán rubbed at his hands that way old people do when they are useless against the cold. 'Hands out now, Seán.' I remembered that first sensation, the way she cradled our hands in the softness of her own. After, when he was crying again and his hands were rosy and stuck deep inside the pit of his arms, she pointed her ruler towards the dunce's corner.

His shoulders continued to shake long after Sister had seemingly forgotten about him and had turned back to speak to the class and even the stupid laughter from Colin Murphy had stopped.

4

The sleeves of Seán's jumper were caked and stiffened with snot. I spied him at break from across the yard, hands set deep in his pockets, alone, head down as if he had lost a precious item in the scrub he was kicking, a patient search. His blond locks blew loosely over his forehead. He was always alone. I noticed him. I saw how he tried to make himself invisible. I noticed everything and found that it was Seán I noticed most.

A group of boys kicked a ball back and forth between them: each one took hold of the ball, imitating presenters off the telly. When the ball was passed to Colin, he paused the game, held the ball to the wet ground under the weight of his foot, and looked at Seán. He made sure he had the attention of the others before kicking. He strained, kicking harder than any of the rest.

Seán must have felt something as the ball torpedoed towards him, the wet orb shedding water as it went. He turned into the line of the ball, helpless as it smashed into his face, loud enough that it caused heads to turn sharply towards the sound. A great cry erupted from the boys as Seán held a hand to his face, looking down at the ball and then across to the laughing children. He stood there unsure, still except for the ribbons set above his ear, pink and yellow like fresh dabs from a painter's brush, fluttering in the breeze. He hadn't taken them off.

Colin screamed something about the ribbons, but the wind robbed the punchline before it came to me and anyway I had swelled with that feeling by then and it was hard for me to hear. I was already halfway across the yard, aware only of the boys' laughter.

Colin's back was to me, his jeans hung low on his thick waist. I rooted him up the hole, as hard as I could and he let out a scream and turned, his hot face, mouth sticky wet with spit. He moved, as if to hit me, but then bottled, says I'm a cunt. Everyone was afraid of Colin. Colin was afraid of me. He knew how my dad was a drunk and how we were nothing and how I didn't care and couldn't be hurt. I stepped closer, put my face close to his. His warm breath spilt out like sour milk.

'What are you going to do?' I say. 'What?'

He stepped back to the safety of the other boys, quiet then, rubbing at his bollox and trying to rearrange his underwear through his jeans. I turned to go, then I saw that Seán was beside me, his cheek blistering red. Just standing there looking, more nerve than I'd expected.

'What you looking at?' I say, about to pass, but we were surrounded. The other children had formed a circle around us, shouting how we loved each other. I felt something pressed into my hand, a warm lively thing, and I saw how Seán had wrapped his fingers around mine, binding himself to me. I looked at his sharp face, his hooded eyes the texture of poppies. They aged him.

'What you doing?' I say, shaking free of his hand. 'Get off,' I say. 'This is why you get balls in the face. And take the fucking ribbons out, dopey cunt.'

That night I looked at myself in the mirror and admitted I didn't like the look of myself at all. I tried brushing my mangle of red hair and spread Mam's cold cream, thick as butter, across my face, not wanting anyone to see the effort, only its effect. In bed, I held my hands above my eyes in the dim chopped light and wished they were different hands. I wished for Sister's long, clean fingers; although I knew they were hands for hurting and cold to touch, they were capable of being delicate, I was sure. I'd seen how they moved the chalk across the blackboard and the lovely trail of letters she left behind. I imagined how Seán would have felt clutching those fingers, and it made my belly warm and hungry.

5

The next afternoon, instead of my homework, I was having a grand old time with Victor Hugo when Mam came in breathless and pulled to one side by her shopping bag. She'd taken a swatch of fabric and found thread to match exactly. Even though that thread would be forever folded in a French seam and hidden, it mattered to her that the colour was right.

'You're a marvel,' I say, and leapt off the settee to take the heavy bag out of her hand. She laughed. I helped her off with her overcoat. 'Sit down, give us that bag, will ya? Sit. Sit.' And she allowed herself to be bossed around. I lit a smoke and handed it to her. She didn't mind me having a cheeky puff when it suited and I was gasping. After she was seated, I gave her the good scissors and her *Evening Herald*, already opened to the horoscopes. She was away then, hungrily reading her sign, her old biscuit box open at her side and the fire blazing. I boiled a kettle and filled a basin of hot and cold water, rubbed her swollen feet a bit and gave them a soak. She let out a sigh.

'Aren't you the best girl.'

'I am.'

I put the fat on the heat and cut potatoes into chips. We ate on the settee and the plates warmed our laps.

She says:

Nothing.

I say:

Nothing.

Mam's radio was set to her favourite show. Her wide back formed a perfect curve as she loaded the first spool of thread onto the sewing machine. It was a Singer, written there in gold leaf across its limb. She'd always owned it. It was the finest thing in our house, the finest thing in the whole estate, and I'm sure everyone was mad with envy, that we, of all people, had one. She set the single task light close to the needle. Her eyes were on the blink and even with her reading glasses fixed low on her nose, she squinted.

I was on the settee, not asleep exactly, but in that halfway place that's neither here nor there. I could hear the machine's motor murmuring in gentle bursts over the radio, as she cautiously fed the material from where it flared, iridescent, in folds across her lap.

Mam's hair was white. It used to be black, coal black, but then as if by fright it turned, all of a sudden. She had leather skin, conditioned leather, soft to touch, and like him the lines of her face were deep as gorges. People said she once had a tinker's good looks. Our Derry had told me that. Mam smoked, setting a fag in her mouth, pulling at it thoughtlessly and removing it only to flick the long ash. As she talked, the cigarette bounced up and down, but the ash never fell without permission. I never saw her brush her teeth, or wash her face. I never saw her dress or be undressed. I knew she did these things, but I never saw. Sometimes, she let me brush her hair.

After ten, I woke to the sound of a dog barking out on the

street, then silenced by a man's roaring voice. My book lay emptied on my lap and the tea had gone cold. Mam was still at the sewing machine, but completely still, save the blue trail of smoke that rose and disappeared past the sharp edge of her task light.

I heard footsteps, more shouting. The door was thrown open and in he came, a lost member of a street carnival. In each hand, he raised a bottle of beer above his head. He began to dance into the room, a tuneless lullaby rattled from his grinning damp mouth. His eyes were nowhere to be seen.

'The hell have you been?' Mam says. He ignored her and continued to dance, his fisherman's cap tilted to one side, raising one bottle and then the next as he sauntered round and round Mam, singing.

'Look what I have, a la la la la. Come on and giz a dance.' His arms reached around her and she recoiled. He tried to pick her up and embrace her.

'Stop that now in front of the child.'

'C'mere to me.'

'Stop it now, do you hear me, that's enough.' She managed to pull an arm free and push him away.

He went to the radio, put one of the bottles down and drank from the other. He turned the volume up, only static, jarring.

'Turn that down, you'll have the neighbours over.'

He danced towards me then, ignored Mam. Pulled me off the couch to my feet and gathered me up. He was strong, then.

'What about you, Juno?' he says, then softer, 'Me auld flower, give your dad a dance.'

I could feel the cold beer bottle wet at my back. His bristle smeared my cheek, rough, pulled back and forth and smarted. He started to sing, took hold of my arm, spun me. Again, again, again. Dizzy.

Mam was shouting, I can't remember what, and I was ... smiling? My body was rigid and I felt numb, except my mouth had somehow folded to the shape of a smile. I was his rag doll. He put the bottle to my mouth and the glass hit my tooth.

'Go on,' he says, 'have some.'

I could taste blood. I could taste blood and his warm spit on the open bottle top and then the spill of beer on my chin. I'd never drink, me. That was my promise.

Mam turned off the radio; silence, then her quick footsteps on the lino. She tried to pull me free but I fell back and her hand slid across my face and her ring caught the skin under my eye and tore. I could feel the blood at my cheekbone without touching my finger to it and looking. No pain, just a warm blood trickle down my cheek.

'Juno, get up to bed.'

'Leave her now, she's fine. Aren't you, love?'

I was running.

Upstairs.

I closed my door behind me and paced a bit and then lay down on the swirling pattern of the carpeted floor and caught my breath. Cobwebs spun in corners hung down the wall closest to the window. Posters bent forward, stiff and yellowed; some had fallen and left behind dark squares. Derry's narrow bed was there alongside mine, stripped bare and dormant years.

Downstairs, she says:

'Stop, just stop.'

It was quiet then – surrender was always quiet – and in the morning she didn't look at me, but put a saucer on the table. Two ice cubes, melting.

'Put that on your cheek,' she says.

6

I sat in the schoolyard, under the metal eaves where the wind carried splashes of rain just past the concrete step. My bare knees touched and a scratchy rung of goose pimples darted down my calves.

My eye hurt. Black and blue it was, that's what they say anyway, black and blue. Somebody, I'm sure, who'd never gotten a puck said it. They hadn't thought it through. Forgot about the red and orange that come later, and the light brown after that and then the piss yellow of rotten daffodils. That's how bruises really are.

The girls from my year had taken to chasing each other across the uneven mounds of grass. Their piercing and delighted cries drew attention from even Sister, who looked on with a shy admiration. Rosemary was at the helm, her strong limbs moving effortlessly as she ran, and even when she was tagged she showed no sign of disappointment.

A summer or two ago, she was my friend. I think she was, really. She was smaller and nervous then and I'd taken it upon myself to see to her welfare whether she wanted me to or not. She was always clean, and even when we played in the dirt, nothing stuck.

I had been nicknamed Annie and Bosco my whole life because my hair looked like it had just exploded but she called me Juno and was amazed by it. She didn't see what the others saw. Once or twice, she even put her hand to my mangle of curls as if it were a flame, as if she could be warmed by it.

She promised one day, after she caught me looking, that she would lend me her crushed-velvet royal pinafore, just like that. I didn't want the pinafore to borrow, but that promise set, like dough on a high shelf. My friend. We'd walk home together and I'd carry her school bag. It was easy for me and a struggle for her, the size of her, hardly up to my shoulder. I was big for my age. Then I stopped growing – a bad seed, says Mam – and everyone passed me by.

In the late summer we swarmed around the chestnut tree, its wide trunk. We'd lob rocks up into the green awning, hoping for conkers in return, and run for cover as the rocks came, meteoric, back down. I was the one who told Rosemary to throw the rock. It had been in her hand an age and she was just stood off to the side, holding it and looking lost.

'You'll be grand,' I say, 'just fuck it in the air.' And so she did, with all her might, right into Maeve Lambert's mouth. Every game stopped at that. It was silent enough to hear the sweep of wind turning the leaves above, and we all looked at Maeve whose face had yet to cotton on to what had happened, but already blood was staining the front of her dress and her mouth swung soundlessly open. My Rosy was in shock, I could just tell, all breathless, a tear and all hanging off her eyelid. She was so afraid of what she had done. I squeezed her shoulder and rattled her head a bit.

'Who threw that rock?' someone was shouting. 'Who?'

And then Maeve started to howl. The screams of her, like

she was murdered, but she couldn't move. She just looked down, screaming, to her bloodied white chips at her feet.

'Me,' I say, 'I threw it, alright? It was a bleedin' accident.'

Nobody says anything to that. They just looked at me. That look. I took hold of Rosy, pulling her away from the tree. I took her to my house first but she got scared there and went home crying.

We weren't allowed out after that and the conkers fell on their own and rubber tyres crushed them into the road before anyone could play with them.

Later, when I knocked on her door to see if she wanted to play, no one answered. I knocked again, and then I knocked again harder. I heard voices on the other side of the door.

Rosy says, 'I don't want to play with her.'

Her ma says, 'You'd better go and tell her then. You tell her your mam said so.'

Rosy came to the door. She says:

'I can't play today.'

She was looking down, her feet shimmied her weight heel to toe, heel to toe, as in the song. She put one finger into her ear, rubbing it like she was just out of the bath.

'C'mere,' I say, and when she looked at me she was frightened. She knew. I was sure she knew, but she came anyway. It took me years to understand the why of that. I lured her round the side of her house and I saw she was crying.

'Me ma won't let me play with you. I'm sorry, Juno. I want to.'

So I hit her. Just like that. I held her hair in one hand, steadied her skull, and with my other hand I boxed her face. Rosy wasn't used to being boxed; you can always tell. That panic, like they're drowning. I held her down, pushed her face into the

24

ground and picked up a fist of muck from her ma's flower bed, buried it past her milk teeth, till she bit me.

See? I thought.

You're not special, I thought.

You bite just the same.

There's a small scar on my hand to prove it.

When I got home, Mam saw the state of me. 'You fighting again?' she shouted up the stairs. She followed me up and lamped me one anyway. She felt bad after and tried to be nice. I got a 99 out of her when the Whippy van came that evening and ate it outside Rosemary's house, hoping her and her ma could see.

I think that was the end. They stayed away from me, the other children. There was no one then.

When Seán walked, his movements were stiff and his fair head tilted forward in what looked like the beginning of a fall and I imagined the struggle his long skinny legs had to keep him upright. He stood in front of me, not smiling. He looked at me once and then away off over the schoolyard.

'Your hands are dirty,' he says, clear blue eyes, no meanness.

'Wha?' I smiled without meaning to and clamped my hands under my knees.

'Yeah,' he says, 'I only noticed. It's nice.'

And then he sat down next to me, close enough that his leg skimmed past my bare leg and it thickened with sensation.

'Look at mine, they're always clean.'

He laughed at himself, held his fingers straight out and showed me the flat surface he'd made, like thin strands of wattling bound from willow.

'Congratulations, clean boy. Top of the class.'

They were clean alright, scrubbed raw. His trousers were

neatly hemmed, the grey fabric folded back and hand-stitched, allowing for a few inches more growth where they could be easily let down and resewn. Peeking through, between his black polished brogues and hemline, were brightly bleached white socks. He was cared for, this boy. Someone made an effort on his behalf.

'That was some kick you gave Colin. I heard they needed a ladder to get his balls outta the tree.'

He lit at that, showed his uneven teeth, his pearly duds, white against his serious face.

'Thanks for standing up for me and all,' he says then, after a bit. He was looking at me, looking inside, I thought, and I didn't like that.

There was a small crack in the black gutter overhead and I could hear the water running off the roof and collecting in the upturned arch before being exposed in big droplets, tap tap tap, falling steady with heavy splashes on the ground.

'Didn't do it for you.'

'Why did you?'

'Why anything? Wanted an excuse to kick him, fat prick. That's the why.'

'I heard the shouting from your house last night,' Seán says. It startled me, made my heart drum and I turned from him.

'Did you now?'

Across the yard, the girls piled on top each other, cries spilling out as their loose bodies fell and they called back and forth.

'Yeah . . .' he says, 'is that why you've the black eye?'

'What, were you spying?'

'No, just walking by.'

'I'm sure you were. I'm sure you didn't stop and have a good gawk.'

It was ugly, my voice – if my voice had a face I'd smash it.

'Not like that, I just wondered,' he says, 'if you . . .'

'What? If I what?'

'Nothing,' he says.

'Yeah, nothing is right. What do you know? Did I even say you could sit down?'

'Sorry,' he says.

'Tell you what, I'll come by yours later, see if your ma's still a loon? See if she's still on the steps scrubbing, waiting for your da. Cos by the way, that cunt's never coming home. Now go on and fuck off.'

'I'm sorry,' he says again, and I thought he meant it.

He stood up slowly, and a drip of water fell unnoticed from the gutter, knocked against his shoulder and was quickly absorbed by the wool fabric of his overcoat. His eyes skimmed over me without stopping, like a pebble expertly thrown across a glass lake. He looked over the yard towards the metal fence, to the old right of way, a disused grassy lane that cows had appeared in one afternoon, having escaped the farmer's enclosure. It caused a stir among the children, who clamoured to climb the fence and see. The animals' eyes shone, huge polished mahogany discs, fretting between their new-found pastures and fear of the screaming children.

The girls had stopped their chasing game and sat contentedly, broken off like small islands, sitting on their coats, lunches on their laps, cheese sandwiches and crisps, or egg or ham, wrapped in tinfoil and greaseproof paper. It looked like it might rain again but not yet, not until the girls had finished and were herded back into the classrooms, then the rain would run in long streaks down the glass and shining litter left behind would blow freely about the yard like jewels.

7

Father tapped his knuckles lightly at the threshold before he came into the classroom, smiling. The children tightened and sat up. He silently placed his hands on the heads of some of the children seated in the front row. He was a big man and his black garb had crisp lines pressed along his legs and up the sleeves of his black shirt. He pulled a chair to the front of the class and, before he sat, tugged gently at the legs of his trousers.

He says:

'What are the seven sacraments, children?'

We say:

'The seven sacraments are baptism, confession, Eucharist, confirmation, matrimony, ordination and the anointing of the ill.'

'Now I hope I heard everybody's voice there, did I?'

'Yes, Father.'

'It is a terrible sin to lie to your priest . . .'

He says this in a mild way, in a voice that was sing-song and could easily be moved into a ballad. 'A mortal sin,' he says. 'And as you know well, even the best of deeds cannot wash away a mortal sin. Isn't that right? Now, you, Philip, isn't it? Stand up so I can get a look at you, Philip.'

He was speaking to a clever boy seated in the front row who shot out of his seat and stood to attention. He looked at the floor between himself and Father. We had not been instructed not to look directly at Father, but we knew.

'Philip Marr, Father.'

'Well, Philip Marr, here is a question you may be asked by the bishop, and all of you would do well to know the answer. I'd like you to tell me now, have we, the children of Adam, suffered because of his sin?'

Philip's hands gripped tightly at the sides of his desk. His mouth was silently moving as he raced through the answer before speaking aloud. When he was sure he had it, he set off with a single speeding breath.

'Because of Adam's sin we are born without sanctifying grace our intellect is darkened our will is weakened our passions are inclined to evil and we are subject to suffering and death.' Unburdened, he took a gulp of air and looked pale and relieved.

'Good, good,' says Father. 'Sit down, Philip, there's a good lad. You will all have picked your confirmation name by now, I hope. Let me see a show of hands. Hands up, please.'

Hands shot up around the class. I was watching Sister, off to the side, having relinquished her classroom to Father, her hands joined loosely behind her back and some other part of her missing, hard-pruned to the root as she looked on with great admiration and attention. She had cast us off to Father's charge completely. I hated Sister just then.

Children said the names they had chosen, the names of apostles and saints. Father approved, until someone said a foreign name. He didn't like that. He considered, smiled.

'Yes, yes. We must remember, the name we choose is very important to God. It is the name we will be known to Him by.

It is a name that must please the bishop. After all, we're not naming our pets, now are we?'

He paused, raised his eyebrows in an exaggerated way, letting us know it was OK to laugh.

The children laughed.

I laughed.

Father was pleased; he took a moment to look down at his patent leather shoes and rotated his foot once. His feet looked dainty, almost feminine, bound in this way.

'Who have we not heard from? Yes, you, have you a name chosen?' He had directed his attention towards me. Faces turned.

Mary, Bridget, Bernadette, I knew them all. In my head just then there was nothing. I was betrayed and there was nothing.

'Dear God,' says Father. 'It's not a difficult question. A simple name, please?'

His patience was stretched; I could not speak.

'You see, this is a concern, for all of us – if this child cannot remember her chosen name here in class, what's going to happen in front of her bishop, in front of her sponsors, her parents and the score of people who will have come to witness her confirmation?'

He walked to my table and I felt his hot fingers grip my chin and I was directed up to his smooth face, his cloudy green eyes, and I saw routed clumps of unruly hair that had been passed over by a blade.

'Stand up,' he says. 'Go to the front of the class.'

I went, feeling suddenly dizzy, and the ground was soft and cushioned, treacherous under my feet.

'Turn and face the boys and girls.'

I saw how Sister watched him, afraid – Sister was afraid. I

found Seán, sitting near the back. He was the only one that would hold my gaze.

'Name one saint, girl,' Father's voice boomed suddenly, as if taking charge at the pulpit and commanding obedience from the dim congregation. My thoughts ground as a dull plough over frozen soil.

'Where is your catechism, girl?'

He slammed his fists on a table and swung the weight of his body round, striking at my empty chair. It took off. I couldn't raise a hand to protect myself and stood helplessly, unblinking. It missed by a good margin and crashed where I couldn't see. He was breathless then. He fixed his uneven shirt, carefully, tucked it back behind his shining belt, pulling his belly in, and ran a hand loosely across it.

'Look,' says a boy near the front. He raised a finger to point. I could feel how it was wet between my legs, how it was warm and cold at the same time and even my socks were soaked. I didn't cry.

'I'm so sorry, Father.'

Sister came to my side. 'I'll take her away, have her cleaned.'

'No, Sister, that's alright.'

Father continued to watch in silence.

'Judas.'

A small voice from the back. Seán, Seán had said it, unsteady. 'Judas,' he says again, stronger, committed.

Father turned quickly. 'Who said that?'

'Me, Father. I think that's the name I'm going to choose.'

And tight as a bootstrap, Father fastened on Seán.

'Stand up.'

Seán stood, not quick enough for Father who was on him, pushing at his back. Seán stumbled and was pushed again towards the front of the class. This time he fell over completely, knocking into a table he had tried to grip for balance, failed, and landed squarely on his back.

'Stand up, stand, I said.'

Seán got to his feet, was roughly moved to my side.

'Sister, your cane, please,' says Father, setting off a flurry of activity behind me. A drawer opened and closed, then another. Poor Sister was in a panic. I almost turned to remind her it was by her Bible under a pile of papers on her desk, that she had placed it there after the break. The ruler was located and handed to Father. He swiped the ruler past my ear several times, wisps of soft air like breath, its swoosh sound. Disappointed, he set the ruler down gently on Sister's table, turned and spoke to the class.

'Not a sound until I return.'

He left the room, not a sound, save the echo of his sharp steps along the dark corridor, a squeak then as his foot turned on the polished lino. He'd pass a crucifix strapped to the wall, life-sized, bigger than life. Bronze, oxidised moss green in the crannies and folds, feet shined brightly by the touch of small hands.

I could feel heat from Seán's shoulder – he had edged towards me. I could feel that. I could feel how he trembled. I reached and took his hand, squeezed it, for just a second. He squeezed too and I let it go. I was not trembling then.

In his spare time, Father had fashioned a baton from a length of curtain rail, just longer than an imperial ruler. He had wrapped it in yellow electric tape. He had named it.

Father returned. He told Seán to step forward first. He called Sister, asked for her assistance, asked that she hold the underside of Seán's hand firmly in position, as if he were about to perform a magic trick. He reminded Seán that if he moved, the baton would strike Sister. That that would be added to his collection of misdeeds. Father held the baton over his head and strained to bring it down with force. When it connected to the skin of Seán's hand, the sound was terrible. Seán let out a cry and immediately stifled it.

'Mary,' I shout. 'Mary, Father, Mary.'

'I'll come to you.'

He raised the baton again.

'Magdalene – I'm choosing Mary the whore Magdalene.'

My face was set aflame, it burned. I fell back, leaving behind wet footprints as I stumbled. Seán, released from Sister's grip, stood in front of Father.

'Leave her alone,' he says crying, his face darkening red.

We were beaten. A sour-smelling odour emerged from Father before he was done. And even Sister's hands were crimson. After, I was taken to the toilet by Sister. She waited outside the toilet door and told me to go in and clean myself. I lifted my legs in turn, rinsing them under the tap. I stuffed tissue down my pants and it created a bulge there like a man. I rinsed and wrung out my socks and put them back on, damp.

When I came back out, Sister wouldn't look at me.

8

Just beyond the scrub, near the high brambles, we laughed, Legs and I; out into the open it spilt – some wariness had been released and we were natural together. My knickers still wet and I didn't care. I'd given him that name for the first time, Legs. I'd simply cried, 'Go wan, Legs eleven,' when he chased me. And it just stuck, as easy as that, easy as the stickybacks he threw clung to my wool. It hung, fixing us. And we ran about, trying different leaves to quell the welts on our hands. Dandelion didn't work, neither its milk nor its bright yellow top. Legs held a nettle leaf in his fist without being stung and we decided dock leaves were best, but really there was no change in sensation to suggest it.

I wanted to spit in Father's face. A day would come when I'd meet him. I would introduce myself, remind him of me; he'd be old then, held by a bentwood cane. He'd smile and laugh and remember me fondly, reach and touch my arm. 'Oh you were terrible wilful, I remember. I can place you now – so many children, it's often difficult, but you, yes, so wilful, I remember well.'

His few strands of grey hair would blow helplessly.

'Good, good to see you now, I like to see the old faces.'

And I'd have a great big wallop of spit ready.

'You got there, eh? You turned out grand.'

He'd say those words.

I'd baulk, begin to stumble. I'd think, he's just an old man: I would disbelieve. It was me, I was a lot, I was too much.

'Yes, yes, Father, we got there.'

He'd say:

'Different times.'

I'd say:

'Yes, different.'

He'd walk on and I'd swallow my ball of spit, aware of his dwindled congregation, how few came and paid their dues: a wedding party, a funeral, barely enough to stem the flow of water, leaking in great drops into metal buckets spread throughout the aisles. His voice from the pulpit reduced, that ludicrous garb, threadbare. I saw, I had to spit, before my spit was gone.

We would enact revenge, Legs and I.

Legs suggested thumbtacks on Sister's chair. I thought about that, about Sister struck dumb while Father bossed her around. Sister had held a raffle, some weeks back. It happened on occasion, if there were some old books or pens or paints she needed gone. It was an old jigsaw, fifty pieces and eleven of them missing. It made up a picture of Notre-Dame, shot through with holes. She stood at the top of the classroom and picked a number between one and ten and the first child to guess would win. Every hand was raised; she chose my hand third – she actually chose it.

'Yes, Juno,' she says.

'Number eight, Sister.'

She looked at me more carefully than I'd ever seen Sister look.

'Yes, number eight is correct, Juno. Well done.'

And the old box rattled when she held it up for me to collect. Everyone looked at me with envy when I went up to collect it, envy, and all that day I carried it in both hands and it never left my side. Sister was good, I was sure.

'No, not her. We'll leave her alone,' I say to Legs.

He thought for a second.

'Agreed,' he says.

Later, walking past an abandoned building site, I saw an unopened bag of Portland cement through the chain-link fence. I slipped through, under the wire. I collected empty crisp bags and filled them with cement that I'd ground back to dust.

At the end of the next school day, we emptied the cement into the toilets. In the morning when we returned, the cement had hardened, clogging every artery of the school's plumbing. I flushed, water swirled and breeched the bowl, running over the edge in streaks, narrowly avoiding my shoes. I ran. Outside, I saw Legs exit the boys.

I winked.

He winked.

The rank odour permeated, had nowhere to go.

'Who did it?' says Sister, red-faced, after she had Legs and me in front of the class. 'Either we have one liar or we have two, now which is it?'

We say:

'It was me, Sister.'

We stood across from each other and watched, beaten in turn. But we couldn't be hurt, not when the other was there. I imagined it was Legs doing the hitting and it wasn't so bad, not when it was someone who cared, even a little.

9

When I came home after school the house was quiet. There was one light on in the sitting room that dimly peered into the kitchen and the radio was off. Mam stood in shadows by the cooker. I didn't think she had heard me, so she just stood, privately pooled in darkness, stroking at the skin of her temple and forehead. A pot boiled on the stove top, and steam billowed and dissolved before reaching her face. I stepped closer. Her neck was covered in that veil of scarlet blotches, that way it did when she was angry, when she had been shouting. There were plates broken on the floor by her feet.

I placed it then, that smell of boiled cabbage; soon the whole house would reek. She looked up and saw me, but only a little. As she stepped in her stockinged feet, her blood dabbed the lino floor.

'Will you be careful where you're stepping, Mam? Look it, Jesus.'

'Don't use that language in this house, Juno,' she says.

She put the lid on the pot and stepped more carefully around the broken ceramic.

'Could yis not have broken something else? I liked that plate.'

'Don't be smart, I'm not in the mood.'

I found the brush and tore a strip of cardboard from a cereal box. I began to sweep. The wedding dress was gone, the mannequin bust that held it, stripped bare.

'The dress? Did your woman pick it up?'

Mam didn't answer. She had moved over to the settee then and with a lit cigarette hanging from her mouth she watched me wordlessly, blinked once, and looked away. The grating sound of shards pushed across the floor, scraping off each other.

'Did she pick it up, Mam? Mam? Can you answer me?'

'She was by,' says Mam, evenly. 'She picked it up. That's enough now. I don't want to hear another word about that rotten article.'

'Did she not like it, Mam? Was she not happy with it? Mam? Mam? Mam?'

'Yes, Juno. Yes, she was happy. She was like a ballerina, mooning about the place. Enough now, Please. I don't –'

'What then? What?'

'I said that's enough.'

'She paid you, right?'

'Yes.'

'But did she?'

'I said yes ... She gave me a deposit.'

'Much?'

'Enough for now.'

'How much?'

'Five.'

'Five? Five pound? Ahh, Mam, all your work?'

'Juno, I swear to God, I'll give you such a wallop if you don't stop after me. That's it now, enough.'

I stood breathless in front of her, aware of the boiling pot, its fluttering lid. Mam sat forward, rested her head in her hands and scratched her scalp. I walked over and took down the worn brown jotter from near the mantel. I opened it and began to read.

'January, Miss F, two pound owed, Missus B, two twenty-five owed, Missus D, six pound owed. Jesus. February –'

'I'm warning you.'

She stood up.

'We're boiling cabbage and everyone in the place owes you? February, Missus B, again, one fifty owed, Missus G –'

She was shouting then, her smoke still in her mouth and her chin in the air. She tried to grab me – I was too fast and ducked out of her way. She caught me one on the back of the head as I ran out the front door. She didn't follow after me.

It was early on Saturday morning. I was still covered by my blanket and I could hear the wind as it leaned against the house, the mild strain on the rafters. I went barefooted downstairs. The boiling kettle made a racket so I turned it off. The telly was gone. It came and went, but just then it was away. There was a sharp line of dust where it had been, and one dead blue-bottle. I fingered through my books. The library opened at nine. Upstairs, a bed creaked and there were footsteps, morning heavy. Me mam, I thought, but maybe him. I gathered the books into a bag, robbed two smokes from Mam's handbag and with my coat over my arm slipped out the door. Outside the world was empty and quiet and my own for hours.

I walked through the Rockies, the same trail I took to school, except I veered off and went up the wooded hill where no path had been cut in or stamped. I was breathless. An old sycamore reached up from the earth and towered high above, casting shade of a thousand leaves. I sat down at the base of the tree. Lit a smoke and settled. Silence, except for blown ripples in the long grasses beyond. A large pigeon cracked its wings as it freed itself from the canopy above. I felt I was being watched, but it was me: I was outside and watching myself.

I foraged around but there wasn't much, just some devil's cheese and rough gorse that cut my hand when I plucked it. I lay under the tree and carefully arranged the flowers on my chest, and stayed in the grass for the longest time. The wind picked up a bit, and in the distance a few clouds were scattered.

Later, I shook myself and ran and through the trees, out onto the main road, breathless towards the library. The librarian was old. She made an effort with me. She liked me, I knew she did. She wore bright blouses, greens and oranges, and every time I saw her I imagined how she discovered them in the back of a dusty shop, delighted with herself. She was not my friend or anything. Nobody knew about me and Missus H.

'You must be getting on great at school with all these books you're reading.'

That was what she said to me, every time.

'Yeah, magic.'

She liked that.

'Well now, Juno, how did you get on with that lot?'

'This was good, this was good, bit shite, massive shite.'

She laughed, put her hand to her mouth, modestly covering it.

'I tell you what, Missus, that *Lord of the Flies*, what a laugh. I have to lord of the flies it in my school every day. Don't need to be reading about them in my spare time.'

'You're a terror, a holy terror.'

She picked the two books I liked from the counter, looked

them over and thought. She had read everything, everything. In her head she could string a line between one book to another, to another and on and on forever, any book; that same way Mam could join up fabrics with thread, that was how Missus H was with books. She was never wrong.

She went off, stepping between sets of shelves built up like barricades on either side, her reading glasses perched on her sharp nose, dipping her neck now and then, delicate as a foraging bird. After a time she came back, holding two books.

'You'll like these.'

She picked up her pen and began to write on the slip inside the cover of one. It had been checked out twice that year; I wondered who by and if I knew them.

'What will you do with the rest of your day?' she says, absent-mindedly.

'Don't know – not much. Have a read, I suppose.'

'You should get out and about, see friends.'

'I buried myself in the woods today. Covered myself in flowers and pretended to be dead.' She raised her pen a moment and thought, then went back to writing in cursive that could rival Sister's.

'You should always wait for late spring to die, Juno,' she says then. 'The flowers are better.'

10

By late morning Mam was sat at the sewing machine. Just a hem on some old suit trousers. She became impatient when I plopped down next to her. I wanted to learn; I wanted her to show me. She says she didn't have time for all that, I'd only waste thread, so I sulked and went back to the couch and watched.

She stepped lightly on the pedal. The fabric moved and throughout the house the sound of the little motor whirred and murmured. Its sound made my eyes drop; my head lolled forward where I caught it and watched again as two pieces were forever joined. The needle is a tool.

When I woke, a patchwork of cut-offs gathered like petals at Mam's feet. White Carrickmacross lace poured over the table along her knee before cascading again towards the floor. She stitched it by hand, her eyes huge behind her reading glasses. It was her wedding dress. She had worn it at the altar and said 'I do' to him. It was first sewn for her own mam's wedding in a co-op in Monaghan. It was to be my confirmation dress.

Without letting her see, I took down Mam's ledger and

some coins from her purse. I went out front and sat on the step and smoked with my collar buttoned tight against the cold.

The catch wasn't heavy on the black-painted gate but, deprived of use, it was stiff and squeaked open almost musically. The distance between the bell ringing inside the house and the first stirring of footsteps was wide enough that I felt like giving up the whole endeavour and walking home and putting sugar on a bread-and-butter sandwich and hiding up in my room.

The door opened: old Missus C, age-bent and smiling. I remembered then, I was a child at her door. I didn't know for what, but Derry was by my side. Missus C had given us each a tomato. A tomato. She had apologised and said that she hated to send children away from her door empty-handed, but there wasn't a sweet nor a mineral in the house. After, Derry had flung hers at a window, a flattened bull's eye, a slow-moving target slinking down the glass. I had sat in the long grass and ate mine like an apple – it was sweet and juice ran over my chin and down my neck and I had felt a strange stirring.

'Hello, yes?' she says.

'Well, yes, hello, Missus C ...'

I looked down at the ledger, tried to steady myself. Missus C was wearing a pale housecoat, forget-me-nots drifted in woven pinstripes. She was frail and the effort to raise her head seemed terrible. She owed seventy pence from January.

'The thing of it is, in January, my mam replaced a zip on a skirt for you.'

She blinked at me.

'Well, as I say, the thing of it is, Missus C, it was seventy pence, and that seventy pence ...'

Her fingers of one hand were stretched over a wooden cane

and she folded her other hand over the first, doubling her effort to remain standing. Her skin was mottled in places and parched dry. She tilted her head slightly; her good ear came closer.

'A skirt?'

'A skirt.'

She was wearing slippers, brown and worn, men's I thought. Her feet were swollen; they bulged hidden underneath the stretched material.

'You see me ma sent me over . . . The problem is . . . You never, she never got . . . She never got the right thread and she wanted to make sure the zip had held alright and if you were happy enough with the job.'

'A skirt?'

Missus F. No answer. Missus G. No answer. The other Missus G had no doorbell – she had a knocker, a polished brass lion's head. She answered and stood in her hall looking at me, top to bottom. She exhaled, squeezed the dish towel in her hands to her hip.

'What?'

'Mam hemmed two trousers in March, you only paid a pound and owe her fifty pence.'

'Wha?'

I held up the ledger and she took it off me, read it.

'Is this right?' she says.

'Yeah, course.'

She turned the pages, silently mouthed the reams of names and then she laughed, one of them laughs people do with their breath, showing they think something is funny without finding it so.

She closed the book and handed it back to me.

'Jaysus,' she says, 'the credit union doesn't carry that much on its books. Hang on.'

I stood at the door and tried to see into her house. I could smell cooking from the kitchen, a stewy smell, good I thought. The door to the living room was closed and, unlike us, they had a hallway carpeted beige, and on a narrow glass table sat a spray of red silk carnations, dust-free like you wouldn't believe. Missus G came quickly back. She put a shiny fifty pence into my hand. It felt heavy and cold and I gripped it tight in my palm.

'Tell your mam I'm sorry to keep her waiting.'

I walked confidently to Missus B over the church road and towards our own house. I held the fifty pence in my hand and gathered the few coppers taken from Mam's purse out of my pocket. Change could be made as needed. Their bell was gold, illuminated by a tiny unseen bulb. A boy from my school opened the door wearing Spider-Man pyjamas. The sound of a television poured out over the step.

'Your ma in?'

'What do you want?'

'I want your ma for something.'

'What?'

'Use your spider senses.'

He stood there, gormless.

'Jimmy, isn't it? Jimmy, if you don't get your ma for me right now, I'm going to bring you into the middle of the road where everyone can see and then I'm going to pull your pants down to your ankles. It'll be a dinkydonk show for the whole street. You think I'm joking?'

He shouted for his ma then alright. She came out wearing an apron. Her hair under a pink net. Already flustered.

'What is it, Jimmy, who's that at that door?'

She saw me.

'Oh, you're dropping shirts back?'

But there were no shirts and that changed her face. But I didn't mind that, I had the ledger and fifty pence and even though I had the page marked I licked the tip of my finger and made a good show opening and reading it just above my head.

'Yes, Missus B. I've come for the three pound fifty you owe my ma.'

'Three pounds fifty? I don't think you have that right.'

'I'm the one has the ledger, Missus B.'

She tightened her face, looked past the ledger at me, thinking she could frighten me off from her high step with her folded arms. I jingled coppers in my hands like I was ringing a bell.

'I can make change if you need.'

'Change? I'll give you some change now across your ear. I owe your mother nothing.'

'Well,' I say to her, 'you better think about that. I have your fucking shirts.'

'Who the hell do you think you are, knocking on my door looking for money? The disgusting mouth on you. Does your mother know you're here? Go wan away, before I lose me patience with you.'

She slammed the door closed. I heard shouting inside and then I lost my temper and kicked a clay flowerpot. It smashed and the soil spilled down the step.

It went quiet inside, then I heard footsteps fast and heavy, so I backed away from the door. Mr B flung it open with a face on. He looked down at the step, the broken pot and the mess.

I ran, but he got hold of me just past the garden wall. He took

46

me by the hair and dragged me across the street. I was screaming crying by the time Mam answered the door. Her face.

'What are you doing to her?' she says.

And as he told her what he was doing he kept swiping me over the head with his open hand. Me, screaming and screaming and screaming, and the neighbours came out onto their doorsteps to see who was being murdered.

The worst of it was that he'd never do it to anyone else. It was safe to do whatever to me. We were a holy show and everyone knew it and they could get away with anything with us.

'Get off her, God's sake. She's only a child,' Mam says.

When Mam freed me from him and got me inside, he stood there telling her off for being some mother, the state of me and that he wanted money for his flowerpot and how he was going to blacken her name, see to it that no one came near her for any mending ever, ever again. Before she came back inside and closed the door, I looked up and I saw Dad's stockinged feet on the landing. He was sat there listening the whole time, just sat there, listening.

11

It was the next morning before I emerged from my room. I crept along the landing and made a silent trip to the kitchen to stock up on provisions. Tins of baked beans, can opener, spoon, then back to my room to feast. There'd be hell to pay when Mam noticed them gone. There were no biscuits – I looked.

After, I slipped out the front door holding my coat under my arms. It was heavy, thick as a blanket, and scratched against my skin. Two milk bottles were sat on the step, the cream had risen just below the top. A magpie had gotten to one bottle, pecked deep holes in the foil cap, then, perched on a high electric wire, was curiously looking down. A jetliner ruled a perfect line in the pale sky.

I walked past Missus B's house to check for carnage. There was none, big babies. The broken pieces of unglazed terracotta had been cleaned and the steps shone immaculate.

I should have been a boy. After Derry left – after she had walked the length of the estate, belly out, finger hoisted in the air like she was a fairground attraction, hoping to catch the first gold band thrown her direction – it was Mam that changed. Suddenly, not gradually. I could have been useful to her if I'd been a boy. I could have been pals with Da, and we would have made her laugh together. Instead, she watched, worried at what I was, what I would become. She didn't have a son, she had a thing that ate and watched back and was moody and growing.

Mam hardly left the house then, except to mass, but sent me to the shops with a modest list of messages written on the back of torn cardboard. Milk, smokes, tea, bread and an occasional bottle for him. All weekend she didn't look in on me or come to sit at the end of my bed. Once I would have gone and found her: I'd stand by wanting to be close, ask if maybe she needed her hair brushed, or a ciggy lit, or a cup of tea.

I knocked at Legs' door – no doorbell here, a simple silver knocker sat above a vertical postbox, polished to a bright shine.

The door cracked cautiously. Legs pushed his pale face through the opening, listless as an old jack-in-the-box.

He says:

'Hiya.'

'Hiya, yourself. You coming out?'

'No. I can't.'

'Can I come in?'

'No.'

'Don't be a cunt, go wan and let me in.'

'Me mam's not here.'

'Yeah, cos I'm dying to see her.'

He opened the door some. Enough. I pushed in, past him.

'You have to take your shoes off,' he says in a panic. I looked down and saw Legs' white feet and long toes.

'Are your feet not frozen?'

'No.'

'I'm not taking my shoes off.'

'Then you have to go.'

49

'Warning you, socks are minging,' I say and one knee at a time rose up and I pulled off my runners.

I saw then how it was plastic that I was standing on. A thin sheet of plastic, cool and sticky underfoot. Above pale carpet the plastic stretched almost opaque through the hall, into their living room and kitchen. It ran up their stairs, covering the banister and the handrail. The chairs in the kitchen looked as if they had been taken out of a box for a doll's house, and never fully unwrapped. Legs was watching me, at how I looked at his house.

'Are youse moving?'

'No.'

'Decorating?'

'No.'

'What then?'

'Mam ...'

'Yeah?'

'She likes ... she likes the place kept clean.'

'Jaysus, wha ...?'

I walked carefully through the small rooms. There were no cushions or pillows or curtains. There were goldfish behind glass. I noticed them but didn't look, orange stains washed by.

'Your ma's a complete nutter, eh?'

'Yeah, suppose.'

'But proper mad, box of kittens, bananas.'

He looked unsure then.

'Like in a madhouse, if they were giving a prize for the big-gest mental case, she'd be a shoo-in.'

From the other side of his serious face came a half-smile.

Legs brought me upstairs to his bedroom. I walked up behind him, his bare feet pulling lightly at the plastic on the stairs, that same way skin pulled behind a plaster. On the small landing there were two bedrooms, doors ajar. Legs quickly closed over his mother's door and stepped silently through his own. The walls inside were bare, painted white and unmarked. There was no mattress on his bed, just a raised frame covered in floral lino. Folded blankets were piled neatly to one side.

I stood at the window and looked out across our estate. It looked empty and unfamiliar, as if I was a stranger there myself. The rows of identical dark rooftops covered all the fixers and menders. I looked for my house, to see it from where Legs saw. Dad's cars and debris stood out against the effort maintained by others.

Legs had dropped down to the floor in a corner of the room, his back pushed into the wall.

'Is that your spot, your corner where you perch?' I say.

'Yeah. Suppose.'

I followed him and crouched down close.

'That what you sleep on?'

Legs nodded and looked out past the half-closed blinds. Clouds, pale at the centre with darkening edges, scraped low across the grey of the buildings. I thought to take his hand and hold it in mine; I thought he liked that sort of thing, that it was somehow natural for him to do, but I was unable just then, so I held back and I watched.

'Bit hard, that bed, no?'

'Get used to it.'

'Who does the cleaning?'

'Wha?'

'I mean, is it you? Your ma?'

'What difference does it make?'

'Just asking.'

'We both do it.'

'Is there a roster?'

'...No.'

'Right ... so ... just clean as needed. Is your ma's bed like that too?'

'Juno ...'

'Just wondering ...'

'She has a mattress.'

'Where's your mattress?'

'Come on.'

'What? Just asking.'

'... Pissed the bed, and it was taken away. Got it now? You happy?'

'...To dry?'

He didn't answer.

'Is it coming back?'

'No. Don't think so; it went to the skip.'

'Right ...You mortified now?You are, aren't you? I can see. You don't have to be.'

'I don't care.'

'Yes, you do ...You sleeping in with your mam?'

'Ah fuck sake, if you're going to be this way you can just go home.'

'Yeah but you are, aren't you? I mean, just sometimes, right?'

'Sometimes.'

'Thought so. Just the type, your ma. Wouldn't worry about it – you wanna see what goes on at my gaff, turn your shit white. Swear to holy God ... I like it in here. I do.'

'You do not.'

'I do.'

'Do you really?'

'Yeah, I do. All clean and that. Ordered. You could start to think straight somewhere like this. Sorry, all the questions, I shouldn't . . . I'm a bit much, I know I am.'

Just then Legs bent forward, put his head between his knees and raised up his shirt, showing the skin on his back. It was red, scorched red, with small pins of dried blood and long scraping lines where something hard had passed over the same stretch of skin again and again.

'Ah Jaysus, Legs. What happened you?'

I reached forward and blew gently against his back, up and down that way, making the air cool through my mouth.

'Does that feel nice?'

'Yeah.'

'She use a scrubbing brush?'

'Yeah, with bicarbonate of soda and vinegar.'

He lowered his shirt then, leaned his head against the wall. We sat that way for a while, with me thinking of something to tell him that would be a comfort, but there was nothing. I think he must have felt that: he turned and smiled at me, letting me know he knew I was useless and that that was alright.

'I thought of a new way to get Father,' he says.

'Did you?'

'Burn his rulers.'

'He's nothing without them . . . hot air is all.'

'I'd love to see his face, waving his empty hands around.'

'He'd make new ones,' I say.

'Suppose . . . Still like to do it.'

'Yeah.'

'Yeah.'

'I think sometimes I want to live with Sister, isn't that mad?' I say.

We were quiet then, just sat with the clean and the silence, except for Miss C's dog locked out again and going mad tied to a post in the distance.

I started into that lullaby 'Daisy'. I remembered Mam singing it. I was young, but really young. It came out of nowhere, not the words, just the tune. I liked the words too, but I couldn't sing them without wanting to bawl crying. Words could be strong that way, sometimes. Off I went humming away and looking down across Legs' pale feet and thinking about how we touched the shiny 'Jesus feet' in school and genuflected. How cold and hard, those feet. I laid my head into the crux of his shoulder. He didn't move or shudder, he just let me, and I felt the warmth of his skin against my cheek and smelt that smell that was him.

When I opened the door into the living room, Mam was sat with knitting in her lap. She didn't look up. Dad had the *Herald* open, his head dipped and hidden in its wide pages.

'Where have you been?' says Mam simply, into the room.

'Out.'

'I know out. Where?'

'Just walking.'

'You're asking for trouble out there. Do you know that? Just asking.'

I went into the kitchen and rooted about. Mam shouted in after me, 'Don't you even think about having your tea, not after your behaviour this weekend! There's nothing on those shelves – nothing coming – thank you very much.'

An empty pot cooled, scraped dry on the cooker. Two plates in the sink. My belly growled. I came back into the room. Da's paper was now folded across his knee. He gawked. Mam counted her stitches, and he gawked.

Upstairs I lay down on Derry's bed. I did that sometimes without thinking. Same as Mam, I was, I suppose, superstitious. I was sending luck to wherever Derry was, seeing that she was out there, asking for trouble.

My room was frozen. The curtains were open and when I turned on the light, my reflection sharpened in the dark window-pane. I stood and watched myself alone in the room. They were silent downstairs, the occasional tap tap of Mam's needles and Da's shifting weight, the creaking of his wooden chair. Mam was first up the stairs. I could hear her steps to the bath-room. I closed my eyes and turned away from the door, setting myself as quick as a knocked mannequin, waiting to see if she checked on me. And when her own bedroom door opened and closed shut, I was all of a sudden alone.

12

By the next weekend, Mam was moving through the house like a bombardier: with no sewing to be done she was lost. She was under everything with the brush and mop. Furiously cleaning, furious. Nothing discarded, just arranged to collect dirt in different places.

Missus B was by to say that she wanted her flowerpot replaced or she'd have the Guards up, that it was expensive, from a big shop in town. She'd kept her promise and blackened our name. In the evening, Mam sat at a loss on the couch, sucking toffee and smoking. The sewing machine and our front door forced into redundancy.

'I'm sick to death watching you lump around the place,' she called up to me. 'Sick to death.'

I sprawled across the bed, some fool on the radio talking, telling the state of the world and how, if it wasn't for him, we'd all be drowned fools. Mam poked the ceiling with the end of her brush.

'Get up outta that, Juno. I'm not going to tell you again. Get up and get dressed.'

I threw my limbs over the side of the bed and thought about dressing.

'Juno?' Mam screamed up. 'Juno? Do you hear me?'

'Jaysus, you shouting at me or someone in Africa? Bloody foghorn ... What?'

'Don't be so cheeky.'

'I'm getting dressed. What do you want?'

'I need your help. You're coming up to Dun Laoghaire with me.'

'Don't want to feckin come up to feckin Dun Laoghaire with feckin you,' I say, but only after I'd slammed my bedroom door.

Downstairs, there was a loud scraping, something heavy dragged slowly across the floor.

'Juno! Juno!'

Mam had her sewing machine and stand pulled into the centre of the room. Its dusty electric cord coiled tight as a noose.

'Give us a hand here,' she says.

'What are you doing?'

'I can't lift it; it's some weight.'

'Where are you going with it?'

'We're going up to John Sr's with it, what do you think we're doing?'

'John Sr's?'

'You take that end.'

'You can't, Mam. You can't pawn your sewing machine.'

'What do you mean, can't? You can pawn what you like.'

'No, Mam, no, you can't. Not the Singer.'

'Take hold of it, Juno, before I lose patience.'

'I'm not letting you.'

'Take that end. Now.'

'I'll get some clothes and there's the radio ... and we'll go through the boxes.'

'Juno!'

She screamed, then seemed to be holding her breath, her head bowed away from her broad shoulders, the kitchen pitched in silence. When she looked at me again there was the terrible damp in her eye.

'Juno, there is no use having a sewing machine if there is nothing to sew, now is there?'

'I'll go see Missus B. I'll beg her.'

'I don't want to hear another word, not one more, I'm warning you. Do you hear me? Nothing to be done about the woman. Now take hold of that end.'

We lifted the machine from its dusty casing: the steel wheels and cogs were heavy. Mam dampened a J-cloth under the tap and carefully set about cleaning the undercarriage and top in long, careful strokes. I watched her, but not long. I tried to remember its sound, tried to place it in some part of myself that would not be lost.

With a hand under each side of the sewing machine, we started off, coats and shoes on, silently half stepping through the estate and out along the main road, the long breathless walk to the bus stop.

'Put your side down and have a rest,' I say, as we waited. She wouldn't: she was afraid the base would scratch off the ground, and then when she looked at the dark sky she began to fret and rearrange the black bin bags we'd secured around it. My arm started to ache, the sharp steel where I'd gripped it cutting into my hand. I switched one hand to the next and then back to the first.

Missus C from our street came slowly into view, her wheelie

shopping cart pulling behind her. Missus C had had her hair done and, under her hairnet, bright pink strands wrapped around curlers like the feathers of a flamingo. When finally she reached us, she greeted Mam and stood off to one side. Mam said hello, avoided looking at the sewing machine, and her eyes dipped to some uncertain place and for a second I could see her as a child, how shy she must have been.

'I'd say that's heavy,' says Missus C.

'Not too bad,' says Mam, and she smiled tightly.

'Going shopping, Peggy?'

'Few bits. Same as yourself?'

'Oh same. Same. I'd say you'd struggle with the shopping, carting that big yoke.'

'Sure, we'll do our best.'

'It's all you can do, your best.'

'That's it,' says Mam.

'I suppose you might drop it off somewhere.'

Mam didn't answer.

'Maybe you'll leave it in a shop or that?'

'Well, that's an idea, Missus C,' says Mam. She looked ahead, out the road to the first drops of rain.

'I'd say that's your sewing machine under there, Peggy? Needing mended, is it?'

'That's right, Missus C.'

'Mmm,' says Missus C.

The bus, when it arrived, was full downstairs. We slowly humped the machine upstairs and Mam insisted on keeping it on her knee where it bounced like a toddler. The ticket inspector, while waiting for Mam to count coppers from her purse, says, 'Should be charging an extra fare for that, wha?'

And as he laughed, his bushy wide moustache sprung, left

and right, across his face. Mam paid and cradled the machine tight to her body, against the jostle of the pockmarked road.

We went through the steel door at John Sr's, our arms murdered, and waited in line behind two others. A lamp was held in the man's hand; in the woman's, a bright oriental-looking vase I later saw was in the shape of an elephant, its trunk the pouring lip.

John Jr was behind the counter. I felt Mam's disappointment. John Jr, unlike his ailing father, was known for trying to make a name for himself, known for his meanness.

The elephant was set on the counter. John Jr looked at it with scorn.

'Ah come on, what are you wasting my time with here?'

He picked it up, checking for a stamp, just in case. The elephant greatly reduced in his hands.

'Fifty pence,' he says, roughly banging it on the glass counter and pushing it back towards its owner. He walked away into the back room before she could defend the article's merit. A moment later, when John Jr emerged, he feigned surprise at the woman still waiting in his shop.

'Do you want it or not?'

'I think it's worth –'

'Then bring it home outta my sight.'

'I just think –'

'Are you trying to haggle? Cos you'll be out of here and don't think of coming back, bringing your elephant's shite and rubbish in.'

'OK.'

'OK, what?'

'I'll take the fifty pence.'

'No – I've changed me mind: out. Bring that yoke with you, go wan, the two of yis, taking up too much room. I mean it: out. Out.'

The woman took hold of the large vase and left quickly, careful not to catch another eye.

'It's in the tradition of Macintosh,' says the man next in line, after placing his lamp carefully down. 'My family brought it from Glasgow.'

John Jr slinked towards the mostly green-shaded glass lamp. He was as wide as a rung of wire, John Jr. A snake, I thought.

'Ya see the sign?'

'I'm sorry?'

'The sign, outside, see it?'

'Do you mean your sign?'

'I don't mean someone else's.'

'Yes,' he says, growing irritated.

'Did it say "antiques"? "Purveyor of rare antiquities"? "Sell posh lamps here"? Or did it say "pawnbroker"? Cheap shite from skint people. Charles Rennie O'Toole's is as far up the scale as we go.'

'You're not interested then?'

'Two quid.'

'. . . OK.'

Only after the man was paid and had left and John Jr had slipped again into the back room and re-emerged did he acknowledge Mam.

'How's you doing, Pegs?' he says, so fondly they might be friends. I see the side of Mam's face, how she didn't like that. How they were not friends.

'Ah, the beast is back. I haven't seen her in a while. I think I was a young lad meself when I last saw her, wha? I suppose you've been taking good care of her. Throw her up on the counter and we'll have a look.'

We hauled the sewing machine onto the counter. Mam's

hands were raw, cracked open like an old wallet. She held them at her side.

'Yes, it's very well taken care of, oiled twice –'

'Yeah, yeah. Now, Pegs, you're not going to like me for saying it, you're not going to be at all happy, but, Pegs, it's the truth, true as God. Nobody, but I mean bleedin' nobody, sews any more. It's all disposable now. I could walk into a Penneys right now and, for the price of a hem, be wearing a new pair of denims. Do you know what I'm saying, love?'

The two top buttons of his shirt were undone and the vertical lines to his collar folded wide. A gold medallion, a Saint Christopher – the one with him holding the lamb – hung low off a thick chain.

'That's the world today, isn't it . . . nothing to be done, wha?'

He swiped his hand over the Singer in rough strokes and I saw how he was looking at me. He held on my hips and belly, over my half-formed breasts, along my neck and mouth. He turned to Mam then.

'This your young one?'

'That's my youngest, Juno, yes. She's twelve.'

'Well, Juno. Haven't you grown up a grand girl?' he says and reached forward and pinched my cheek until it hurt and I pulled away from him. 'She's a cheeky one, I can tell,' he says and laughed. He tapped the machine a few more times, thinking. Then says, 'Five. I'll do it for five.'

I saw a tremble in Mam's hand. She was shocked, looking at the machine, her jaw tightly clamped.

'Your father always gave me twenty-five, you know that,' says Mam. I looked at the floor, away from what was becoming of me mam. 'He would give twenty-five,' she says, 'and add an extra five, call it luck money.'

John Jr looked at Mam, fuming then.

'Yes, he did. I do remember you taking that little excursion on his coat-tails, more than once. My father, you see, was what is called fiscally irresponsible. Now, I know you don't understand what that means, but in plain language, he was a soft touch.'

Mam was not looking at him: she fixed across the burnish of his Saint Christopher. The patron saint of travellers had her mesmerised.

'Thank you, that's fine,' she says.

John Jr took hold of the sewing machine and made a point of dropping it on the ground, where it landed in a heap by his feet. He dug into his pocket and pulled an impressive roll of notes and counted out one, two, three, and at four, he stopped. Put the remaining money back inside his pocket. Mam looked at the four notes he had lined up side by side on the glass counter. She waited and for the longest time did not speak. John stood on the other side with his fingers fanned out across the glass, lit from underneath, pink fingers with hairs and tightly bitten nails.

'That's four. You said five,' Mam says.

He picked up a pound note from the counter, put it back inside his pocket.

'The first one is a haggling fee. The second is for arguing,' he says.

Mam looked at the three notes, transparent above the light.

'Ahh, Peg,' says John, and he smiled and reached inside his pocket and held one pound note up. 'Here's your luck money.' When she went to take it he pulled it away again. He says, 'You ever mention my father again and you'll be wearing that rusted lump of shite home, you hear me?'

He scrunched the pound note up into a ball and flicked it

across the room. It sailed up over our heads, dropping silently near the door.

'Have your little bitch fetch it.'

Mam didn't move; she looked on with growing confusion and horror. I took the three notes from the counter and pulled at Mam's arm.

'Come on,' I say, taking her with me. I dipped down and picked the balled note from the floor.

'That's it, fetch,' I heard behind me.

'Go wan, ya cunt, and fuck off,' I say.

'Oh I like you, you can come back any time.'

I opened the door and shoved Mam through it, her empty hands clutching at the air.

'That man . . . I don't understand.'

She looked ahead, searching.

'You're alright, Mam. You stay here, I'll be right back.'

And I left her, one arm pressed against the wall, and went back through the door. He lit upon seeing me and says, 'Missing me already, princess?'

I went searching for something I'd seen earlier. A small brass bust, the size of a fist. I took it in my hand, its cold smooth nose and chin, and, as hard as I could, I hurled it towards him. As he ducked out of its way, he slipped, falling over, and I heard glass smash behind him.

It was dark by then and the shop windows seemed to blaze. Light shined up from the damp streets. People, tightly packed, inched forward along the path. Mam struggled to navigate the crowds and was bumped again and again and each bump she absorbed with fright. I put my arm through her arm and pulled her closer to me. When we arrived at the long line at the bus stop, she whispered, 'We can't, Juno.'

'Can't what?' I say.

'Money for the bus – we need to keep it.'

'We're not walking.'

'Yes,' she says, so I spun her around, back past the shop lights and sounds. She stepped, determined enough, until the path finally darkened and people thinned and no longer passed us. I looked up and saw our bus, as bright as a carousel, rumble by – if Mam saw it too, she never let on. She marched the long way home keeping her back straight and chin high and I struggled at times to keep up.

'I never thought I'd be happy to be here,' I say to Mam, as we rounded the final corner into the estate. She looked sideways at me. She'd not spoken in some time and I saw how I'd never know her thoughts.

'Go on in, Juno. I'll be along,' she says once outside our house.

'Where you going?'

'Just do what you're told, for once.' She untangled herself from me and started across the road. I watched as she unclipped Missus B's front gate and it swung noiselessly. I couldn't hear the words, but Mam reached inside her purse and notes were passed.

Our door was knocked some nights later. I listened from upstairs to a woman's voice. She wanted some mending done, some patches, elbows and knees worn from her children's clothes. I heard Mam say her machine was on the blink, she offered to do it by hand, said it was the best way, and after all, we were sewing long before those auld machines anyway, and she laughed in a way that made me want to cry. The woman didn't want 'by hand' sewing, so Mam recommended a shop on the main road.

13

'You shouldn't be doing it, Juno, you'll be seen,' says Mam.

'It's coming – I hear it,' I say. Stood at the window, I saw its headlights.

'Close the curtains,' she says. I went to the door and was about to run. 'The bag, Juno, don't forget the bag. Please God, be sure you're not seen.'

Underneath her worried face I could see a small hint of excitement and, as we were doing it together after a fashion, I knew I could do anything, frightened and all as I was.

'I won't be seen.' I gripped the bag and darted out the front door. The small truck passed and brake lights came on as the driver slowed to a stop, spilling out all that red light onto the wet road behind. The truck lurched a little and pebbles of coal fell from the back. I heard the handbrake pull as the driver emerged, went to the back of the truck and, as he opened the hatch, a few more pebbles fell. He took hold of a sack and effortlessly heaved it onto his shoulder, walking it up Missus G's path.

I ran, dipping under the truck, quickly gathered up the small lumps. But in the dark the road's black and the coal's black were the same black and my fingers keep scraping off the wet tarmac. I got what I could before running back to the safety of the path. When the driver walked out of Missus G's I thought he saw me but he said nothing.

Missus D's. I heard the idling engine rev and could smell diesel and the truck rolled on to its next stop. I walked past again, watching. The driver rested Missus D's coal on his shoulder and used his free hand to sweep coal from the back of the truck and let it fall, tap-tapping at his feet like tunes from a miner's axe. He began to whistle then, up the garden path, continuing that lullaby and alerting me to his whereabouts.

I ran again and bent low, working through the small mound, wet coal dust as far as my sleeve, filling my bag to bursting. A moment and the man, not whistling now, was standing over me, peering down, his face peppered with grey-white stubble. The bone of his cheek high and sharp. I couldn't say the colour of his eyes, but they shone in the dark.

'You missed one,' he says and reached across the pallet and plucked an enormous rock from the platter and put it in my bag. 'Been saving that one.' He walked around the truck, whistling again.

Later it was glowing hot in the grate, and I'd scrubbed my hands as clean as they'd scrub and I'd decided my nails would never be clean again and gave up on them. I hadn't told Mam about the man, wanting for her to think of me as her hero. She took down her wedding dress, and had me put it on. This material she handled differently than other material. She took it in her hands and carefully unfurled it like an old secret history: the celebrations and the crises, the embraces and departures.

She opened the zip, and I raised my arms over my head. The smooth of the satin passed down my body, falling in places it should not fall. I was reminded Mam was a woman and I, I was not. Still, as the fabric touched my skin I was overcome. When Mam's back was turned I ran my hands along it, coal dust still bedded under my fingernails, pressing it where my flesh was bare. I thought of the scores of girls who had stood as I stood, with a secret feeling, set ablaze in their mam's kitchen.

Mam knelt before me and started to shape and pin. I tried to remember the last time I felt me mam this close, but I couldn't. I remained silent, lest I say the wrong word and ruin it. After she had me pinned she told me to walk the length of the kitchen and she watched, she really watched. She was thinking about something else when she said casually, a small hint of surprise, 'You're a pretty thing, Juno. Not beautiful or that, pretty.'

14

I knew there were kitchen tables with fresh flowers, with knives and forks that shined on both sides of colourful plates, and Granny's white linen heirloom that ran like spilt milk over the edge. I boiled two kettles, one after the other, and poured them into the kitchen sink with big squeezes of washing-up liquid. I left the water just hot enough that I could put my hands in for a moment without scalding them and no longer. My hands were scarlet. I started on the table, scrubbing with a sponge till its surface was sopping wet and I was almost out of puff. I set about polishing once it was dry, and although the varnish remained drab at the worn places we sat, it gleamed in others. The metal draining board was pocked with rust and even with a Brillo pad it could not be removed. It was the same with the cooker and grill, where the white enamel was chipped beyond. The grease and layers of fat I'd scoured.

Mam had gone to bed the night before, after the dress had been taken off and carefully folded away and packaged. She'd stood at her bedroom door and I'd stood at mine and she says, 'Goodnight, Juno,' in that old way and smiled, turning to her door. I had lain in bed and felt as though I were still swaddled by the satin fabric.

When Mam came down, ragged with sleep, she was silent but put a hand on each hip, looked at the immaculate table and was delighted. I was about to give her the tour, but the moment was taken when she caught sight of the dress, bound in brown paper, that way she did for customers. It all tumbled back, how there was nothing to be sewn, how she could go no further by hand-stitching and how her wedding dress was, that morning, being brought to another seamstress. It galled her. 'Ma, come and look at the cooker, it's shining. Ma, look.'

She was searching the nowhere in the middle of the room and raised her hand to her face, rubbed it, then glanced briefly back at the bundle before allowing herself to be led to the kitchen. 'Look, it's all white. I got the muck off the corners and the sink, Ma, look at the sink.'

'That's great, Juno. It's . . . Put on that kettle, will you please?'

'. . . Yeah.'

She was away, gone inside herself and from the next room I heard the brown paper crinkle as the package was set on the table. When I walked past her, she was at the coat-rack, sorting through woollens, in search of her own. I was on the stairs when she says, 'Did you put that kettle on?'

'Don't have time, Ma. Don't want to be late for school.'

'What?'

She was bulling then, shouting after me about how ungrateful I was, how she was only bringing the dress to Dun Laoghaire because of the trouble I'd brought. I waited at the head of the stairs and watched her go to the kitchen, the fluorescent light flared and she paused under it, motionless, elbows across the counter, her wide back rounded. I ran down the stairs and from her purse took two cigarettes before opening the front door. I slammed it hard behind me and sat on the steps in a mood.

The rising chill of the concrete and a damp feeling pressed me. I lit a smoke, then thought to go back inside. 'Sorry Mam,' I'd say and sit her down and mind her, with tea and toast and great wallops of melting butter. I wanted that, I did.

Spring, the turncoat, was bringing a strong creeping light over the rooftops and the sky was clear and blue. There wasn't a peep in the estate, except for someone's light footsteps coming along the road, walking a dog. I could hear the animal's nails quickly scraping at the path. It was one of those black-and-tan sausages, and it stopped at our gate and looked back anxious and comical to its master before pressing forward in its frenzied manner. I almost called to it. I followed the leash from around its neck to its holder's hand. Father, just then, dipping down to reassure, his great hands sweeping affectionately across the full length of the animal.

'That's it, that's it. Good, good girl.'

A voice I could not fathom had emerged, a wallop of kindness, tender like you wouldn't believe. He must have felt me watching, that mysterious way people do, cos he turned and saw and straightened and in an instant his demeanour was recast and it was Father again. I'd seen something I was not to see, I knew that, and in my unsettled state I'd forgotten to dispose of the smoke that lolled about in my mouth. I dropped it quickly and stood. A long soundless moment passed between us, he looked at me, up and down, just to let me know what he thought, before he allowed himself to be drawn forward by the small restless creature.

I watched after him, as he continued down the road, and he knew I was watching and so remained aloof and never allowed that softness to return. I was about to sit and collect myself when I saw how Father paused at Legs' gate. He opened it and went up the scrubbed steps, then he gathered the dog tightly on its leash, before a cheerful knocking was heard. The door was so quickly opened by Legs' mam, she'd plainly been stood on the other side in anticipation. 'Not playing hard to get, are you, missus?' I thought, picking up my still smouldering cig and leaning across our gate to watch.

I'd hardly taken a second draw, when the door was flung open again and Legs emerged, his school bag wrung about his neck, frantic. He seemed set to run off, as though a string had been pulled at his back and he was fully wound. Frustrated at having nowhere to go, he quickly paced around the tiny garden and then ran to the side of the house, free from his mam's front window, and began kicking at the wall to the side. Without thinking, I opened our gate and ran. His head was pressed hard against the pebbledash, and when he turned to me, his forehead was marked and red and he had tears flowing down his face.

'Juno?' he says, embarrassed by his crying and wouldn't look at me then.

'What's happened?'

'Nothing, nothing's happened.'

'Legs . . .'

'Seán, me name's fucking Seán.'

He began to pace again, this Seán, this boy in well-hemmed grey slacks and a starched white shirt buttoned to his thin neck.

'He's just a bastard, is all. A mean bastard.' He says it in a whisper and checked over his shoulder, that he'd not been heard.

'What's he doing here?'

'He's always on to me mam, saying stuff.'

'What stuff?'

'I don't know, just stuff . . . and she gets wound up and

then ...' He turned back to the wall, kicking at it again. 'My mam hates me.'

'Your mam doesn't hate you.'

'She does, I think she does.' He started going then, really crying.

A modest bit of light folded in at the side of the house, cut a straight line over the tips of his leather brogues and made them sparkle, made me expectant of him bursting suddenly into dance and how wonderful.

'You,' he says, 'he tells her about you, sometimes.'

'Oh.' I didn't ask what was said and felt myself shift uncomfortably, rearranging my jumper, pulling at my skirt, and hiding my hands in its fold.

'She knew you were in the house.'

'Smelt me, did she?'

'Course not.'

'I was joking. Jaysus.'

'I want to kill him.'

The sun was still low in the sky, somewhere unseen, casting shadows that sketched long across the estate. My front door was opened and closed and me mam came out carrying the dress bound in brown paper and tied twice with twine. She paused at the gate to fix the buttons of her coat and then moved off, slowly, gravity clutching at her shoes a little tighter. I watched her, and felt in my belly an ache. I hated when Mam was cross with me. It sent me off to the bed with a knot in my stomach and a restless feeling taken hold.

'Do you want to see where I buried myself?' I say.

'Where you what?'

'Buried myself.'

73

He looked at his house, lifeless and sombre; the two of them in there, decisions being made, bad ones, I was sure.

'Yeah,' he says.

'You might wipe your nose or something, Jesus.'

He ran his sleeve over his nose and there was the start of a smile.

'Can we go the long way? Me ma will be looking.'

Walking the estate, he hugged the inside of the path, looking down, and his fingers scraped through the bristle of hedgerows. We turned down a high-walled lane that led to the grasses. Sounds of our footsteps went up the wall, fell back and echoed.

'I have a spare smoke – you can have it.'

'Don't smoke.'

'It's easy – I'll show you.' I led him through the small path. The sky had started to grey and it made the green stand out more green. Legs walked a few paces behind, stopping now and then to notice. The first flushes of bluebells had come in and clustered together just past the shade. Missus H was right, the flowers were better. When we arrived at what I thought was my spot at the base of the sycamore tree, there were a few branches, colourless, buried in the grass.

'It was here, I think.' I looked to see if Legs was disappointed.

'What did you do?'

'I'll show you.' I lay down quickly and folded my arms across my chest, looked past the great trunk to where its cardinal limbs swayed high above.

'And then you put flowers across and close your eyes.'

Together we found dandelions, sorrel and Queen Anne's lace. Burning drops of fuchsia. Some brambles I'd no name for: they had the smallest white blossoms and tiny lines inside of the palest pink, although you had to squint to see. We took turns at being buried, and when I lay down, I felt his hand take hold of my arm and pull it towards him. The sleeve of my jumper was raised as far as my elbow. I let him. He was holding a marker he'd taken from his school bag and asked what was my favourite flower. 'Poppies,' I say, without thinking. He nodded and thought and his face was serious. He pursed his lips in concentration, and with the tip of his marker pressed. I felt the curves and the straight lines, I felt his hand holding my forearm steady in his own for some time, then small dots for seeds, I think, four or five. When he let go my arm, it flushed with sensation. I opened my eyes and looked.

'How did you do that?' I say. There on my arm was an arrangement of poppies, as if he'd just plucked them from the ground and set them down, their long narrow stems and docile blooming leaves, so real I imagined they could be moved by a small breeze.

'But how?'

'I like to draw, sometimes,' he says, as if kneeling in the confessional, unburdening himself. He looked away, shy then. 'Do you think it's good, really?'

'If I could do something like that, just once, I don't know, I'd just never have to do anything ever again, ever.'

Legs lay down. I told him to close his eyes and I arranged a bouquet across his chest. He laughed out loud when I tickled his neck. Not once did we mention Father, or his mam, or even my mam, and although they were in the air around us, we never said. When Legs settled into his resting place, his face was serious and set like plaster.

'Am I supposed to do anything?' he says. His eyes didn't open.

'No, you just stay like that until you're bored.'

He was quiet for the longest time. In the places we'd trodden, I watched stems slowly spring back and right themselves.

'Can I be Legs again?' he says.

'Nah, you fucking ruined it.'

'Go on.'

'Don't move, you're supposed to be dead.' I followed his eyes as they moved up through the budding pale green canopy.

'I don't want to be Seán any more,' he says.

'What do you want to be?'

'Legs,' he says, 'I like that.'

I lit a smoke and puffed hard to get it going before laying down beside him. I offered him a drag, but he said his ma might smell it and go mental.

'Why was Father at your house this morning?'

He looked down the hill to where the shade ended at the tree line, the blocks of houses sitting in the middle distance. I thought he was going to say, but he took hold of the smoke instead, unnatural between his fingers, and brought it to his mouth and coughed at his first inhale. I thought about how when we were old we could be married and although I had never thought about it before, it would be something, having this feeling all the time.

'Do you believe in God, Legs?'

He looked at me squarely with those practical eyes.

'Yes,' he says, without hesitation.

'Right.'

'Don't you?'

'Not as much as you, I don't think.'

'Let's not go to school today,' he says in a sleepy way, but thinking about it, he sat up. 'I've five pounds. We could go visit my granny?'

15

I'd never been on a bus without Mam, and Legs seemed unsure and suddenly scattered. We'd stood at the bus stop for so long, worried we'd be seen, and he panicked when the first bus arrived and insisted we must take it. In excitement, we ran up the stairs to the front seat where the view was best and plopped down and only then checked around us for any neighbours or familiar faces that might tell and get us in trouble. It was mostly empty up there; nobody took any notice. We looked at each other and I could feel all of that, back there, drifting away as the bus pushed on further into town and we were filled with a different sensation, giddy, we were giddy.

Legs kept his five pounds in his hand ready and when the ticket collector came along, he looked at us, our bags and school uniform and knew. He said nothing.

'Where are you going?'

'To see me granny,' says Legs in a flap.

'Mind she doesn't eat you. What stop is Granny's?'

'The one in town.'

'There's half a dozen stops in town. Do you know where you're going?'

'The river.'

'OK, Eden Quay so, last stop. Single or return?' Legs looked at me unsure.

'Return,' I whispered.

'Return,' says Legs, 'two returns.' And he handed over the five-pound note, and it looked huge in his hand, the size of a tea towel.

Mam didn't go into town, she didn't like it, it frightened her. She knew the shops and shopkeepers and streets in Dun Laoghaire, she knew herself, she'd grown up there. In town, she shrunk; the wide boulevard of O'Connell Street, its hectic and unfamiliar bustle, filled her with alarm.

She'd brought me in only once, on my communion day. Me, Mam and Derry. We sat downstairs and I was given a whole seat to myself, my white dress ballooning left and right, filling the whole seat. I had been lent a small leather satchel. It was white too, and it bounced on my knee, empty, while Derry and Mam sat on another seat watching. The conductor said I could ride for free and wouldn't take money for my ticket, and each time he passed by, he asked if everything was alright with my journey. And when I couldn't answer except to giggle, he kept going, saying if there was anything I needed, anything at all, just come and see him.

'Legs?' I say. We'd passed Monkstown by then, and Blackrock village, and the view of the sea had come and gone and returned. 'Legs, does Father visit a lot?'

'Not a lot.'

'Right, and your mam, does she take up the plastic, before? Like when she knows he's coming, does she run around, quick, Father's coming, take up the plastic?'

'No. She leaves it.'

'And does he ever say?'

'No, never.'

'Jaysus, does he bring a pillow or that? Something to sit on?' He smiled.

'He brings Percy and she hates that. She cleans after he's gone. She hates when he brings the dog, thinks it's dirty.'

'Percy?'

'Percy.'

'Ahh Father, Jesus! I thought Percy was a girl?'

'She is.'

'He's good with that dog though, isn't he? Loves her, like he really loves her.' And I thought about that moment where Father had been someone else, just for a second, closer to a creature himself, filled with that same stuff. Kind, I suppose, innocent maybe? I didn't understand.

'There's a school up in the north,' says Legs, 'Belfast, I think. He's after Mam to send me there.'

'A school?'

'Yeah, a special one.'

'What's special about it?'

'Don't know,' he says, but I think he did.

'Is she going to send you?

'Don't know.'

He was less inclined to speak then and I worried at the side of his face.

'Belfast?'

He looked away, out the window, catching a last glimpse of Dublin Bay before it disappeared and the bus made its approach, past the red-bricked and stone mansions, all the way through Merrion and Ballsbridge. Our lessons would be starting. I could see Sister, before prayers, how she'd look to our seats, empty, and maybe smile to herself. She'd know at once. I hadn't cared before, but a type of disquiet had crept in unnoticed, a hollow disquiet like when you'd forgotten something so important and had just remembered and it would always be too late.

The bus stopped at the Quays and because everyone stood and made their way down the stairs, we did too, stepping off the bus into all that activity. Legs turned and beamed. 'Look,' he says, 'I got us here.' As if he'd driven the bus himself. He paused on the path and searched for any familiar sight and was quickly brushed left and right by fast-moving passers-by. 'It all looks different,' he says, taking hold of my hand and pulling me forward against the flow of the people. On the bridge, Legs stopped, searching. 'Look, the Ha'penny Bridge. I know where we are!' And we walked quickly, close together, our shoulders bumping along O'Connell Street. He whispered as though telling a great secret, 'We've enough for six doughnuts. Just here. Granny brought me once.' And we stopped under a red-and-white awning and six doughnuts, still warm, were wrapped and handed through the small glass opening. Unnoticed in a doorway, we sat and silently ate in a kind of stupor every last lick of sugar and jam, and from that low vantage, looking up, it seemed if we sat there long enough all of Dublin would pass.

We walked up and down nameless streets, getting to the end of one street only to discover we'd already been and had simply circled back to where we'd started. We did that for hours. I suggested asking someone for directions, but Legs didn't know the name of his granny's street. We paused to look at bright shop windows on Grafton Street and we knew not to walk inside.

Later, our feet in tatters, we sat near the pond in the park and looked at the ducks. Some auld one was feeding them, wearing a long stained mac and several woolly hats and she was talking to them by name. 'Rita,' she says, 'you've already had enough. Let Marilyn and Audrey have some too.'

'That your granny?' I say, and we laughed, and worn out from walking, decided to abandon our search.

'Pity though,' says Legs, 'she's great. She plays the piano sometimes, sings and everything.'

'Does she?'

'Yeah. She was my da's mam, you know?'

'Right.'

'I mean, I don't remember him or anything, but she has pictures and that, she always takes out.'

Just then, the woman in the hats put her paper bag of bread-crumbs behind her back and stopped moving. She looked reproachfully at the ducks and suddenly walked away, saying, 'I'm worried sick, Sophie, just worried sick.' Some of the ducks followed.

Legs took hold of his school bag, set it on his lap and opened it. He took out a small stack of A4 papers, yellow and white, and held them. He looked at me quickly and then off across the water.

'I was thinking I could leave these at my granny's, but eh, do you think you could mind them for me instead?'

'What are they?'

'Just pictures, they're stupid. I just don't want me mam to find them, show them to Father. I'm not allowed at home.'

'Giz a look,' I say. He passed them to me and I leafed through the papers, unfolding these familiar images, in dark ink and marker.

'They're all religious.'

'Yeah.'

'How'd you learn to do it . . . I just can't believe it. It's mad!' The crucifixion, Saint John the Baptist and even Lazarus.

'Would they be alright at yours?'

'At mine? Oh yeah, they'd be grand there alright. Me da would trip over them six times and still not bother to look. I tried keeping a diary, dying for someone to read it, so I was. I even left it on the kitchen table a whole week, nothing.' When I put them in my bag he never looked.

'They're really brilliant,' I say.

'Thanks, and thanks for minding them and all.'

'Yeah, course.'

'I think it's getting late.'

'Yeah.'

But we didn't leave, not right away. A quiet had settled over us both, not a bad one, just quiet.

We found our way back to the Quays and without hesitation knew we had boarded the correct bus. It was stuffed with people, their bags filled with messages, some looked tired and watched out the window and others chatted in low or excited tones. There were no seats upstairs so we stood at the base of the stairs, holding on to the pole and swaying.

'Tickets please, tickets now, please.' The conductor paused beside us. Legs went into his pockets, the first and then the second and continued, gaining pace before starting back at the first. The conductor looked to the other passengers as if he was on the stage and the bus was his theatre. His mouth tightened and he rolled his eyes. He reached up and pressed the small red button we'd been so curious about before. A bell sounded and the bus drew to a halt at the next stop. 'C'mon on, the two of yiz off.' He herded us through the congested aisle. We never protested, not once. One woman caught my eye as we stepped off the bus and looked so sorry that I'm sure she'd have bought us tickets if she could spare the fare. The bus pulled away from the path, disappearing under the burgeoning chestnut trees that lined the street. Legs and I, stunned at what had happened and so quickly, howled with laughter, clutching at each other like falling-down old drunks.

It was a long walk home, and after so much walking that morning, my feet were sore. I'm sure his were too, but he never said. At first, we didn't understand just how far it was and remained cheerful. But as the afternoon stretched into early dusk, we fell silent. The other children would already be home from school, sat at the table or out playing on the street. I thought about me mam that morning, my way with her. She probably walked all the way to Dun Laoghaire, her feet sore like mine, except her feet were already banjaxed and hurt all the time. I imagined her watching out the window at the children in the street, searching for her own. I quickened my pace, Legs too, as if outrunning the same thought.

We didn't speak for the whole rest of the walk, not when the street lights and car lights came on, not when the path had emptied and people no longer passed.

From across the green, I saw an amber glow of light in my window and I wanted to cry, but I held it in, saved it up inside myself, and before I took to running, hard and fast over the uneven ground, I looked once at Legs' frightened face. Then I ran, fast as I could, until I came bursting through the door, breathless for me mam.

He was slumped across the settee; he looked up from his newspaper, casually surprised and then uninterested. I stepped further inside the room so I could see into the alcove of the kitchen. The light was off and it was empty.

'Where's me mam?' I say.

'That's what I'd like to know,' he says.

'Is she not here?'

'Close that door, the cold's coming in.'

I closed the door and swept the room again, expecting she would appear, that I'd missed her the first time and he was playing a trick. I ran up the stairs, searching. He was still talking: 'I thought she was with you. I've been sat here on me own and nothing to eat all day.' I couldn't think. I swung open their bedroom door, just street light, it blared across their well-made bed. 'She's not up there, couldn't hide a mouse up there, God knows.' I came slowly down the stairs, numb and confused and trying to think, piece it together. 'Juno, stick on something for me supper, would you, pet? Me poor tummy's growling.' In the kitchen, the fluorescent light flickered on and I saw her upturned cup, draining at the sink. I made him something, I must have. I remember him sitting at the table with a steaming pot and a fork in his hand and noise coming from his chewing that made me sick.

I tidied up after so the place would be nice, and I filled the kettle, ready for her, and even put two tea bags into her cup the way she liked it, strong enough that the teaspoon would nearly stand up, and then I sat, waiting. I even attempted a book at the table, distracted by the slow rounds of the clock. Da was across the couch, seemingly untroubled, as he stretched his stockinged feet. But I was sure as the news came on the radio, I caught his eye move towards the clock. And as the seconds, minutes and hours dragged on, the silence we shared thickened. I stood finally and went to the window, pulling the curtain aside and peering out past the windowsill with dusty geraniums and busy Lizzies, their almost leafless stems stretched arthritic towards the glass, the window so black I only saw my reflected face. When I opened the front door, he barked again about the heat. I pulled the door behind me and walked outside. The street seemed longer, eternally stretched on both sides. Every twenty yards or so, street lights caught specks of misted rain spilling past the empty glow.

I thought of her out alone, her deliberate step, monotonously beating forward, winter coat buttoned tight, and her shoulders and back pressed into the damp wool. I knew something was wrong. I thought of all the places she must pass to come home, where boys waited in the dark, holding bicycles and bottles and brown flagons filled with soapy warm cider.

I went inside and sat back at the table in a panic. I began to pull some words from the book, but they just rolled about and could not be swallowed and again I was watching the clock. I slammed the book down, making more noise than I'd expected, and turned to him.

'Where is she?'

'Who?'

'Who? Me mam!'

'Must have run off with a sailor.'

He showed me his teeth and when I was not charmed, he glowered from the other side of the room. A while later he was up and putting on his shoes as if engaged in the final act of a tragedy. He started around the kitchen, pulling at tea canisters and sugar jars, looking inside, and putting them back on the low shelf.

'Where's your mother's spot these days?'

'Where she keeps her coppers?'

'Yeah, where she keeps her coppers.'

'What do you need that for?'

'Are you going to start with me?' he says.

'No.'

'Then where?'

'Behind the picture.' He smirked at that, finding something funny perhaps in the photo of Mam, younger, sitting in the doorway of a caravan, her bright face tilted towards the sunlight. He located it, tipped up the tin can and coins, not many, tinkled into his hand.

'Are you going to look for her?'

'What does it look like?' he says, that way.

I slept on the settee that night, not wanting to face the hollow of the house from upstairs. In the sitting room, the last of the embers' glow rolled red into the room only after the lights were out. And I lay with my eyes fixed on them, not sleeping. Hours later, I heard a key in the front door and lit up. It was him. He passed by and dragged himself to the top of the stairs.

In the morning, there was an insistent hammering at the door and I leapt to my feet, still dressed. It was a young Guard, capped and standing to attention, with another policeman who did all the talking.

'Can we speak to your father?'

'Why? What's wrong, what's happened?'

'We need to speak to your father.' I backed away from them slowly, scrutinising their faces, then I ran, screaming up the stairs for Da. He was splayed like a thrown sack across the bed.

'Da, Da!' I was shouting. He didn't budge, so I lamped him across the head with the back of my hand. That shifted him.

'Da, Da. Guards downstairs, Da, get up, the Guards are here.' He swatted me away.

'Alright, I'm up.'

I ran back downstairs. The two Guards were planted where

I'd left them, gawking in the doorway through to the sitting room and small kitchen.

'He's coming,' I say and stood there closely staring. I could learn nothing from their faces. Sounds came from that fool upstairs, falling over himself for the sake of a sock.

'It's me mam, isn't it?' I say.

'We can talk to your father only.'

'Is she alright?' But they wouldn't answer and found places where I was not to look. And as they did, I felt that terrible sick and fury and helplessness. I screamed.

'Jaysus fucking Christ, is she even alive, will you just tell me?'

'She is.'

I came away from the door and all the night's panic flushed through me and wet my face. He lumbered down the stairs towards the door, and stood almost to attention.

'Gardaí, will you come in?' They wouldn't. They preferred to stay at the doorway with their caps and uniforms pressed flat.

The bus that jumped the kerb and hit Mam was carrying a dead bus driver, his heart stopped beating right at the wheel. She bled on the inside, but was being made comfortable above in the hospital. They felt they should let him know; they felt he might be worried.

He closed the door, scratching himself as he went to the kitchen.

'I want to go and see her,' I say.

'That's enough,' he says. 'Give me a second to think.' I gathered up my coat and hat until he roared at me then.

'What did I say, eh? What did I just tell you? Sit feckin down on that chair – till I have a think, you're going nowhere.' He sat in a plume of smoke and sipped tea. His hands trembled. I sat. For as long as I could, I sat.

'She'll want to see me,' I say. 'She'll be worried on her own. She'll have missed her horoscope – she hates that.'

'Juno, shut up, swear to God, shut it. You're not going anywhere near that hospital.'

'I want to see me mam.'

'They don't let children into hospital. Don't be so stupid.'

'I want to see me mam.'

'She doesn't want to see you. She wants rest.'

'She does, she does want to see me,' I say, but I swallowed the words and what remained was soft and uncommitted. It was then the pains started for the first time, deep in my belly, almost causing me to double. I wriggled on the chair and the pain moved down my back.

'She's comfortable.' He kept on saying it, over and over. Comfortable. Comfortable. Comfortable. 'She'll only be in a day or two,' says Da. 'You're just going to have to keep the ship on course here and I'll go see –'

'Fuck!' I scream with the pain – it surged again and again. 'Fuck!' It startled him. 'A fucking bus! She was hit by a fucking bus! Go wan and see her, for Jaysus' sake!'

I'd have said more, but he went for me then, knocked the table and teacups and all. I made it up the stairs away from him and hid, listening to his banging and screaming through the floorboards. I knew he was rooting around down there, in search of hidden money, and before the door slammed shut he shouted that I better have the place cleaned before he came home.

There was blood on my knickers. I knew what it was, I wasn't a fool, but some part of me was not ready and I was in shock. It might have been better if I had had me mam, but I couldn't be sure. I'd tell her, I need those things, for down there, I'd point, and they would arrive in my room later, wordlessly, except the words to say nothing in front of your father. I washed the knickers in the sink, but they'd stained beyond. I binned them and stuffed a new pair with toilet tissue. I thought to have a bath, but the worry I'd continue to bleed and be surrounded by stained bath water was too much. I imagined myself on my knees later, scrubbing at it so he wouldn't see. I imagined the blood rushing down the drain. I imagined Mam's blood on the busy street, with people's feet crossing it as they stepped off the bus. I imagined her waking to that rough fool's face and thought how I shouldn't have listened to him. I should have gone myself, of course children are let into hospitals. Fool fool fool, me.

16

Dad came in late, wet boots scraping like breeze blocks over the lino. Under his arm, he carried a brown-paper bundle tied twice with twine, and dropped it at the base of the stairs where it sat taking a breath and crinkled. He walked past me then, up the stairs to the bed, stopped on the third step and turned with some small thought in his head as if he'd forgotten to turn off the gas or take the keys from the door.

'Your ma's gone.'

'Gone? Where?'

'Heaven, suppose, isn't that what they say?'

'Wha?'

'She's dead, Juno. Your mam is dead.'

17

I was alone in the shop, separated from John Jr by the glass counter. Outside was dark and I blinked under the glare of hard fluorescent. He had a wide grin, kept it on his face from the first.

'You were very, very rude the last time you were in,' he says. 'Very nasty mouth on you.'

'I'm sorry about that,' I say. And it galled me.

'I heard about your ma,' he says and he waited to see the effect. 'Little orphan now, aren't you? Little orphan Annie.'

'I have a da,' I tell him.

'Where is he? Why are you here and not him?'

'He doesn't know I'm here,' I say, and wished I hadn't. 'I want me mam's sewing machine back.'

'Do you now? I'd be delighted to see the back of it. Takes up more space than it's worth.' He went into the back room; I could hear the sound of scraping metal on metal shelves and he came carrying it out of the room, lumping it carelessly on the counter. When first I saw it, I bit down on the inside of my cheek, hard enough to taste blood, a bitter rusting taste. I saw how the machine was buckled at the base, where the fabric slips along before reaching the downward stroke of the needle. It had been flung with great force, across a room maybe, meeting a wall on the other side.

'There you are now, Annie.'

'You've smashed it.'

'I know, stupidest thing I've ever done. You upset me and when you left, I just threw it.' He leaned towards me as if in confidence and says, 'Destroying me own stock, imagine! I was doubly upset.' He laughed, showing off his small teeth, and a sour smell pushed past his mouth.

'Fifty pound, my love, and you can take it away.'

'What?'

'Sixty pound.'

'But you've banged it all up.'

'Seventy pound.' We're both silent then, and he gawked at me, that way.

'Do you want it?'

'Yes.'

'Do you want it?'

'I said I did.'

'I know you do, Annie, and I know you don't have seventy pounds. For God's sake, who has seventy pounds these days?' He walked casually, flipped up a wooden section cut into the counter, and pushed out a small door on a sprung hinge. He passed me and stood at the entrance. 'But look it, we'll not worry about that now. There's always another way, right?'

A plastic sign hung on a string in the centre of the door – it read Closed, and was framed by blue-and-red piping. He reached and flipped it. Open. He locked the door.

'C'mon.' His left arm was raised and without touching, he

guided me, gently, past the swingy door towards his tiny back room. At its crest I stopped, one step down to a stained concrete floor and shelf upon shelf filled with bric-a-brac, the objects people could just bear to part with. I felt slight pressure at the small of my back and stepped forward. I went to the farthest point of the room, finding only a corner, and turned. John Jr had stopped, two foot from where I stood, watching, his sharp eyes darting so quickly around me I couldn't keep up.

He was wearing tight jeans, the palest blue with a huge belt buckle. There were grimy dark stains at the mouth of each pocket. He rubbed his hands together, and blew air inside his joined fists.

'Now, let's see if we can get some value for money outta you, seventy pounds, the pressure.' He undid his belt and I could see on the large square buckle a cowboy astride a horse, and behind him the colour blue, for the sky. And with John Jr's belt open, it looked as if the world had tilted on its axis and the little cowboy would tip and fall from his horse. Both his jeans and his pants were drawn down to his knees: he moved towards me, hobbled and ludicrous. And I thought: he can't run now, and I looked around for anything to smash his head, enough times that he'd never recover. I even saw within arm's length a brass lampstand, free from bulb or shade. I took to laughing – even as I looked at it I knew I couldn't, that my body had calcified. My bones, my thickening blood and, just then, my heart, I felt, had stopped.

His prick fell to the side almost buried in its platter of dark curled hairs.

'Give that a good pull, there's a good girl.' He gripped my wrist, pulled it towards him, and the back of my hand knocked against it. 'Come on, girl, pull it.' But I wasn't following the commands fast enough for his liking; I couldn't keep up, couldn't hear. He called me names and boxed the side of my head, and so I did, I pulled at it and I thought, no, not just blue, what's that other name for blue? That sometimes blue of the sky. The back of my knee smarted from where he had kicked, putting me on my knees, and my hair was pulled so tightly that I wanted to cry out. I didn't cry out. But before I did what I knew he wanted me to do, I heard the door of the shop open, the bell sounded and a voice called into the back room.

'John? John, is that you in there?' John Jr froze with a look of panic and quickly zipped himself up, pulling at his jeans and buckling his big belt. He squeezed my mouth with his fingers until it hurt, and with a warning look, whispered, 'Not a fucking peep outta you.' He stepped away, and tucking in his shirt, he called out, 'Are you looking for me, Dad?'

I heard their voices from the shop. John Jr was telling him not to worry about something, he'd come along upstairs in a while. I imagined him manoeuvred out of the shop and how it would start again. I stood up and steadied myself, making my way slowly to the storeroom opening and looked into the shop. John Jr already had the door open and was ushering his father through it.

'Hello, Mr Simon,' I say. It was hardly a voice, more a whispered sound. He didn't hear or stop. 'Hello, Mr Simon,' I say again, and banged my hand on the glass counter as hard as I could. He stopped and turned. 'Who's that, John? You didn't say anyone was in.' I could feel John Jr look across in a silent rage.

'Juno, Mr Simon. Peggy's girl.'

'Peggy?' He came back into the room and slowly walked towards me. He went to press my hand but I quickly pulled away. 'Juno, I heard about your poor mother, I'm so very sorry.

Is everything alright, is there anything that we can help with?'
I reached across the counter and took hold of the sewing
machine with both hands, pulling it towards me, and closely
cradled it.

'I just came in to get this back.'

'Yes, yes, of course. Goodness, I know that machine very
well, as well as I knew your mother, I suppose. It's heavy, you'll
need help?' I edged out from behind the counter, slowly
towards the door.

'Let me give you a few bob for sweets, I've nothing, John,
give her a few bob, will you please.' I felt a tear drop to my face
and I'm sure if I wasn't clutching so tightly to the black steel of
the machine my fingertips would dance and dance and dance.

'I don't want anything from your son, Mr Simon. Nothing.'
Mr Simon looked at his son, I didn't. Not once did I look at
John Jr's face, not until his dad told him to open the door, and
only then, with my exit secure. I hated him and looked at him
with hate. I wanted him to know.

The walk home holding the sewing machine took an age, and
when I got inside and set it on the kitchen table, I dropped. It
was only later I saw in the mirror that I had a slight shiner and
the collar of my shirt was torn.

Mam called the mirror a glass, imagine. She must have heard
it somewhere and liked how it sounded. A glass. 'Juno, state of
you. Do you never look in the glass?'

'I do, after I've turned off the wireless. Jaysus, Ma, how old
are you?'

'What, what are you saying?'

'Nobody calls it a glass. It's been a mirror for a while. I think
Jesus was familiar with the term, Moses was, no, Adam and

Eve, particularly Eve, she was a demon for a glass, loved watching herself eat an apple.'

'What? What are you talking about? You're not too old for a puck.' If Mam saw my collar she'd think me awful and I was glad she'd gone.

18

The house was silent. Da wore his dark suit and in a plume of Brylcreem and Old Spice he left, gone all afternoon and evening and then it was late into the night and still not home. He was sure of free drink, today of all days: he'd probably passed out in a bush at some halfway point between the pub and home, perhaps dead, who knew. I cared so little.

I took hold of the package at the bottom of the stairs, where Da had dropped it. A paper pillow torn in places. I snipped the string: a satisfying snip. Mam's brass scissors, so sharp, and heavy and cold in my hands. I cut the brown paper too. Folded inside was my confirmation dress, her wedding gown – mostly intact, it had ripped and grazed in places. There was some gravel and a few loose pebbles embedded. I kept one, put it in my pocket and for years would transfer it whenever I changed my clothes. I don't know where it is now, lost.

I spread the long dress out across the table and it seemed to glow under the kitchen light. Not exactly white, but some other white – ivory maybe? I approached it slowly, unsure. The first cut into the satin felt brutal and frightened me. I cut the wounds from the fabric, the torn and frayed threads, avoiding the Carrickmacross lace, pleased it was saved. The dress needed to be shortened by the thickness of three fingers: Mam taller than me by half a head. I took after my father's side, runts. She had pinned it and folded and marked with chalk, leaving me a map, signposts: no, not that way, Juno, go this way.

I'd gone into Mangers' shop and stood with my hand across a wheel of dark silk. Mr Redmond had come to my side and said he'd remember Mam fondly. He had briefly clasped the tips of my fingers, soft tailor's hands, and said he was very sorry. He asked if I needed some of that material. 'Yes,' I say, but I thought it would be too expensive. He cut more than a yard of it and said it would make a fine slip. No charge.

'She stood where you're standing now, and we'd always talk.' He was cutting absent-mindedly. 'She could say if a swatch of linen was from England or France, just by sight. In a different world she might have done anything,' he says, and then laughed at himself when he saw I didn't understand.

The sewing machine was unyielding. I tried without any real success to straighten the base, plugged it in and turned on the task light. I rested my foot on the pedal, and put my hands on the limb of the machine. Even with its banjaxed base all crooked and bowed, it sparked up, still lively, that whirling sound. I knew what to do, but I couldn't, not like her. I took it slow, did my best for hours bent over that table of hers, my back aching until it was done.

I filled the sink with dye, and folded the white dress carefully into the dark water, steeped it for hours. The fabric clasped upon the dye and it held well enough – when I pulled it free, it was transformed. The water dripped onto my bare feet, staining my toes as I hung it on the line and the wind kicked and punched, but it wouldn't dry. I went back out to the line every few minutes and felt it again, squeezing the fabric in the pink of my hand till drops of water emerged. Finally, I attached the dress to a hanger and strung it above the hot oven, leaving the door open so the warm air would flow out beneath the hanging dress. It seemed to sway as if to music, one of the old songs; its final memory of a first dance.

The hearse would arrive at ten, then the procession would move past our house, around the estate and on to the church road. Da had not returned as I struggled to move the zip up my back. I watched myself in the mirror in a stupor. The dress hung in places it should not; in others the still-damp fabric clung too tight. The dye came from the dress onto my skin, marking it. I made tea, and sat and smoked, defeated and already mortified.

Near ten, there was a firm knock at the door, and although I knew what was coming, the sight of the black suits and the shining hearse beyond and the bowed heads of neighbours shocked me.

'Me da's not here yet,' is what I say. The funeral director peered down at his watch, perturbed, but looked then – the shock of my face. Pitied me.

'I'm sure we can spare a few minutes.' I closed the door over and didn't know where to put myself.

The day before, when the funeral director had been round, he had sat at the table across from Dad, moving a cereal box and milk aside for a better view. I'd been cleared off upstairs so the men could talk, but I didn't clear off. I sat on the top of the stairs, bent forward and listening.

'There are a couple of final questions, small last details, very quickly,' he says to Dad. 'Did your wife have a favourite flower?'

'You mean ones she liked?' asked Da, and I could feel my

eyes roll. 'Well,' he says, 'she wasn't really a big flower type of a person.'

'Lilies,' I shout down. 'But only white.' There was silence in the kitchen then.

'Will we say white lilies then?' he asked Da, eventually.

'Yeah, yeah. That will be grand . . . Are they expensive? The white ones?'

'No more than any other colour.' Upon Mam's death, a cheque was drafted from Royal Liver Life Insurance and sent, to Da's dismay, directly to the funeral home. Mam had diligently maintained the tiniest of weekly payments, all the women in our area had, and Da hoped for change.

'Music – unless you want additional players, flute or string – we suggest using the church's organ. We have a player that is excellent.'

'Grand, that's grand.'

'Is there a particular hymn that Peggy or the family liked?'

'Well, best leave it to herself, sure she's the one that'll be playing it.'

'Very good.'

'"Ave Maria",' I shout again. Silence.

'"Ave Maria"?' says the director.

'Well, sure if, eh? Yeah.' Da was boiling, I could feel it and was delighted. When the director left, he had screamed up the stairs and I scattered. He'd put on his coat and I heard the door bang shut. Through the upstairs window I could see he'd caught up to the director and had hold of his arm, Dad's head tilted forward, talking directly into the director's ear as if it were a microphone.

The door was knocked again.

'We must proceed, even without your father in attendance.

The church is booked and the priest will not thank you for keeping him waiting.'

I looked over his shoulder at the gathering onlookers and I found I couldn't go out at all. I started to pull at my dress, losing confidence in my work, although I'd followed Mam's instructions exactly.

'Juno,' he says, 'your mother would be very proud.' He knew my name; he'd taken time to learn it and say it to me in case I'd forgot myself completely. He held out his elbow, teapot fashion, and I threaded my arm through, as if gaining some piecemeal of propriety. He helped me off the step, past my little pile of butt ends and down the garden path towards the waiting car. I held tight, not wanting him to let go of me. I saw no one. I never took my eyes off the wet ground, but just before he opened the car door and I folded inside, a white hand appeared in front of my face, clutching a tiny bouquet of daisies, their green stalks drawn together with fine white thread. I took hold of them and Legs stood before me. I threw my arms around him and he held me for a long time, there, right in front of everybody, he just held me. The director's arm came across my shoulder, tugging gently until we sundered.

I was manoeuvred into the car and before closing the door the director put his head through the opening and said, 'On the other side, you just wait in the car. I'll come get you, OK?'

The inside of the car was enormous – it took a moment to realise there was a driver, sitting in the front of the car, face forward, his hands lightly touching the wheel. There was a second row of seats, empty as Tuesday night's last bus. We pulled forward slowly, smoothly, as if the tyres were weightless against the road. I looked up for the first time: Missus G, Missus B and dear old Missus C, cane in hand, head bowed.

The car lurched to a sudden halt. There was a commotion further along, someone was shouting and moving towards the car.

'Is that your dad?' asked the driver, raising his voice to be heard.

'Yeah, that's him.'

He was beside me, breathless. His shirt-tails out over his pants, stained, tieless.

'I can't believe youse were going without me, Juno. It's my wife we're burying, don't you forget. Might be your ma, but it's my wife.'

'Tuck in your shirt,' I say, 'and button that top button.'

The smell of drink seeped from him, catching at my nose and making me gag.

'I won't be dictated to by you or anyone else ... It's ... it's ... it's the significance of the day, nobody else seems to grasp.' He tucked his shirt and buttoned his collar.

We took a first turn as the long car glided out of the estate. From the back seat all the way through the front glass, I could see the hearse in front. And for the first time, the yellow of the stiff pine.

'Oh fuck,' I say, 'I can't breathe.' Something had hold of me, a strangling hold on my breath, and I was suffocating. I doubled over in the seat trying to pull at the air.

He started to pat at my back. 'You're alright, your dad's here.'

'Get off, get fucking away from me,' I say.

'Suit yourself,' he says and began to sulk. 'Am I alright for a smoke back here?' He shouted all the way to the driver. He didn't respond. 'Just the nerves have bate back here, you know?' The driver was looking in the rear-view mirror. 'No, you can't.' Da pretended he couldn't hear, turned to me. 'Who's your man with the hat think he is? Wha? Postman with a driver's licence. We're paying him, you know, not the other way round.'

And so we went, what a pair, like loose change rattling around in the back of the big car. A pocket full of sixpence, we all fall down.

We came to a final halt outside the church. Da, gasping for a smoke, sprung from the car.

'What are you waiting for? C'mon,' he says. And slammed the door shut. I looked neither left nor right. I waited and finally heard the latch on my door give. The director had remembered me. He reached inside the car and took my hand. When I was standing, he said, 'That's the girl. You just keep your head up. Make your mother proud. Watch these steps here.' He'd made me cry, but I did as I was told. Even when climbing the steps and even when I saw Sister's lifeless face and the sea of children lined behind her. He led me into the empty church and set me down in the front row. 'Here's what's going to happen: they'll bring your mam's coffin through and then everyone will come in behind it and sit. And then the mass will start and you just sit there and think of the nice memories you have of her. Yes?'

'Yes.'

'I'll come back for you when it's over.'

The organ started. The clean and beautiful refrain churned. It was awful, grinding. I turned to see Mam's coffin rolled up the aisle. Four men, strangers in black, each had a hand in navigating. Da followed slowly behind. The rest spilled in behind and when scattered throughout the church the congregation seemed meagre. I felt crushed under the scrutiny – the sideways glances and the whispers. The coffin passed, naked as a winter garden. Just four resting palms, and once set in place, removed. When Da sat in beside me I looked at him and tried to think of the cruellest word I knew and found I had to make do with bastard.

Bastard for a white lily, bastard.

Bastard.

Bastard.

Father began. He raised his arms, as if himself crucified. 'Let us pray.' And everybody stood. I didn't stand. I wouldn't stand or kneel or pray, this God, this God reduced to the size of their meanness would not hear from me, ever, and I hoped that Sister was watching. That I caused her eyes to pop and knees weaken. Father says Mam's name, Margaret. That was what he said. Margaret? Margaret to Maura to Meg. Meg to Peg to Peggy. I sat on the hard seats, in the frozen church, and listened and he went on as if he knew her, but he didn't know and left everything out.

I wanted to scream.

'Me and my Peggy met on the shores of the Shannon. A little look across and I saw her and she saw me, we were very shy back then, but still that day our lives changed forever and for the better, the only time in my life, I was looking the right way . . .' That's how he began, Dad. And I felt the congregation swoon a bit, and I had to wonder was he making it up as he went along or had he actually prepared? 'It wasn't yesterday, or the day before, but here in this church, this house of God, we took simple vows and we kept to them, in sickness and in health. You might say we were lovebirds, me and Peg. Sorry, Father. A man couldn't hope for a better wife and I think, in my own way, I did her proud. She could cook and mend too. And together we reared a family. I was with her at the beginning, and at the very end. I was with her when she drifted, as in a dream, she held my hand and I said, "Peggy, keep the door open a little, I'll get our Juno raised and I'll be along." She smiled, she says, "I know you will, I know." She'll be missed, by me for one.' He paused there and bowed his head. 'So eh ... there'll be drink and sandwiches and that up at Smites after. All are welcome.'

I wanted to scream.

I don't remember the director's face. If I'd met him the next day, I'd have passed him like a stranger. I know he wore a small band on his wedding finger and a gold signet on his pinkie, sitting just off to the side. The sleeve of his dark overcoat was fine wool, softer than any I'd felt before. Crisp white shirt-sleeves, poking out in penguin fashion, bound by dark polished cufflinks.

He led me slowly back down the aisle, in step with the coffin, but I dropped his hand without a thought for him after I looked up and saw Derry standing there, watching me, her hands curled around the handle of a baby's buggy. I ran, pushing through mourners, shoving through their slow-moving shoulders and hips until I was close enough to see her face more clearly. But in that face of hers, there was no Derry. It was as though she'd been scrubbed clean of us and was now watching the approach of a chair or a teacup. I stopped short, all that momentum crushing into me.

'You came,' I say.

'I'm here so I must have.'

She smiled tightly and was distracted by the child. She had popped its dummy into her own mouth unconsciously and then pushed it back into the child's. The collar of her anorak was frayed and she seemed frozen.

'Look, it's Mam's dress,' I say, 'her wedding dress, I dyed it.'

'Yeah, I can see that, Juno, I know what it is.'

'Did you want it? Sorry, of course you should have it and I've gone and ruined it.'

'I don't want it.'

She looked at me, looked past me, she even looked up into the rafters – I was too much for her, I could tell. I tried to see her, past the new mask of her face. I could see only glimpses of Derry, as if a face could be buried underneath another face and I had to hold my memory in front of her to see. She looked like she was the other side of tired. Old maybe. Is twenty-six old? Her hair was bleached, with inches of dark roots, making her skin more pale, and even the freckles that dotted her cheeks had now spread and covered her face with dark brown marks. She had applied a run of lipstick, uneven dabs stuck in the corner of her mouth, thick and coagulated.

'You're growing up, aren't ya, kiddo?' And she reached her hand as if to touch my face, but didn't quite, and stroked the air before me. A million rings on her fingers, shining.

'Suppose . . .' I say, embarrassed then.

'That da of yours can make a speech. Can really paint a picture with words, wha?' She looked away, remembering the child. 'I better be getting along. He'll need a feed,' she says.

'Don't,' I say. 'Come in the car with us. It's huge,' I say. 'It has leather seats and all. You can fit the buggy. You could fit your house.'

'Nah,' she says, 'I'm not going up to the grave. I've seen enough.'

'I'll come with you then.'

'What?'

'I'll help you, feed the baby and all.'

'You're alright, pet, I'll see you.' And her knuckles whitened as she began to move the buggy on. I grabbed her arm, stopped her.

'When? When will I see you?'

'I can't now, pet. Not now, I can't . . .' And she looked at me.

'C'mere to me.' And I folded into her arms and I started to bawl. 'Please don't leave me, not with him, please – I'll do whatever you say.'

'You're alright, you're alright. Look it, go on, go and bury your mam and be strong.'

'She's your mam too,' I say. She pulled back and untangled us.

'Yeah, me mam alright . . . I'll see you.'

She pushed the baby, disappearing into the last of the crowd. Later I told myself it was because of the child and how I'd never said anything nice or made a fuss.

At the graveside, it rained. We stood in a circle and I refused to throw my handful of wet muck.

19

I didn't go to school. Without Mam, there was no one to make me. The habit had been broken and the thought of returning filled me with panic. I stayed in my room mostly and time passed without order. Without Mam's intention, the house sat idle, drifting, time only punctuated now and then by him rattling up the steps or a mug falling from his loose hand and crashing to the floor downstairs. We spoke little, him and me – we had gone to our separate parts of the house, but I don't remember him being there much. The house was quiet beyond quiet. A fat and thickening silence settled over the curtains, between the plates and over the sewing machine. It left the horoscopes uncut, and the kettle unfilled. It dripped from the draining board, the chairs and unset table. At times I'd pause while dressing, thinking I'd heard Mam's footfalls downstairs.

Legs knocked our door every day, once on the way to and once on the way from school. I didn't answer. I didn't know how to see him and every day after his second knock, a small drawing was dropped through our letter box. Poppies, always poppies.

Word had spread to the library, and although she never mentioned Mam, at the counter Missus H changed her way with me. She looked at me with great sympathy and no longer said what a great girl I was reading all these books. Something was expected of me, a new way of being, mournful maybe. I didn't understand and became quiet.

I'd stay late at the library, sat at the table near the window. For the first time reading had become difficult, still I found I could contentedly look out the window at the impossibly narrow branches of swaying saplings filled with colour and caught in the wind. Missus H would circle past and, as if casually, drop a book on the table. *Charming Tales for Girls*, or some such. 'Come on, Missus H. Who are you trying to fool?'

I'd taken some needles and brightly coloured thread from Ma's drawer at home, and would spend hours embroidering loose swathes of material, raw linens or muslin, sometimes a nice bit of lace with a spray of loose thread at their edges. It was crude, my needlework, inexperienced and halting stitches, but later became unhurried. I didn't know how Missus H felt about this break from reading, she never said, not even when she would put an occasional sandwich in front of me, saying, 'Would you ever eat that, it was left over and I hate to see it go to waste.'

By late afternoon, when the windows had blackened, I'd help Missus H tidy up, collecting stray books and putting chairs under tables.

'Safe home now, Juno,' she'd say when I was on the way out the door. 'Safe home.' And I could feel her eyes on my back.

The walk then, through a thin blanket of dusk; blurring mirrors of street light pooled at my feet, past all the brightly lit rooms, before the curtains were closed and their play began. Walking over the lumpy green, my house lay dim beyond. Letters from the State scraped across the lino when I pushed the front door. 'Come back to school,' they insisted.

Sunday morning, and I watched out my bedroom window, drawn to it by the ringing of church bells. A father and mother walked along the path, pulling a girl my own age behind them like a string of laughter. Her full-sleeved dress, the shaping of the bodice loose and drawn to her waist by a simple belt, finished with a ruffle trim. It bounced carelessly as she danced up the road; her alabaster shoes gleamed.

Soon the street was alive with them: short balloon sleeves and high necks. Pale pinks and mauve, chiffon and velvet. More emerged from behind closed doors, their parents in Sunday's bright best, conveyed towards the crisp sound of the bells.

There was a knock on the door downstairs, lightly first and then insisting. I moved to the landing and watched down the stairs and waited. I went cautiously down and stood to the side of the door. The letter box was pushed open and pink fingertips could be seen.

'Juno,' came a voice. 'Juno.' I opened the door finally and Legs was there, a little man suit, three-piece, three buttons, brown and falling like boiled bacon, loose off his shoulder.

'Well, look at you,' I say.

'Well, look at me.' He walked inside and twirled a few times, delighted. If he'd noticed the dreariness of the place it never showed.

'It's today?' I say.

'It's today.' He took a silk hanky from his pocket, an aqua blue that shimmered in his hand. He pressed it between his fingers and roughly folded it to a triangle shape.

'If I wear this in my pocket here, will I get beaten up?'

'You will, but look it, you're used to that.' He stuffed it into his breast pocket.

'What have you done? Jesus God, the way you have it.' I

took it back out and there was quiet between us as I refolded it and carefully tucked it back inside with its silk tongue protruding just right and stood to attention.

'They used to call it your ticket pocket, for going to the theatre and all. Was it your dad's?'

'It was, yeah.'

'It's good, with the brown.'

'It is, isn't it?'

'Yeah.'

'Come on, you ready?'

'Ready?'

'For the confirmation.'

'No.'

'Come on, I just ditched me ma for you. I'm not getting murdered for nothing.'

'Are you joking?'

'No, I came to fetch you.'

'I'm not going.'

He went and sat down on the couch, settled in, content to wait. I heard myself laugh, nervously.

'I'm not going,' I say. He looked at me then, stern.

'Do you think I'm joking – you're not making your confirmation?'

'I don't want to.'

'So what?'

'So why would I if I don't want to?'

'Cos you're not scared of them.' When he said it, I felt my eyes smart.

'I am. I am scared of them.'

'You'll be with me.'

'I can't, Legs, I can't.' My face hot and flushed and I took to sobbing and felt ridiculous, running up the stairs, shouting, 'I'm not going.'

And in my bedroom, I heard, 'I'll wait for you here, so.'

I looked at the black dress, but couldn't bring myself to put it on, though it was what Mam had wanted. It had been beautiful, and I had destroyed it. I had only one other dress, too small by years. It was a colour that faded, no longer that fresh pink – time had made it neither that colour nor another. The dress had meant something to my mam, something she hoped I'd be but I wasn't. I pulled it on. It was tight.

When I came back downstairs wearing it, Legs stood silently and watched me.

'You look . . . magic,' he says.

'Go wan and shite.' My face was burning. 'This is mad,' I say.

'A bit, yeah.'

The dress was riding up as I moved; I pulled at it every few steps. 'Fuck, me shoes.' I found them by the door where I'd last flung them. Dark flat sandals, scuffed at the front.

'You'll stay with me?'

'I will.'

'Will you do me zip?' I turned around and felt his fingers search out the zip, and the cold of his skin, a knuckle maybe, brushed between the blades of my shoulders. When I turned, I didn't meet his eye.

'I got you something,' he said, and reached inside his pocket. A black satin ribbon. He pinned it to the sleeve of my dress, saying, 'Cos you're in mourning and that.' And it poured down my arm.

Before we opened the door, I thought to bring him to my room and show him, floor to ceiling, his beautiful poppies so that he would know what they meant. But I'd grown shy by then and never did. We stepped from the dim of the kitchen outside into the sudden daylight. Legs pulled me forward and we flowed along, like a minor estuary heading out to sea, in step with the others. They gawked; they twisted themselves stupid to look. Then one would tap the other closest, point, and they would have a go at looking and turn back to the first and then the laughter would start.

'Fuck them,' I say to Legs, 'just fuck them.' We passed one family, their heads craning – I say, 'Do you want me autograph?' And Legs even spat on the path, one of his useless spits, but still the effort was made, catching in the wind and some landing on my dress.

'For fuck's sake, Legs, me good dress.'

We'd forgotten ourselves entirely. We'd forgotten his ma. We'd forgotten Sister and Father. The cruel looks from neighbours and God. It was only when we turned a corner and the church's great spire could be seen that I felt Legs hesitate and his body stiffen beside mine. Then it all came tumbling back.

'Oh fuck, fuck, fuck,' I say, and I froze. 'I can't do it, Legs, I can't.'

'You'll be grand,' he says, but he'd faltered himself and I didn't believe him any more.

'I fucking can't.'

'Come on.'

He took hold of my hand and I was pulled to a gravel pathway left of the church. It was soft at my feet, still damp, and a pale sandy mud covered our shoes. I pressed my back into the side of the church, and could feel a chill off the stone. There were long grasses running to the side of the wall; I remembered running through them in late summer. I must have been small: the grasses ran waist-high, until I returned one morning to find them cut and stacked and the fresh shorn bristle darkening. The ornate edifice at the front of the church did not extend to that side of the building – the stonework was plain and unremarkable and the colours of the stained glass could not be seen from outside.

I rolled a smoke and saw how my fingers trembled and without thinking I offered him one. He shook his head and stood off to the side, suddenly remote.

'You don't know what to do with me now, do you? You're starting to regret it, coming and getting me and all.'

'No,' he says, and I pulled hard on my smoke and felt the first drop of rain.

'Is your ma going to reef you when we go in?'

'Probably.'

'It'll be worse when you go home?'

The sky had blackened, and the rain started down, heavy. His head tilted up, watching the sky, and big droplets fell onto his face. My smoke had become sodden then, so I flicked it off the building.

'It's just how are you going to stay with me when you're off having your ma bate lumps outta you?'

'I don't know,' he says. His suit was darkening from the rain and his pocket square was being battered limp.

'Oh, Legs,' I say, 'your good suit. Quick.' We took off again, along the side of the church.

'My world, my world,' I cry.

'Melting, melting!' says Legs, and we laughed again, running through the full car park where the last of the stragglers could be seen, collapsing their umbrellas and disappearing inside. By the time Legs and I came to the steps, we were drowned, rain-drenched faces and my hair stuck to my cheeks like wet straw.

We stood breathless in the vestibule and I held my arms out away from my dress, sodden.

The tall double doors were open and the organ music spilled around us. We shook like old dogs, producing puddles at our feet. The music paused as the bishop stepped onto the altar, flanked by several altar boys with raised burning candles. He was visible from his shoulders. I could just make out his damask choir cassock, and how his neck flowed into his assured chin. His mitre, bejewelled in the sign of the cross, gave shape to an otherwise very round head. The congregation rose and the organ started up again.

I saw Father moving swiftly past the Stations of the Cross, his head down, determined. Legs hadn't seen yet and was searching in a frightened way for his ma. Father appeared before us and set about closing the giant doors; he really had to push and gave an audible groan. When the doors were closed, his faced burned with effort and fury.

'What do you two think you're playing at?' he says. Legs and I were dumbstruck. Father's gold vestments fluttering like magnificent wings, laden with shining hand-stitched thread, a gleaming chest-plate of armour, the Eucharist and a lamb.

'Do you think you are coming in here dressed like that? Do you think that I'd ever allow you to bow before the bishop dressed like that?'

I saw how it was that he looked at me and felt how my wet dress rode high up my legs and it clung tightly to my backside and I filled with shame.

'Seán,' came a voice, a sharp whisper. I saw his ma had come by way of a small side door. Like Legs, she was tall, a tightly bound, ferocious lank. She stood, her still-dripping rain mac and a mute-coloured dress showing in a straight line at her front. She must have stood outside in the rain fretting over Legs, and I felt for her. I felt the worry of all mams' waiting.

'I'm so sorry, Father, I'm so sorry,' she says. And stepped towards Legs, an arm raised as she calmed him. 'With your permission, Father, I'll take him inside now.'

'Do you see the concern you are causing your mother? The trouble?'

Legs looked away from Father.

'Yes, Father.'

'Do you think your actions have no effect, no consequence?'

'No, Father.'

'Bring him inside, Mrs McGuire. We'll talk after.'

His ma pulled him towards the side door, but he resisted and wouldn't let himself be drawn.

'Seán, now,' she says, 'this instant.'

'What about Juno? Can't she come with us?'

'She cannot,' says his mother, pulling at him then. 'Now, I won't tell you again.'

'She can't be left. It's not fair.'

'It's OK, Legs, go on with your mam.'

He was relieved, I was sure. He allowed himself to be taken away through the small doorway, dipping down to pass under. Passing through the eye of a needle, I thought, isn't that it? The choir began and could be heard though the opening, a drift of voices inside rising up.

I was an affront to Father: he hated me, a real hate. He made me stand, a shield from the cold wind that whipped in through the vestibule. I had no words for Father, and though my eyes stayed planted on his face, I'd stopped watching him.

'Who do you think you are?'

'No one, Father.'

'No one is right. Did you think you'd get the best of me?'

'No, Father.'

'No. Now, where is your father?'

'Don't know.'

'You don't know. Well, aren't you a fine lot, with your mother just resting in the earth and her soul in purgatory, awaiting God's judgement. Running around here dressed like a banshee. Are you not ashamed of yourself?'

'Yes, Father.' I was desolate with an unknown feeling, my voice a stranger and my teeth all a-clatter.

'Please, can I go home now, Father?'

'You'll go when I say you can go. You tell your father that he's to come and see me or I'll come find him. And, Juno, Monday morning, if I don't see you in school I'll be up to your house. Now get out of my sight.'

I turned slowly and looked out. A single magpie pecked silently in the grasses beyond the tarred road. Mam would be furious at that: she'd stand out like a looper, waiting for the bird to be joined by a second or, at worst, a third. 'Have you no one belongs to you?' she'd call to the bird. 'A single magpie, Juno, nothing but sorrow, and we've enough of that, thank you very much.'

20

The one day I didn't want him up, he was up and around. Da.
Jesus God, I thought when I saw him in his undershirt, his
trousers hanging, standing in the kitchen. I stayed out of
his way hoping he'd go back to bed, but he didn't. He clattered
around the place and then stood watching me stuff jotters and
books in my school bag. He had not heard when I'd first come
down the stairs, barefooted and silent, but I'd heard him.
Crying. A childish sob he was trying to swallow up; it made his
breath sharp and he gulped at the air, drowning. I froze on the
landing and watched around for where to put myself and then
tiptoed back to my room to recover. I took a moment, and
then started a racket, both in my bedroom and back down the
stairs.

'I want to get in there and make a cup of tea,' I say.

'Who's stopping you?' He didn't move and he knew well
only one at a time could fit in the alcove kitchen without
knocking into each other.

'Well, will you move then? I want to get in.'

'Where's your mother's reading glasses? I have my own
broken.'

'They're not in the kitchen.' I tried to get past but he stood in my way. 'Try one of the drawers in the cabinet.'

He moved as far as the couch, where he bent himself L-shaped with a groan and stared at me.

'They're not on the couch either. Do you want me to find them?'

'If it wouldn't kill you.'

'Would it kill you to ask?' I rooted through the drawers in the sitting room and quickly found the glasses. I kept them in my hand longer than I intended, rubbed my thumb back and forth, not a caress, not in front of him, never. I held them to my eyes for a quick moment, as if I could see what she saw, as if I wanted that, as if. The glasses needed a good clean – no wonder she went around half blind. They were red, Mam's glasses. And they made her look elegant almost. The way they framed her face made her seem worldly, as if the life she had was a different life and with customers, the posh ones, I was less ashamed of us.

'What are you in such a fuss about this morning?' he says after I've handed them over and he had them sitting low on his nose.

'School, Da, I'm going to school.'

'Aren't you very clever. The mourning period has ended so?' I walked back to the cabinet and picked up a stack of let-ters and handed them to him. He wouldn't take them in his hand, instead he peered down at them over the rim of the glasses. I dropped them on the arm of the chair.

'That's why I'm going to school, cos the Guards will be around if I don't. And it won't be me they're after.'

'Wouldn't be the first time you've had them calling.'

'And Father is looking for you.'

'Father? What's he want?'

'He wants to shake your hand and tell you what a marvel you are. Probably give you a prize.'

'Watch it now.'

'Same as the letters, he wants to know why I'm not in school. Tell you what an abomination I am.'

'Doesn't need tell me. I know all about it.'

While the kettle slowly boiled, I went in search of pens and stuck them in the front pouch of my school bag. My bag was an alien to me, a child's possession. I took my tea and when I passed him, he says, 'Maybe you can get through the day without causing havoc.'

'Poor thing,' I say, 'you're lost with no one to fight with.'

'You'll get a good puck, without your mother to cry to.'

I opened and closed the door behind me, then settled on the step and sipped my tea. The morning was wet and unexceptional. Some teenagers ran past, shouting. And I could hear him, inside. Fool.

I saw the top of Legs' head bobbing up and down as he walked slowly on the other side of a hedge. He hadn't seen me yet; his head filled with serious thoughts. He stopped at my gate and looked at me, and smiled with all of that feeling he tried to hide still planted on his face.

'I was coming to get you.' He opened the gate, and came through and sat next to me and says nothing, then reached for my cigarette and took a long draw.

'Well, look at you, smoky McLegs, a fish to water.' He was an awkward smoker. 'Jaysus, I hope your mam doesn't see you, big penalties for sitting next to me.' I looked at him and thought how I was always looking at the side of his head, only ever at one side. 'The confirmation was a howl, wasn't it? I suppose you and your ma had a great day after?'

'Yeah, great.' He opened his bag and reached in and showed me a yellow bottle of lighter fluid.

'What's that for?'

'For Father's rulers.'

'Yeah,' I say and I heard myself laugh with meanness. 'I don't care about them, Legs. I don't.'

'Yeah, but just to show him he can't do whatever he wants to us.'

'Yeah, he can. He can do exactly that, whatever he wants. Is your ma going to stop him? Is my ma? Fuck's sake, Legs.'

'I was doing it for you.'

'Were you? Thanks. Will you please not do anything for me? Like, don't lose bus tickets and make me late home for me ma, and please, don't be bringing me to a confirmation so I can be made look like more of a fucking eejit. You want to burn something? Fucking burn him.'

He put the bottle back into his bag and slowly zipped it. I wanted to say sorry; I didn't.

'They're sending me to Belfast.'

'To that school?'

'Yeah.'

I closed my eyes and gathered my breath and slowly allowed it to leave my body. The world gone dark and I felt nothing.

'Course they fucking are.'

I couldn't ask him more about it and he didn't offer. I stood up and began the walk to school, with him trailing behind, his bag slung loose over his shoulder.

We stood in the yard in silence. I was early for once and the other children stopped their games and watched, mouths hung, the younger ones fidgeting. In class, if Sister was surprised at seeing me, she well camouflaged it. Legs and I sat together until Sister saw and swept us to the far corners of the room, but Legs held my gaze like before, and in spite of myself, I felt the start of a smile before sitting. Poor Aisling O'Neil was not happy about being put next to me and pointedly sniffed the air and folded her legs, looking into the classroom as if for help. Later, when I sneezed, I aimed at the side of her head, blowing her long conditioned hair like feathers.

Sister told us about Zacchaeus climbing the sycamore tree so he could better see Jesus. She turned to the blackboard and began to write, the chalk firmly pressed and white dust cascading in the air and down her wrist. She turned back and asked questions of the class, slowly cutting her way through the arms that bobbed and swayed tall as sunflowers.

She drew a long line, a stem, fanning out into the five fingers of a sycamore leaf. Her drawing was perfect, but when I thought about Legs' poppies, weightless to the page, the way you could be confused into thinking they needed for water and maybe light, suddenly Sister's sycamore leaf became a prisoner of the blackboard, and when I looked at it all I could see was its wish to be outside. How I'd loved it when Sister told us stories. How I'd have listened to her voice for days. But not now. I saw everything, and it was ludicrous, everything, right down to the rustling folds of Sister's long gown and her dancer's quick tapping steps.

At eleven, Sister made us pray. There was a rattle of chairs as we stood out of our seats and found places to kneel. She told us to give thanks for our parents and priests and teachers who watched over and protected us. My bare knees were chilled and pressed to the floor, the paltry shape of kneeling, even with our hands flat together and pointed like a cathedral. She demanded we shut our eyes. But I didn't shut my eyes: I watched as Sister led prayers and paced back and forth, with the secret thoughts of someone left alone. The children prayed, but not me, I didn't pray. I found I no longer wanted to be knelt down. I found I no longer wanted to pray for our parents and teachers and priests. And as the children said 'Hallowed be thy name ...' I unfolded my hands and stood.

'Juno,' says Sister, 'kneel down at once.' I stood and watched her. 'Juno,' she says, again, 'this instant, or straight up to Father's office.'

'No,' I say.

'No?'

'I'm not praying any more.'

My cheek burned after that. Sister, having struck me, stepped back as if to watch its effect. One or two of the children continued with prayer, but an increasing silence took hold, their eyes popped open and they looked on, frightened I'm sure. Sister was livid, her face flushed hot with anger, her arms raised again, not to hit me but in an attempt to push me back towards the floor, she was pressing on my shoulder. She soon gave up and changed tack, pushing me then towards the door: 'Get out! Get out! Up to Father's office right this instant.' But there was no need for that. Father, either stirred by the commotion or happenstance, stood in the doorway.

'That's alright, Sister, I'll see to this.'

And he stepped inside the room bringing with him that dark air that seemed to travel with his garb; that tight air of a small and hateful God.

'I'm sorry, Father, but this child is refusing to say her prayers.'

'I see,' says Father. He looked at me almost kindly, but not so kindly as his dog. 'We must make allowances – after all, this child has been through a great deal, have you not, Juno?' His honeyed voice strummed lightly, as if from a well-crafted and ancient instrument. I wasn't fooled, I knew what kind voices were used for. I knew all the meanness in all the world begins with a kind voice.

'Pack up your things now and come along to the office, everything will be sorted there.' I bent, reaching past Aisling O'Neil, and lifted up my bag from where it was heaped on the floor. I was about to leave when I saw how Legs had moved to his feet and positioned himself between Father and me, his own bag low on his shoulder. His face was pale and I was reminded how it was for me a face I could happily watch and for a long time. Forever, maybe. Not from the side, but like this, just in front of me. Legs' face, that normally held so much worry, seemed at that moment only calm and sure, and I thought he even gave the smallest smile, as if he'd remembered something he liked, a favourite memory or that. And then he turned and walked past Father and out of the room.

Father looked shocked and, for the first time, unsure. He had to pause to think. He'd lost interest in me entirely; it seemed Legs was the bigger prize. He went out the door and turned in the direction Legs had gone and followed after him. His quickening footsteps across the hard floor could be heard from the classroom. Sister walked into the corridor and watched after them, then quickly came back and directed the children to retake their seats. The children, as if wakening up, moved slowly and no one spoke. Their eyes on Sister in case of further instruction.

'Juno, you too. Sit.' I sat.

I saw how I was not without feeling then, as the clock turned and my body tightened. It was then we were forever bonded, Sister and me, the moment we heard that howl. An animal sound. It was me she looked at, and I at her. Sister was afraid – I looked to her for help, but she was afraid. Another howl, terrible and agonised as the first. I bounded from behind my desk, with Sister making chase. We were out in the corridor together. A bright flare came charging into view, lighting up the whole corridor. It came towards us fast, arms outstretched, wayward. Flames fed from its left side, boots to bonnet, brilliant licks of amber, red and blue, sailing high above as it cried out. Then I saw how it was Father's polished shoes, reflecting every gorgeous colour there at the centre of the fire.

Screaming, screaming, screaming.

A moment later, Legs came running, rounded the corner and leapt, knocking Father to the floor, their bodies convulsed together. I went towards Legs to save Father from his endless crashing blows, but as I neared I saw it was Legs stamping out the flames, his own skin and cloth raked black.

Father lay on his back. He'd stopped moving and Legs, sitting astride, nearly so. His face downcast, exhausted. The corridor was drenched in smoke and the flames around Father reduced to a smoulder. Sister moved to his side and knelt. She began to pray.

She believed. Sister really believed.

I think she cried.

Children spilled out into the corridor and they began to spin around and panic and scream. A teacher must have called for an ambulance because I could hear its ding-a-ling as it came in the distance.

The skin on Father's left hand and face no longer looked like skin. The heat had so affected the area that the white of a molar could be viewed through his cheek. I put my hand to Legs' face and said his name once.

I dipped towards him, my hand firmly on his shoulder. 'Legs,' I say.

His head turned towards me, there but not there.

Sister was shouting: 'It's him, over here, it's him that has done it.' She kept saying it. Bright light appeared through the smoke, torch beams fouetté across the ceiling. Huge uniformed men appeared and Legs was pulled like a rag doll clear from Father.

In the chaos, I chased after Legs. I called his name and pulled at his limbs, but I was pushed back again and again. I watched as policemen took possession of him and pulled him to his feet. His head fell forward and his arms were pulled back and handcuffed. He was away then, in rhythm with the polished jackboots.

The ambulance men worked hard, attending to Father. I hoped for his death, a slow one, please, and turned my back and walked away. But he wouldn't die, Father, he'd spend his life convalescing out of sight.

21

We were herded outside, away from the smoke and the stench, through double doors, the yard's silence broken by the tapping children's feet. I covered my eyes against the noon sun. The nuns scurried quickly, roughly pushing at the backs of dazed children, calling back and forth to each other like prison guards after an escape.

Once placed in our rows, we were made silent. Sister said she would lead a round of the rosary, and offer it up for Father's swift recovery. She began, 'The Lord is my shepherd, I shall not want . . .'

Her voice, though loud, was strangled by emotion. A lock of her hair had come unbound and fell loosely past the binding of her veil. The lightest of breezes took it and each strand caressed her forehead. Sister's hair was black. Jet black, blue black, coal black. The concrete yard echoed with the children's prayers and sobs. Another nun walked through the rank and file and manoeuvred lost ones back into place. A small one near me suppressed her sobs, so much so she struggled for air. I thought to comfort her, but held off; later I felt sick and dampened by my resistance.

Behind Sister, the double doors softly opened and a Guard came and stood by Sister's side. He lowered his head and removed his hat, tucking it under his elbow until prayers had ended. Then he addressed the assembly, saying that we were unable to return to our lessons, that the school would need to be closed due to the smoke. Our parents would be notified and brought in to collect us. As he spoke, I saw blue lights in the distance and a police car slowly pulled forward and moved out of view.

Children peered through the railings with longing, staring out to the main road, willing their parents to appear. I watched Sister; she caught my eye and gamely walked towards the Guard. She called my name.

'Hurry up now, Juno, this way, please.'

I walked past her into the corridor. It was dark and the sickly burning smell caught in my nose and I could taste it at the back of my mouth. A policeman stepped out of the class-room, looked towards the burnt floor and says, 'Inside.' I stepped around the doorway and peered in; the room was empty.

'Inside,' he says again.

'What do youse want?' I say, and felt his hand move me.

'Go and sit down,' he says. He called to Sister; he wanted her in the room too.

When Sister came in, she glanced at me. 'Sit down, Juno, stop making a show of yourself.'

The policeman was talking, but at that moment I couldn't hear what was being said. I looked to his mouth, the soundless movement of his lips. I closed my eyes and buried my face in my hands. 'Would yis just fuck off!' Silence, seconds of it, before a rough burning at my shoulder, as the policeman flung me back into the chair.

'You listen to me. Do you think I've time to be wasting with the likes of you? You start behaving yourself or I'll haul you off so fast it'll make your head spin. Do you understand?' He stood and looked shyly at Sister. 'Sorry, Sister, it's the only way with this crowd.' I looked at Sister; her wayward strands had been located and hoisted back into position and she stood there, still and lovely.

He says:

'Do you know what happened here today?'

I say:

'There was a fire.'

He says:

'Do you know who started the fire?'

I say:

'I do.'

He says:

'Who started the fire?'

I say:

'Me.'

The church bells chimed as I walked home slowly through the haze and scrub. I had always loved the sound of the bells, until I was told the bells in the church had years earlier been replaced with a recording and I felt betrayed by that, like someone was playing a trick.

Once, coming home this late from school, after Father had kept me back, I'd been upset and rushed in the door for Mam. She'd been waiting and looked at the cut of me and says, 'What happened, what happened you?'

I couldn't speak – I just stood in front of her and flooded with tears.

'Jesus, Mary. What's happened to you?' She took hold of me, led me to the couch. 'Sit, sit down. What is it, pet? What's happened?'

I stretched an arm around each side of her wide hips, pulling her to me and pressing my head against the rounds of her belly, sobbing. She stiffened, but didn't remove my hands.

'Father hit me,' I say.

'What did he hit you for?'

'Nothing, he just did.'

'It can't have been for nothing.'

'It was, I swear.'

'He must have had a reason,' she says.

I thought about the times I'd tried to tell her how it was with Father, but all she kept saying was, 'Not Father, not without good reason, that poor man, a man of the cloth.'

I'd finally screamed, 'No. Not poor Father! Not poor bastarding Father! Poor me, Mam, poor me!'

The fingers of one of her hands rubbed across the fist of another and lay on the lap of her dark pleated skirt.

'You go into school tomorrow and apologise to Father, do you hear me? I don't want him knocking my door.' I could feel the drying tears harden on my cheeks. My head hurt and I shyly looked away.

'Yes, Mam,' I say and went upstairs without being told.

When I woke it was late, though some light from the street had snuck in past the open curtain. I was not unmoved by the tray of cold food I found sitting nearby, or the thought of Mam preparing and carrying it up, or how she must have stood, tray in hand, watching me sleep from the end of my bed, before gently setting the tray down and tiptoeing from the room. I didn't know what I was if not awful.

The policeman must have said 'Seán' a thousand times. I told him, 'I have no idea who that is.' I wanted to be there, wherever he was now. I'd be brave and take his hand and even hold it to my face in the filthy back seat of that car, among the stains and the smell of drunks. I'd take my chances, even with the pigs gawking into their rear-view mirror. I wouldn't be afraid to let them know I cared. They said Seán was in big trouble, that the best thing I could do was just tell the truth, so I took to singing 'Daisy', words and all. Sister whispered to the policeman about my mam being dead and all, and the Guard looked at me like I'd come a cropper, happy to see the back of me.

22

Father's door was blackened and sealed, his presence quickly diminishing in the loose steps of the children, their open laughter. The whole day had passed before Sister brought it up at all. She says, 'A terrible act of violence was committed here yesterday. A cowardly act.' Cruel and barbaric and unlike anything she had seen or heard of in her lifetime. She says, 'Father is stable and recovering and in need of our prayers.' She told us to come out from our desks and kneel and pray. Chairs and boots scraped, knees were pressed and eyes were closed, but not my eyes. I remained defiant, and stayed at my desk. And without the threat of Father, Sister let it go. I knew it was an accident, I knew for sure. I saw it, he was putting out the flames.

Sister started, 'Our Father who art in Heaven . . .' When finished and the bell had sounded and we were clearing off our desks, Sister says, 'Juno, I'd like you to remain.' Each student looked at me in turn as they left. Sister stood very still in the silent room, her hands bound at her front. 'Take a seat,' she says, her voice like an invitation and not a bit cross.

'I'm grand.'

'Take a seat,' she says, more sternly. Her decorum, thin as

crêpe paper, wrinkled at her feet. Sister came from behind her desk and with the flat of her palms smoothed over the wide folds of her gown. She pulled a chair close to mine and sat. Sister rarely sat and never close to me.

I could chart for the first time a rise and fall of her small chest. Her pale oval face protruding from her veil, the web of tiny lines clinging left and right of her eyes. The smile lines, the worry lines. Her pale blue eyes hooded like drawn-down silk, translucent and keeping nothing out.

'Tell me, Juno. How did a girl like you come across a name like Juno?'

'Wha?'

'It's a very pretty name, but unusual, don't you think?'

'Me mam liked it.'

'Well, she must have to name her daughter it.'

'Suppose.'

'You suppose . . .' And she gave a little laugh, and her small mouth folded back. Her teeth were uneven: not straight, and not unpleasant. They were yellowing, and I wondered was Sister a secret smoker. It accounted for her crankiness later in the day – Sister, halfway through prayers, gasping.

'She was a Greek god, did you know that?'

'No, Sister,' I say, but I did. Missus H at the library had given me that ages ago and even a book to read. She wasn't one of the big ones, Juno, no Zeus, no Helen of Troy.

'Well, there you go. They say you learn something new every day, isn't that right?'

'Yes, Sister.' She paused then and her eyes softened – I felt them, scraping through the dank of my hair, across my face, down to my blunt fingers twitching on my lap. Sister was appalled by me, I just knew.

'Yesterday was a difficult day for us all, traumatic. And of course, Seán is your friend, I know that, and how awful to watch a friend blacken his soul with sin.' And she reached and took hold of my hands, cupped them in her own. And I felt first the cold of her fingers but then the shy emergence of warmth created by our joined hands. I was overcome; I began to blink, and felt how my chest had tightened.

'That was a terrible show, before confirmation. Isn't that right, Juno?'

'Yes, Sister,' I say.

'Seán had asked for you to be let in, and you weren't let in, were you?'

I didn't answer, but my head slightly bobbed once to the side.

'I'd say Seán was very annoyed. I'd say you both were, or maybe disappointed?'

'Yes, Sister.'

'Now, Juno, it's time to be honest.'

'Yes, Sister.' I whispered it.

'He had the lighter fluid that morning. Brought it in with him, didn't he?'

'I ... I'm not sure.'

'It's alright, you don't have to say. We already know, he's told us himself. I'm just trying to help, just making sure what he said was correct. He's very confused, as I'm sure you can imagine.'

'You spoke to him?'

'He's in terrible trouble and I think, Juno, you and I are the only ones can help. Do you understand?'

'Yes, Sister.'

'So, he had the lighter fluid that morning, and he showed it to you?'

'Yes, Sister.'

'And why on earth did he bring lighter fluid to school if not to burn something?'

'Father's rulers, Sister. He was just going to burn the rulers and that's all.'

'And yet the rulers are intact, and Father, badly burned.'

'Yes, Sister.'

'Seán was very angry at Father?'

'He didn't want us hit any more.'

'He was angry.'

'I suppose, yes.'

'Maybe you encouraged that anger, just a bit. You might have suggested something? Be honest now, Juno.'

Silence had fallen across the school, its dim corridors emptied of children, and even the late shouts and cries across the yard had softened. There was only Sister then, her pale watchful eyes, the warmth of her hands and the rare lambency of her attention.

'No, Sister. I didn't.' That's what I said, and something I didn't understand drifted away from me.

She squeezed my hand gently and says, 'Juno, it's alright, Our Lord already knows the truth. I'm only trying to help you and help Seán.'

'Yes, Sister.'

Tears fell and I wiped a hand roughly across my hot cheeks. Sister's expression never changed. She stroked at my hand with her thumb, that way a mother might, to comfort or that, if a child were upset.

'But, Sister,' I said, 'he never meant for Father to be burnt like that. It was an accident. He was trying to stop him burning more. You saw that, you were there.'

'I did,' says Sister, 'I saw.' And she stood then and walked to her desk, taking hold of a white sheet of paper and pen.

'Would you like to see Seán?' she says.

'Yes, Sister, can I?'

'I think I could have a word in the right ear. He must be terrible lonely and frightened. I think it would do him a world of good; it would do well for you both. Now, let's put this whole matter behind us.' She began to write, that writing of hers, that I had tried to mimic and failed.

When she passed the paper to me, she says, 'You read that, Juno, like a good girl, and tell me if there is anything I've forgotten.'

I read: she had recorded my words precisely.

'But, Sister,' I say, 'it doesn't say about Seán trying to help Father, with the flames and all.'

'Oh,' she says, 'that part will come later. One thing at a time, isn't that what they say?'

'Yes, Sister.'

Sister was lying. I knew.

I was lying. I knew.

I had saved myself.

I didn't want to sign then, but it was too late. I felt myself committed to some agreement that could not be broken, lest Sister would show me her great disappointment. I signed.

Never ever mistake what is beautiful for beauty – I read that somewhere, not understanding at the time. Sister stood again. She brushed her gown as though after lunch some stray particles of food had embedded in the fabric. She worked at it with her nail, perturbed. She wouldn't look at me then. She held the paper close, checked it was in order and went directly to open the door, saying, 'Alright, Sergeant.'

Two Guards walked in. The tall one from the day before who had spoken to me, and a fat one, uniformed. His trouser cuffs sat high off his shoes and gave him a ridiculous air. But they weren't ridiculous – they had all the power in the world, and had been waiting just outside the door, listening. I imagined the shorter one punching the air as the ink dried on the paper. They huddled together reading over what Sister had gifted them.

'Go on home now, Juno, that's the girl,' says Sister. I left the room as the policeman was telling Sister she was in the wrong trade. He had a good laugh at that, they all did.

Days later, a new Father appeared, much like the old one.

23

Legs was let out briefly on remand. I tried to see him, but nobody could see him. I stood in front of his house, I suppose the same way I had stood in front of Rosy's house holding my 99. I stood there and showed him my freedom. I thought I'd caught sight of him one morning, peering from the upstairs window, but I couldn't be sure.

I woke in the dead of night, quite suddenly. My eyes bolted open and I sat upright, attentive to the dark and silent room. I heard movement outside. A slight raking of gravel underfoot. I went to the window and down below, lit by the yellow street light, was Legs. I ran, in only my pants and long T-shirt, barefooted down the stairs. Outside, I could feel the cold on my already wet face. I wanted to touch him, hold on to his slight frame. But I didn't do those things. I'd ruined it.

He was pale with trenches like dark circles beneath his eyes. His fine, capable hands were bandaged with white gauze. He didn't speak, so I didn't speak. I found myself looking away when I didn't want to look away. I was aware somehow of the time; that this was it and that I had no courage.

Legs leaned towards me – I didn't make that up. He didn't

reach out and touch my face, but he leaned, tilted his head a little closer to me. I wanted to scream how I was sorry but that poxy word carried nothing, and I wasn't brave like that, not when it mattered. I wanted to kiss him, even on his forehead, but I knew nothing of kisses like that and felt a sudden chill. He was already gone and couldn't be touched then, and with him away what I'd felt before would return.

TWO

'But the landscape of devastation is still a landscape.
There is beauty in ruins.'

Susan Sontag

1

Dear Legs,

I was going to send a cake with a nail file. But I ate it. The cake.

I saw your ma at the shops, the screeching wagon made me cry. She howled at me, says it's all my fault. She's not getting a prize for figuring that.

Sincerely, Zelda wicked witch of the ... well, you know where I am.

I wanted to send it.

I didn't.

I went on.

Dear Legs, please forgive me if I forget.

Everything.

I had heard how Legs cried when he was sent down and his long legs finally buckled when he was dragged from the dock. That the judge called him a sadist and a gurrier, said he'd be locked away in juvenile detention until his eighteenth birthday.

I just went on.

There were no nuns or priests in secondary school; the teachers were mostly men in nylon shirts that gave a stale smell by afternoon. Some were kind and would try to encourage us.

There were days I went to school, days I didn't, and nobody bothered. I didn't finish. One morning I stopped at the school gates and simply decided to go no further. I turned around and went to the library instead.

'I'm finished with school,' I told Missus H.

'I wouldn't let that trouble you, Juno,' she says. 'Haven't we better books here. Sit down.'

I could feel her watching me at times and wondering and I found it was a great comfort that even in our silent friendship I knew she worried after me.

I'd begun to choose my own books. She would pass by, glance down and approve or disapprove. She'd lay a book on the table.

'You might take a look at that,' she'd say.

'You're some compass, Missus H, some compass, alright.'

In these books, she'd set a course, France or Russia or America. She brought me to Spain once and had me stand on its southern shore and wait until out from the medina drifted the scent of spice and tanners, warmed by the sun and blown across the straits of Gibraltar. I'd close my eyes and I swear to God I could smell that smell.

But as the chairs were stacked and the lights, one by one, went out, the books closed shut and I'd return to that haze.

'Goodnight, Missus H.'

'Goodnight, Juno.'

One evening walking home from the library, I saw Dad in a kebab shop, nursing a styrofoam cup. With Mam gone, his body had quickly fallen to rack and ruin. Bristled face, hollowed gaunt stare. He could be picked up with one hand. I saw him as if he wasn't mine, through the plate glass marred by blinking neon, my own reflection with the evening light draining behind me.

Two grinning teenagers sat close to him. One of them blew the paper from the tip of his straw, catching Dad in the ear. Dad swivelled on the plastic chair, took a look at the boys and turned away. The second teenager copied the first. Dad ignored it this time, just sat there, the boys laughing.

I walked on.

Once home, in the usual way, I set out the table, his plate and cup and cutlery. I ate on the couch and read and before he came home I was away up the stairs. He was by then tamed, domestic. We both were. I'd taken control of the money, enough of it to keep the house afloat. Like my mam, I'd walk him every Tuesday to the dole and stand in line and wait for twenty pounds. He drank the rest. I made him his supper every night. I washed clothes in the sink and hung them out on the line. I took to cleaning the house and found Mam's shadow everywhere.

In the morning, I'd clear him off: 'I don't want to see you back till dark.' He'd look at me, doe-eyed, downturned mouth. 'Go on, I won't tell you again.' He'd turn on his heels, look away across the estate, as if towards the gallows. He'd walk, his shaking hands plunged inside his big pockets, fingers trembling like strings on a violin, so much that at times he was unable to button his own coat.

'I know you have money hidden,' he'd say.

'I might.'

'There are men have died in my condition.'

'There are.'

'You're terrible cruel to your father. I'm the only one you'll ever have, you know.'

'I know,' I say, closing the door. Left alone then.

Alone. Alone, alone.

Dear Legs,

I walked this morning and walked and walked. And stamped and stamped and still I could hardly feel my feet on the path. I'm neither here nor there. Nobody knows, and that shouldn't matter, but it does. At the strand there were big gulls, low-flying things, the screams of them, like all belongs to them gone. I wanted to reach up and pluck one from the sky and pull its wings asunder and say, 'There, that's how it feels to be floored.' Isn't that a terrible thought? When some are pretending to care and don't, and others pretending not to care and do. Caring is the worst, Legs, I hate you for that.

I didn't send it.

They fade, memories, even good ones, the ones we want. I'd practise my favourites, learned as if by rote. But no matter, you end up with memories of memories: you get tar from coal, not diamonds. I sat outside of things. Time, quick as a drum roll, flew past. Then I was sixteen. Then I was seventeen.

2

Da was approached, while sitting adrift on the church steps one morning, by Brother Philip and another man. He was low-hanging fruit even for that brigade, Jesus. Then, dipped into the sweet tea with plain digestive biscuits, slurped and drank. The warmth of the sacristy, hard chairs, a gentle invitation.

I came home from the library; the front door was open by a few inches. Hearing voices, I pushed it the rest of the way slowly. Da sat at the table, flanked on each side by these neatly suited men. I set my bag at the base of the stairs. Da was already pushing himself up, his chair dragging on the floor.

'Juno, Juno,' he says. 'Juno, c'mere and meet Brother Philip and Brother em – Brother Jack.'

'Were youse born in a barn? Left the front door open,' I say.

'This is my – my daughter, the apple of my eye, isn't that what they say, wha? Hmm, Juno, this is Juno.' Both men stood. The taller of the two, Philip, came around the table and stood before me: a sharp smooth face, eyes deep and blue and wide as a fisherman's net.

'Juno,' he says. And my name had never sounded so fine. Once fallen from his mouth, I wanted to catch it, bundle it between my arms and cling on. 'I'm so happy to meet you.' He smiled then and watched me and I felt a sudden obligation that I didn't understand. I found myself wanting him to see me, the best of me, and to have that best approved.

'Juno keeps us going here at home, don't you, Juno?' says Da. 'That is, she's very good with the housework and that, the meals, you know. Keeps us fed.' He took to laugh and stopped. 'And she's strict too, keeps me right, the right path.'

Da scuttled back and forth: an insect, he was in their boys' jam jar, among the twigs and dead leaves, and on occasion they rattle him for fun. He says, 'Will you, will you join us, here at the table, pet?'

'I've stuff to do,' I say, and stooped for my bag and went to the stairs.

Brother Philip, whose eyes had not left me, says, 'I'm glad we have met, I can put a face to the name now.'

'Can you?' I say flatly. And he showed his disappointment as if he'd pulled back his plaster on a flesh wound. The three men wordlessly watched my ascent. When I reached the top, I could hear the chairs move as they settled back at the table. A rich timbre of male harmony flowed around me and I thought how it would be; surrendering to that sound.

I lowered my head, listened as Brother Philip read text and spoke to Da about 'the way'.

'That's right, that's right,' Da kept saying, 'that's me, that's how it is for me, you see.' And whenever he tried to really explain, he became confused and his words stumbled and Brother Philip would catch him, and say, 'Perhaps, this was the way it was.'

'Yes,' Da would say quickly, 'like that. That's right!'

Before they left, Brother Philip welcomed Da to the flock.

And when he said, 'All are welcome, all who seek to find truth and hope and eternal life,' I saw how he knew I was there, listening, and how he was sending a dove, flap flap flap, up the stairs.

Dad was off the drink, a crucifix around his neck, knees reddened by breakfast. He held a stack of pamphlets and knocked at the neighbours' doors. He wanted me to join him. I wouldn't. I tried to encourage him, but I was unwilling. I was angry at his peace, so much so that I fucked his Bible out on the wet road when he left it down, then sat watching as he searched high and low.

'You and Jaysus having a go at hide-and-seek?' I say.

And he knew.

Then, they came to me one morning, Philip and Jack, tapping the door just minutes after I'd heard the church bells. They stood smiling, unreadable.

'Good morning, Juno,' says Philip. 'We wondered if we might trouble you for a few moments of your time.'

'Might we come in?'

'No, "we" mightn't.'

'How are you this morning?'

'You seem upset.'

'I'm busy. What do yis want?'

'We are worried about you.'

I laughed out loud and that serene look they'd cultivated was quickly dropped, the way I might drop an egg and then catch it again at the last second.

'We know the atmosphere at home has been very tense lately, to say the least. It has your father very down on account of it.'

'Depressed,' Jack says.

'He's depressed?'

'That's right. We know he has not always been a model parent, of course we know that, but who hasn't failed and sought forgiveness? You must see great changes in your father.'

'He has made room in his heart for the Lord, and has found peace.'

'We have come to invite you, Juno.'

'To open your heart.'

'He's been forgiven? You've forgiven him?'

'Anyone who has come to Christ, sincerely, is forgiven.'

'Even you, dear.'

'Even me?'

'No child is without sin. We are born of sin.'

'You're right,' I say. 'You're right.' When they saw the wisp of a tear, they smiled. They had broken through. A crack, wide enough that some small vermin, a rat say, could scuttle through.

Is this the world? What the world believes? I couldn't ask it aloud.

I closed the door. I think they were talking still, their voices choked out by the thickness of it, the click of the latch. I went up the stairs, took to the bed. I lay under blankets and coats, that same way Mam had, when there was nothing to look forward to on the other side of a long afternoon.

Da stood at my door casting a long shadow and promised he'd pray. For me. And voices carried up the stairs: a vigil. They sat around the kitchen table, holding hands maybe. And through the floors, their prayers pressed me.

Then the kettle boiled, the ping and rattle of cups. Dad had found the good saucers. Someone's wife was sent up to sit by my side. A great big culchie with freckled face and flapping arms. She put her hand on my forehead, and then pressed a damp tea towel. A shining gold crucifix dropped from her neck. She began to pray. Her voice as pretty as a song and I took hold of her hand and she let me rest it back on the cold towel on my head. I remembered when Mam would sit in the evening and watch her shows, and how sometimes I'd curl up into her on the settee, close to her, the roughness of her over-sized wool cardigan. She pushed me back one day; it seemed sudden, the way you would with a cat that was driving you mad. Without turning to me she says, 'That's enough now, you're too big for that.' I didn't feel too big, I felt the same, not small or big, just the same voice inside.

'Can you sing?' I asked the woman, and she quickly took her hand off my head.

Even the saved have their day jobs, and one by one the vigil drew down. I heard Dad at the front door, seeing off the last of them.

3

In the morning, I dressed and opened the curtains, humming some tune I didn't remember knowing. Downstairs, the kitchen looked like someone else's, bursting with cornflakes and milk and fresh bread. Dad was sitting, shaved, a new Bible open on his lap – watching me. I opened the presses and fridge until I had got the lay of the land.

'It's good to see you up,' he says.

'Is it?'

'How do you feel?'

'I feel like a smoke. Where's me bleedin' coat? Youse have everything moved.'

'I would like it if there was no more swearing in the house.'

'You're a hoot,' I say. 'Couldn't make you up.'

Outside, the road was quiet. On the way to the off-licence, a few cars splashed past cold, and the careless drizzle hardly wet my clothes; it pecked at my face and made me blink.

'A naggin of your wildest Irish rose,' I told the auld lad behind the counter.

'Is himself off the wagon?'

'He fucking will be.'

'Thank God for that,' he says. 'The lights will be off without him.' Chuckle chuckle chuckle.

'I'll tell you when something's funny,' I say to him.

'No need to be like that, just a bit of gas.'

'Yeah, gas alright.'

I stood on the steps of the house with a smoke. All of that, boxed inside behind me. It waited, years of us, crushed into years of us, settled, thick as jam. I felt the cool of the glass bottle inside my coat pocket.

Back inside, only his thumb had moved, maybe a page or two. I didn't say a word, just put the bottle on the table and went in search of a good glass. When I found one, I held it up to the light. It was cool to the touch, polished by the hands of God. I sat at the table. The click of unscrewing the cap, and I tilted the green bottle on its side. The glass filled up with the pretty amber like cough syrup. I held it under my nose and the fumes made me gag.

'The feck you playing at?' he says from across the room.

'Language, Daddy.'

I gulped down the first glass, feeling the ugly shape my face made and a dreadful burning inside. I gripped the glass tighter, trying to swallow all the way down. Like learning to smoke, you were only sick for a bit. I felt warm suddenly, light-headed. He came sniffing over, sat across, watched. He took to praying. The words were so new to him, he soon stumbled and faltered like an old drunk.

'You look awful thirsty, Daddy.'

'I'll give you some hammering, you keep this up.'

I filled the glass. He prayed louder, but even at full tilt, he was only puff and hot air. His head bowed low into his clasped hands. He stopped then, gave up I suppose, and the bitter moment that followed made me feel what I didn't want to feel. He started to cry.

'Oh dear God,' he says, 'dear God.'

When finally he did reach for the glass, the joke was on me: I didn't want to let it go. I held on to it, tight, or it held on to me, anyway we grappled a moment, until he gave up and instead slapped my face and took the bottle and like a child ran to the toilet. I heard the door lock and wondered if he was pouring it down the drain. It might have been his plan, until he got himself alone with it. It was a long time before the door opened. When it did, he was changed. We both were.

4

I struck a match and lit the candles, one pink, one blue, set ablaze. I watched them a while, the glow and heat around the quick melting sticks, the flickering light they gave. Make a wish, I thought, make a wish. I opened up the drawer that held Legs' poppies.

I made a wish.

I didn't go into their room often. But that morning, along with the birthday candles, I had bought a naggin of vodka and was bolstered by the drink. I was bored and curious and I suppose looking, just looking. There were a few of Mam's small trinkets left untouched in a bowl on the dusty wooden dresser. The dresser had belonged to my granny. Three large drawers that needed waxing: the rails they sat on caught hold of the drawers and could be opened only with great effort and a stop–start motion. Inside, next to the modest pile that half filled the drawer with hosiery, woollens and skirts, were two handles that had, I think, come off in her hand and were never returned to their working position. A mirror attached to the top was water-stained deep inside, where the glass looked rusted at the edges and in long drip lines. It swivelled on an axis, and when I stood looking down, I became almost frightened by my unnatural reflection. This was how Mam had seen herself, in the morning, at night, slipping back between the covers, waiting like a bookmark.

Of the remaining trinkets, there was nothing to be said.

Some clothes clung loosely to hangers in her wardrobe: cardigans, a few blouses and two Sunday dresses I'd never seen her wear. He was always saying he was going to box them, bring them to the pawn.

I reached in and took a dress from its hanger; its metal rattled against another as I returned it empty. It was a beautiful dress really, dark navy with printed yellow bows, a high-buttoned neck and Peter Pan collar. I undressed and stepped in carefully, the polyester catching a little on the hairs of my shin. It ballooned about me; the hemline fell below my knee. I tied a belt around it and looked at myself in the glass, and pulled the belt tighter. My head tilted, hands on hips. What sort was I?

At the side of the closet I saw an old photograph; it was stuck with a tack to the wall and showed a younger me, smiling. I neither remembered it being taken nor shown to me when it was exposed. And when I wondered about Dad or Mam sticking it there, I was a little overcome. I sat down on the side of the bed, defeated as if by a sudden wound. I stood again and unclipped the picture for a closer look. I saw then how there was a hole in the wall behind it. With the picture removed a rush of cold air flowed in; I felt its chill on my fingers. Cold. I had to laugh then – me, used to fill a gap.

By late morning the house seemed more cramped than ever. I sat at the table; I sat at the couch. Up and down the stairs, the walls tightening around me. I drank from the naggin and watched the bottle empty by degrees. Music played on the radio and I danced like a wild thing. The house had come undone from our neglect; it moaned with carelessness. There was so little left; even in the bathroom, the scarcities continued. An evening paper torn in strips, the news fractured, lay in reaching distance of the bowl. One bare light bulb dangled from a hook in the ceiling. I turned it off, stood in the dark, and waited for its heat to escape, then I unscrewed it and felt my way through the unlit pitch, reversing the operation in the kitchen.

I walked to the pub. The early house smell: days-old tobacco washed with hops and barley and something else. Daylight was strictly held back by heavy shutters. I saw him there, Da, sat at the bar. A cigarette burned in his hand, his eyes away somewhere unknown. There were a few around, scattered, backs turned in isolated pockets. I kinda skipped towards him, put my smokes and matches down, claiming a few inches of the bar. He was boiling then.

'Hiya, Da,' I say, all cheers, a lit smoke between my teeth. 'Hiya, Pops, Father of mine, Daddy, Dad Dad Daddio.'

'What are you doing in here?' he says, eyes cast down to the stretch of no man's land between us. He never looked at me. The barman came across, the white sleeves of his stained shirt cuffed above his elbows, forearms sinewy and hairless.

'An orange for me and whatever thirsty here is drinking.' He took a moment to understand the relationship, that way barmen do. He blinked once, had us and moved off; we weren't a challenge. I put a tenner on the bar.

The barman brought the drinks and I waited for his back to be turned before pouring the vodka I had hidden into mine. Da saw but pretended he didn't. We sat then, unmoving. I watched the barman without interest as he stocked the cases with bottles of porter. Da ran his finger across the smooth surface of his cigarette packet, the flat of his other hand pressed into his cheek, pushing the loose skin up and making a funny shape of his left eye. He took hold of his glass, as if he'd been resisting the urge or savouring it. We had only the silence, a confession-box silence, sitting in the dark telling of yourself to an unseen face, to an abacus, counting up sins for punishment. I thought about something to say to him, I really thought.

'What does your da do?' That's what people ask; they ask it early.

I thought of how easily I could get a rise out of him. I could just say the word 'Mam' and sit back and watch and laugh. But I didn't. The drink had caught me and I felt washed out suddenly, and anyway, the word 'Mam' was too much for me.

'He'll have another one,' I told the barman and he pressed a small glass under an upturned bottle. As he walked the drink over, I turned to Da.

I say:

'I fucking hate you.'

I'd timed it perfectly, just as the drink was set in front of him. Da gave me his best big bad look, but he was already holding the glass.

I got up from the bar then, after he'd had a few sips. I took my jacket off and before I went to the loo, Da looked at the dress I was wearing. He was raging.

'Where did you get that?' he says.

'It's my dowry.'

I walked to the loo, looks from auld lads stuck like chewing gum to my arse. The toilet was frozen and covered in piss. I stopped at the mirror and looked and talked at myself: that way, heavy with drink, declarations were made and then forgotten as I walked out to the bar.

I sat back beside Dad. He didn't like me watching him drink. No witnesses. I played a game. The rules were, the first to speak lost. I got elephants drunk. No winners. The money was gone, spent. As soon as Da finished his last sip, he got up from his stool and walked out of the pub. It was so quick and decisive that I watched the door expectant, his presence still felt and it didn't matter that his chair was empty.

The barman cleared the empty glasses and from the other end of the bar he silently watched. He thought for a moment and came back. 'Probably time for you to be going home.' I stared blankly.

'She's alright, I'll keep an eye on her.' I turned to see a man, grinning, not Da's age, not yet. He reached and touched my face with his fist, the tip of his knuckle gently grazing past my chin.

'Juno, yeah?'

'Yeah.'

'I knew your sister, long time back. Derry.'

'Me too.'

He laughed. I took hold of his pint and I drank it so fast that I felt I might be sick.

'You want another?'

'Yes. Is it raining out there?'

'It's sunny,' he says.

I looked at the shutters and tried to imagine. I'd read something that morning, something, something, what was it? 'Not for a long time have I felt such a keen desire to be happy,' I say.

'What are you talking about?'

'It's from a book, written in 1934. Imagine that.'

'You're a bit off your rocker, aren't you?'

'Am I?'

He gave a grin. He liked it quirky, that's what he was saying: I was a bit of quirky game, but he could handle it.

'Maybe I'm completely normal and you're off your rocker.'

'Cheeky little bitch, aren't you?'

'Oh, you say the sweetest things, let me go and get me knickers off.'

'You'd want to watch your mouth.'

'Good one, I've never heard that before, dumb fuck.'

'I'm warning you.'

'Another cracker from the hymn book. You buying me a drink?'

The barman asked him if I was old enough and between them it was decided that I was. He thought I was a dandy, this one, a hoot. All that I said he found charming and he bought drink after drink and listened and listened, and although I knew what he was after, something in me opened to that lost warmth of a companion.

I was coming out of the stalls in the women's toilet and he was waiting. He says how he used to fuck Derry in there, he says where and how. I swear to God, his voice was so casual, it unfolded like a shopping list. There was a heart on the wall, scratched with a penknife. 'Micky and Bonner, true love.'

5

'What a pair,' I say to Da. It was evening by then, fully dark and I sat facing him from across the kitchen table.

'I don't want you wearing your mother's stuff,' he says.

'No? I don't much feel like wearing it any more.'

'Good.'

'I'm going to make tea, you want a cup?'

'Go on then, I will.'

When I stood I could feel at my hip where that man had grabbed me, pushed me against the stall and pressed himself so I could barely breathe. He lifted my dress and his fat hands were everywhere, rough, inside and out. Then he changed tack and kissed me on the cheek, tender and all, brushed his hands over my hair and my face and I think he'd expected tears, but I wouldn't cry for him. He said he liked me, he wanted to see me again, he'd give me a ride like I wouldn't believe, that that's all I wanted for. He left the stall and when I came back out to the pub, he was gone. I walked through the busying bar to get my coat off the chair and the barman for the first time wouldn't look at me. I'd walked home, trembling, the sound of roaring traffic at my side. The glow of street lights misted over in the fog. I'd got indoors and went and washed myself. My face and down there. The cold water smarted, but not without its own relief. My hips were marked where he'd held on, bruising me in the usual colours.

I put my hands around the kettle as it boiled, but only for so long. The tea stains where we dropped used bags had inched slowly out of the sink and along the draining board. Mam used to push back at them with a Brillo pad.

'We need to buy Brillo pads,' I tell Da when I sit back down.

He looked at his tea, disgusted. 'It's black,' he says.

'Well, you should have gotten milk,' I say.

'Maybe you should have gotten milk instead of playing big shot up in the pub.' I looked at him then, armed with a thousand replies. But just then, I couldn't. I just couldn't.

'Is your leg at you?' I say.

He pressed his hand to it then, remembering.

'Well, it is, a bit. Yes.'

'You should make a hot-water bottle.'

'I might, yeah.'

I heaped three teaspoons of sugar into my cup and stirred. The drink had been slushed about my body, it'd spilt from my head and collected in heavy pockets around my limbs.

'Tell me happy birthday.'

'Wha?'

'Tell me happy birthday.'

'Is today your birthday?'

'Yeah, today.'

'It's not?'

'Just bleedin' say it.'

'Happy birthday then.'

'Thank you.'

'What are you now?'

'I'm not going to answer that.'

'Suppose you'll be leaving me soon.'

'Only if there was a God.'

'That's not funny, not funny being left on your own. Left to die with no one to know or care. Just like your sister, up and left one day without a word.'

'Yeah, I'm just like her now alright.'

I rubbed my eyes and my head felt heavy in my hands.

'She broke your mother's heart.'

'You broke my mother's heart.'

'Your mother loved me.'

'I know she did. It's the only way to break a heart.'

'She was only out cos of the trouble you'd caused. The trouble you'd brought to this door. If you're looking to point fingers, start there.'

'You're right, Dad, you're right.' I think it was by then I'd started to cry. I couldn't see properly and I was confused. 'There's nothing about us that's good. We're just nothing.'

We didn't speak, we sat for a long time – the house lay silent, and we were both trapped at that table. But then he was talking; he was rolling a ciggy. His fingers shook and strands of tobacco fell to the floor. His wet tongue shot out his mouth and licked the length of the paper cylinder. 'She was a vision,' he says. 'A vision.'

Something, years ago, when they rented a caravan in Cortown. A warm morning, wind pushing the long grass and the cold sea beyond. She was walking towards him in a summer dress she had made out of leftover fabrics. She was a beautiful patchwork of colour. Back when she had a waist, back before me, and it was pulled tight with a thin white belt.

Wellies on, cutting just below her knee. She was holding a basket, bread and milk and duck eggs with feathers stuck to the shell; she had gone to see the farmer before Dad had woken.

I craned my head to look up and caught the glare of the naked light, tightly closed my eyes. Pink, red, flesh.

Fairy tales, he was telling me fairy tales.

'I remember,' I say. 'I remember Cortown. Me, Derry and Mam and you.' As I spoke my voice was calm in a way I didn't recognise.

'You were too young to remember.'

'I do. It rained, every day it rained. I remember how we sat for three days, stuck in the fucking caravan, waiting for you. You left us on a Friday and it was Sunday evening when the farmer knocked, telling us you were on the main street, that we better do something before the Guards were called. Mam's face.'

'You've no idea what you're talking about,' he says. 'She loved me.' He shouted it. 'Loved me she did. Then you come along – Christ, you're not a daughter, you're a wedge. If it wasn't for you, my God.'

I opened my eyes and from the hard wooden chair I looked at him. A crisp line of smoke rose up between his hands; his long strands of grey-black hair, matted, fell across his forehead, covering his eyes.

'I miss her, Juno, I loved her. You know that, don't you, pet? I loved your mother.'

'I miss her too,' I say. 'At the end, did she say anything?'

'I suppose she might have.'

'You suppose?'

'Well, how would I know?'

'Because you were there.'

He looked at me: vacant, then confused, then guilty.

166

'You told me you were there, you stood up in front of the whole church and you said you were there. Please God you didn't leave her die on her own ... Da ... Dad?'

He started to speak, but by then it was too late, I knew. I was bent over, I put my head on the table and was saying no, no, no, over and over.

'I loved her, loved her.'

'Don't say it again. If you do, I swear I'll kill you.'

'You don't understand, I loved her.'

I stood and went into the dim alcove of the kitchen. The little peeling knife was in the sink, just a few inches of it. I thought about putting on the kettle again. I told myself, just make another cup of tea, extra sweet, and bring it to bed. But then I'd wake up in the morning and have to go on. I didn't know myself then; I knew no kindness.

I picked up the knife and ran at him. He was so frightened, poor man. He raised his arm to shield his face, his neck. The blade stopped above his elbow suddenly and wouldn't go on. Skin and bone and sinew are tough – I kept at it, I wasn't afraid. That's freedom.

I must have caught a vein and I suppose the blood collected at the bend in his raised arm, because when he lowered it a splash of blood poured out as if from an unturned glass. He ran.

Outside, the doorsteps filled like stalls on an opening night, the faces of neighbours washed blue from the sweep of ambulance light, sucking on the commotion like sweets. Dad was put on a stretcher and rolled along the street.

6

Derry walked into the house; she seemed rattled by the small step over the threshold, though she never let on. She stopped at the table, and looked around as if for something, years earlier, hidden. She removed her thick blue woolly hat and her hair was matted close to her head in some places and spiked in others. She shook it out between her fingers until it settled. She looked rested since I'd seen her: pretty, I thought, and I wanted to tell her that. But after closing the front door behind her I just stood, shy, not knowing where to put myself with excitement.

'I got milk in. Do you want a cuppa?'

'No,' she says, her slight voice pushed into the room carefully as if not to disturb. She continued to watch, her eyes panning, deliberate strokes in search of what was familiar and what was different.

'Same as you left it, nothing changes here.'

She nodded.

'Do you want to sit down?'

She walked into the small kitchen, cautious, her hands pinned to her side.

'You don't have the kids today?'

'No, they're with their granny.'

'They're gorgeous, aren't they? I mean the one I saw was. I'm sure they all are.' And I laughed and tried to swallow my laugh.

'Sit down,' she says. 'I need to talk to you.' She had full command of me, and I remembered how that was with Derry and me. She could be kind and she could be cruel, and either way, I would come to heel. I sat down.

'It's frozen in here,' she says.

'I've the heat off, sorry.'

'Why have you the heat off?'

I was mortified; the bricks in the house had not felt a flare of heat in some time and ached with chill. 'Just is,' I say.

She pulled a chair out from under the table and sat. She had lovely eyes, Derry, the loveliest, I was reminded as she pulled closer. A nameless blue. I'd looked for it a thousand times since, and every blue was wrong except for Derry's blue.

'Dad's not going to press charges,' she says.

She looked flatly at me. Her nail tapped the arm of the wooden chair like the hollow pecking of a bird. They were painted red, her nails: they looked as if they had been scorched by great heat, and before they had dried she must have touched off something. The varnish had dried in uneven clumps on one nail and I wondered if she'd noticed and it made her furious at her own stupid clumsiness.

'Is he coming back?'

'No, not here. Not at first.'

'Where?'

'They're going to put him in a home, leave him dry out for a bit.'

'And then?'

'Back here.' And I thought about the handful of days I'd have the place to myself, how the hours rolled out and felt like a blessing. At times I had thought the Guards were coming for me; I'd stand near the door and listen with my head lowered as a car pulled up to the house, or the sound of sharp steps like a marching band. And even at that, I knew it was worth it.

'I need the house now,' she says.

'I need it myself.'

'I have three kids, a husband and his ma. And now I have Dad to take care of, thanks to you. I need it more.'

'Where would I go?'

'You should have thought about that before you started stabbing people ... I'm not sure, maybe down here with his ma. We can get you a mattress to pull out or that.'

'I don't mind that.'

'She might.'

'I could look after the kids.'

'No, his mammy does that.' She stopped and thought. 'Look it, we'll try make it work.'

'I can sleep anywhere. You can put me in the bleedin' garden, I wouldn't care.' I reached across the table saying her name, it was a question. My fingers swept though her hair and I meant that as a kind of comfort. Her head pulled back, as if from a blow.

'Don't do that,' she says.

I quickly took my hand away. 'It's a shame,' I say, then, 'what with him gone and all, if Ma was still around, imagine? We could help with the kids and that, we could have a laugh.' I waited to see if she'd say anything, but she just sat, silently, that level stare. 'You know that bastard left her die alone up in the hospital,' I tell her. 'Stood up in front of the whole church and lied.'

She was fixed on something unseen and her scarlet finger-tips ran down her face and along her neck.

I say:

'Derry.' Come back to the room with me.

'Derry.' Come back to the room.

'Derry.' Come back.

'Derry.'

She smiled a bit, a smile I wished was directed towards someone else, one of them smiles that told the person talking that they were a bleedin' clown for believing what they believed.

'You just don't like me, do you?' I say.

'What?'

'You just don't, I know — it's like I always did something wrong.'

She had leaned back from the table and looked at her hands resting gently in her lap, on the verge of speaking, and through the walls I heard a scraping from next door, Missus G cleaning out her grate. She did it every day at the same time. It was four o'clock.

'She chose you and I suppose I was jealous and I hated you at times, I did and I'm sorry for that.'

'Chose me? You weren't here, you'd fucked off.'

'Is that what you think, really? When I sat there at sixteen and told Mam I was pregnant. I finally get the courage to tell her ...' Derry wasn't looking at me and she'd stopped looking about the room, she was there and not there and her words, long-hidden, crept out. 'Mam just sits, watching me. She's not angry or anything, she's ... disgusted. She was ashamed of me. "I knew it," she says. "I knew you were a bad egg. I knew it from day one, since that day up in the grasses."'

Her words, now freed, came more quickly and she looked at me then.

'It took me a second, before I realised she was talking about that day I was attacked. She thought it was my fault, I'd always felt it, that she blamed me. But I thought, no, that's just too mad, but she did … She goes up and gets the priest, and her and Da and the priest have me sit off over there while they all decide what's to be done with me. And it's Dad, Dad is the one who says, wouldn't she be better off at home? Dad says it. But she keeps telling the priest, "I want her out of this house, I'm not having her going around the estate with her big belly." I'm to be hidden away somewhere and the baby will go up for adoption. And I think, fuck this, and I take off with me fella and I have me baby and I pushed that pram up and down the road almost every day, right past the house, right past the neighbours. I made sure they could all see me. And not once did she come out, not once … That's your mam, Juno.'

It looked as if she might cry, but she didn't cry, instead her face sealed over, closed shut again and I couldn't see how she felt at all.

'My mam wouldn't do that.'

'Your mam was a miserable wagon, dying alone was too good for her.' That's what Derry says, she was breathless and pale after it was said. We sat for the longest time at the table saying nothing, until I slowly picked myself off the chair.

'You're always a shit big sister, you know that? Just shit. Take the house,' I say, 'just fucking take it. You, your bet ugly kids and his cunt ma. You're welcome to each other.' I walked slowly past her, upstairs. In my room, I gathered what was within arm's reach and put it into a bag. I opened Mam's tin box, filled with her horoscopes, and took Legs' poppies from the drawer and lay them carefully inside. When I came back down, the front door was wide open and Derry was gone.

I stepped out into the street under the cloudless sky. The road was quietly adrift in its ordinary late-afternoon routine. I looked back into the empty sitting room and kitchen where Derry's chair had been pulled out; memories crowded. I pulled the door closed and posted the keys in through the letter box.

THREE

'And suddenly in the crowd, you meet a human glance, and your burdens are made light, as after a communion. Isn't it so?'

Andrei Rublev, Tarkovsky

1

I had become nervous – my fingers fluttered like small feathers – and I was awake, always. My eyes drooped for minutes at a time, but never fully into that restful place before they would snap open and, unable to find a way back, I would watch, I would listen.

I didn't have a pile of stacked bricks to surround me: I was exposed, and the days were made long with hunger and cold and that awful thing of being alone. But it was the cold for me, that bastard cold I did anything to ward off.

I found a refuge under a staircase in an uncared-for building. I would creep in after dark, huddle down in my sleeping bag. I had a small plastic transistor radio, stolen from a shop to sell, but found I was unable to part with it. It was white, palm-sized. I would hold it to my ear, set it to a whisper and close my eyes.

Above me I could hear the first echoes of families waking. Shoes sparked off each step in heavy descent. Somewhere a front door was opened and closed and the hallway fell silent. I closed my eyes and must have drifted.

'There's another one here, Jim.' A woman's voice.

'What?'

'Another one, under the stairs.'

'Junkie bastards,' says Jim. His voice spilled down through the concrete stairwell. I opened my eyes and she stepped back, as if I were a stranger's mongrel. At her side stood a child of maybe three or four. The child glanced at me, uninterested, two wet fingers in her mouth, and says the word 'crisps' at the empty packets littered around. I started to move then, quickly kicking my sleeping bag away from my feet and gathering up my possessions.

'Sorry,' I say. 'I'm going, missus.' My rucksack was overfilled and I had difficulty packing it.

'She's getting away, Jim.'

Jim's steps came closer, uneven steps, where he'd paused here and there to get an arm into a shirt or buckle his belt and then they'd quicken. I tried to stand then, but I was under the stairs and bent to the shape of its arch. She wouldn't stand aside to let me out.

'Crisps,' the young one says again. I tried to smile at her but she clutched tighter to her mother's leg. Jim then.

'Every fucking morning,' he says. 'I'm sick to death clearing up after you bloody junkies. Come on,' he says, 'get out to fuck.'

'Get outta me way then, so I can get out.'

'Move.'

'I'm not a junkie.' My glass naggin fell from my pack, smashing on the hard floor. A sweetly sick smell of alcohol.

'Who's going to clean that?'

'I'm sorry,' I say, and I dipped down and raked the broken bottle with my fingers. Glass embedded under my nail. I panicked, picked up my pack and ran.

Outside it had rained and stopped. After checking both ways up the street, between a Fiesta and a white van I hunched low and pissed. I had sixteen pence and stank of drink.

The park was emptied of all but a few runners, an occasional nanny pushing a pram. The trees were long cleared of their leaves and so thoroughly it seemed impossible to imagine their return. I sat at a bench in front of the pond and expectant ducks carved perfect lines towards me, their ruffs catching light and shimmering. A man passed along the gravel path behind me and stopped. Suit, tie, overcoat, scarf. He arrived after the first ducks, who once ashore had shed all elegance.

'Are you well?' he says, sitting down, legs wide and loading an arm across the top rail of the bench. His clean fingernails hung loosely and a slight spray of dark hair ran from the knuckle of his little finger to his wrist. I looked away – across the pond where the foliage was thin I could see the flat lawns and further, where the dark beds began, bulbs dormant, tulips and daffodils, and restless crocuses that found their way first through the softening ground. Mam knew the names of flowers: hyacinths and wisteria and night-scented stock. Her mam, half tinker, had named them on walks through country lanes on the way to mass. She'd come to the church late, my granny. A zealot, Mam said, who had later stopped talking about natural things. Granny looked at me mam one day, she says, 'Weeds don't grow up to be flowers, they're plucked and torn asunder.'

'I said, are you well?'

'Yeah, great,' I say. My pack was on my lap; the weight of it pressed down on my legs and I felt its damp when I pulled it closer.

'I think I've seen you before around here,' he says.

'Have you?'

'I have,' he smiled.

Sometimes they expect me to move a certain way, at my hips. All loose and everything. I can't. The music I hear is not the music they hear.

I went to a fast-food chain on Grafton Street, bypassed the line and went downstairs to the loo. I was followed, quick steps from behind the counter.

'Excuse me, excuse me . . . Where do you think you're going?' he says. *Alan*, his name tag reads. *I'm Alan,* it says, *Manager, Ask me a question.*

'Going to the jacks,' I say.

'Are you now? Well, the toilets are for our customers only.' He was about my own age, oily skin and pimples.

'I am a customer.'

'You're not. I know you – I've had to ask you to leave before.'

'I am.'

'Have you ordered anything?'

'I'm going to.'

'Come on, out.'

'I'm going to order, I'm not going to order and sit and eat when I'm bursting, am I?' I reached inside my pocket and produced my remuneration, a crisp five-pound note.

'Look it,' I say. 'Look, I have money.' Alan looked, and I could see he didn't want to go back to his colleagues empty-handed after making such a fuss of chasing me down the stairs.

'I need the toilet, and I'll be up to order after, OK?' I turned and continued down the stairs. Once inside, with the door closed and locked, I breathed deeply and fell along the wall to the floor.

The water was warm through my fingers; my eyes closed as the sensation filled me. Warm. The clear blue soap dispenser was empty but still I washed my hands and face and around my neck as best I could. The door was knocked then, doggedly, as I was cleaning the splashes off the floor with toilet paper.

'There are people waiting. Do you hear me?' Alan. He'd stayed outside the door, waiting.

'I'm just coming.' My tummy was wrecked and I didn't know if it was the hunger or the drink. I didn't know the day of the week or what month exactly. I wrapped a wad of loo roll around my fist, again and again, unceremoniously stuffed the tissue down my knickers. And a second wad folded in my pocket for later.

With the door opened, Alan faced me; behind him a woman was just taking the last step on the stairs. He saw her and says, 'There are people waiting.'

'I'm not waiting – I just got here,' she says.

I sat at a table in the far corner. The room smelled of bleach and the Formica tabletops had a wiped layer of grease. I opened the styrofoam box and felt the heat off it rise up before taking a first bite, before eating most of it in an instant. Then, I stopped myself, setting a small amount back in the box, I rolled a cigarette from tobacco dust left in my pouch and played the tip of the fag off the brightly coloured tinfoil ashtray. Three teenagers folded into a table close by, their green school uniforms pressed and crisp shirts a shocking white. They looked over, but without interest. Alan continued to circle, and at one point tried to take the beige-gold shining box.

'I'm not finished with that,' I say. It was already in his hand. He looked at the bite of food that remained and reluctantly placed it back in front of me.

I went to a library where I was not known, too shy by then to return to my own Missus H. I had circled past one evening and saw her through the glass, blazing yellow blouse, books stacked up her arm. I went and stood inside the door. My pack was pressed on my foot, the sleeping bag roughly stuffed inside and ballooning out the top. When she saw me she paused; I'm not sure she recognised me at first – I was just something blown in off the street. She came closer and paused a second time, her hand going to her mouth but stopping short. She said my name and I ran.

I claimed a table with two books I'd quickly taken from a nearby shelf. As long as I didn't sleep and was seen to be reading, they left me alone. There were a few of us littered around throughout the day, time drifting, valueless creatures. We looked on at each other in secret and thought, at least I'm not as bad as your man, and we tried to align ourselves with the others: the collegial, the housewives or the staff.

By four, the staff started to gather up, keen to be home. The dim afternoon light had for a second given way to the warmest colour, it flared through the stained glass before darkening. Outside it would be cold again, the buses filled and the city emptied out. I ran down Exchequer Street in time to catch the off-licence. I hid the bottle well before I left the shop. Outside, two lads looked like they could kill for it.

It was nearing seven when I went back into the fast-food restaurant. Alan was gone and the night shift had begun. Before going to the counter I stood back and looked at the brightly lit sign. I held my money,

'You alright there?' A young fella behind the counter. His uniform was stained and his waist stretched the polyester pin-striped pattern.

'Yeah, I just wanted a cup of tea, but I've only thirty-five pence.'

'Oh,' he says, and looked, as if for the first time. 'Yeah, right enough, forty pence.' He began wiping the nothing clean off the counter and then leaned his forearm into the wet.

'You wouldn't give us a cup for thirty-five?'

He wasn't surprised at being asked; I didn't think he minded. 'Nah, sure they count the cups in this place.'

'They what?'

'The cups, after the shift, they get counted and the amount has to correspond to the till roll.'

'Oh ... right. Thanks. You wouldn't spot me five pence, would you?'

'Eh, yeah, if I have it.' He dug around in his pockets, his pink fingers whitening. He patted his pockets then.

'No, sorry.'

'That's alright,' I say. 'Thanks for looking.'

'Hang on,' he says, 'I'll check me coat,' and disappeared out of sight. The street beyond the plate glass was almost emptied and a drizzle of rain coated the path. A woman threw her arms around a man and he was trying to play it cool but was delighted. They kissed then, not for long, and walked on. I thought about having to go and plant myself outside, hand out, hoping for five pence. That was what I'd say: 'Can you spare five pence for a cup of tea?' But I'd never be believed.

'You're in luck,' he says. He put a silver five pence on the counter. Happy, as if we'd achieved something together.

'Thanks so much, thanks so much.'

'Tea, is it?'

'Yeah, please.'

I took six milks and four sugars and disappeared to the seats at the side, out of view. Opening the lid, I poured a good belt of drink in. It tasted sweet and warmed my inside.

I'd sat an hour, maybe two. Couples had come through and an occasional man on his own; they ate quickly and wished to be somewhere else. The upright shape of the seats had my back murdered and I could feel its dull calling under the shape of the drink. The boy from behind the counter came past, binning boxes and wiping wilted lettuce and ketchup stains.

'Thanks again,' I say.

'What's that?'

'For the five pence.'

'Oh yeah, yeah.' He stood for the moment, uncomfortably, holding a tray tightly against his belly, as though it had been flung at him at great speed.

'Pain in the hole this or is it alright?'

'What, working here?'

'Yeah.'

'It's alright, I mean ...'

'Yis hiring?'

'Don't know, I can get you a form, an application – they have them behind the counter.'

'That would be great. I need a job, you know ...' His eyes were almost green, but hadn't been imbued with anything crisp or immediately striking. They, like his face, were ordinary. But he was kind and through those plain eyes there was no meanness. He went off then, his shape ill-fitted to his uniform. I'd forgotten to look at his badge. When he returned, he put the stapled form in front of me. David.

'I wasn't sure if you had a pen,' he says, and put a chewed biro on the table.

'I do,' I say, patting my huge bag. 'I've me bleedin' whole house. Like a snail, me.' But I'd made him uncomfortable.

'Right,' he says.

'Thanks for this,' I say. The cheer had left my voice. 'I might take it with me, look it over properly so I can answer it right and all.'

'Yeah, fair enough.' He went to walk off then.

'Cos, you know the way, you're in an interview or that, and you say the wrong thing and they look at you like an eejit, and then they're saying that that's not what you said on the form. I mean, it's not like I'd be called in to an interview. I'm not being big-headed or anything. I mean, if they did that would be great and all, but no worries, of course, I'm not ... Where do you live, Davis?'

'David.'

'David, right, David. Fucking Davis, what am I like? Does it drive you demented when people you don't know talk like they know you cos they know your name? Where did you say?'

'That I live?'

'Yeah, do you live on your own, have you flatmates, what's the story?'

'I'm sixteen – I live at home, with my folks.'

'Right, yeah, course, course you do ... thanks for this, this form and all. Thanks.' He stood there looking at me. I nodded and looked away, pretended I was reading the form.

'Good man,' I say. But he didn't move.

'I need that pen back, or I'll be in trouble.'

'Yeah, of course, yeah yeah. Take it.'

It had started to rain outside, and the wind had picked up. I had held on as best I could but David circled twice before saying, 'We're closing now.' I thanked him and told him that that was great, that I was going to see a friend now, anyway. I folded the form then, carefully. Said I knew the manager, Alan, I'd pop it in to him first thing in the morning, and I knew I could never go back.

I snuck into a car park where the chain link was loose. There was a hut, lit inside, its eaves hanging wide around it. I slipped around back and heard the light dragging of the security guard's boots. Silently, I unpacked my sleeping bag, unfurled it and wiggled inside with my back pressed hard against the hut's wall. I settled then, the dripping rain off the eaves, and in the distance the flutter of plastic bags caught in the chain-link fence. I set my radio to one, half of a one, and held it tight against my ear and I heard a voice and I drifted and woke and drifted.

I didn't dream. It was dark and I didn't dream. I rocked back and forth – gently at first, but it became more insistent. Then I felt it, heavy and hot and painful at my side. I'd been kicked. A man was there, standing over me, milk light spread out from his wide shoulders.

'Fuck, I thought you were dead.'

'I'm not fucking dead. The fuck you kicking me for?'

'I just thought you were. Scared the shite outta me. What are you doing there? Christ. You have to clear off, you'll have me shot. Go wan.' The security guard. Last night his feet dragged about inside and his body settled against the other side of the wall from where my body had settled.

'I'm going, I'm going. Would you like to wake up to a boot?'

'You can't be here. I mean it, go on, get!' He stomped away, still talking, giving out, and I could hear him, back in his box, his footsteps and the start of a kettle boiling.

The wind had blown rain against the back wall: it had

dripped down and found its way into my now-drenched sleeping bag. I rolled the bag up and I tried to think where it could be hung out to dry but there was nowhere.

I needed a piss then, and wondered if I'd time before he came back out checking I was gone. I squatted quickly behind the hut, and halfway through as I felt the first relief I heard the door swing open. I pulled my pants up and ran around before he could see.

'I'm going,' I say. He was holding a mug. Clean, shorn face and balding sandy hair. He was the age of someone's dad.

'Here,' he says. 'Drink that.'

'What?'

'It's a cup of tea, drink it. And there are a few biscuits too.'

'Yeah?'

'Yeah, go on. Sorry for kicking you and all, just got a fright.'

'I got one myself.' And he laughed a bit and his body swayed and he looked away off, and I followed his eye – it was nothing he was looking at. He was shy then, as I took a sip of tea. It was milky and sweet.

'Can I keep the biscuits till later?'

'Course, do what you want with them. Feed the ducks, if you like.'

'Not giving away ginger nuts.' He looked at the ground, at his boots, and the toe of the right foot rose up and tapped a little on the tarred ground.

'You have heat in that hut?'

'There is, yeah, a little blower one – it's not bad.'

'Can I go in, have my tea in there?'

'No, not allowed anyone in there.'

'I won't touch anything.'

'I know, I'm not allowed.'

'I won't tell anyone.'

'Ah, they do check-ups and that.'

'Right . . . You don't have a smoke, do you?'

'I don't smoke, thank God. You're a bit young to be smoking.'

'Yeah, I suppose I am.' I gave him back the mug after I'd finished. 'Thanks, mister,' I say.

'Sorry again about before.'

'You're alright.'

'I'd give you a few bob if I had it, but I haven't a bean.'

'You're alright, honestly.'

'You'll be OK, you will?' he called after, just as I'd gotten to the wire fence and the noise of the road overwhelmed the last of his words. I switched the weight of my pack from one shoulder to the other. It was only trucks at that hour, violently loud moving steel. The concrete along the path uneven and rutted with weeds and slowly correcting itself as I came closer to town. Large trees then, bare and webbed overhead.

At the top of Grafton Street, the shopping centre gates were open. I went in, wandered its empty, brightly lit and wide corridors. Music piped in and played on a loop. It took a moment, and I almost sang along, 'Santa Baby', but then it dropped like an anchor, rooting me to the spot. Christmas. I began counting on my fingers. How long since I'd had a home? Not a year, not yet, I knew that.

I stopped at window displays and looked and looked. Polished articles beamed at me, double-stitched wool coats that flared at the hip, deliciously coloured dresses, and pots and pans boiled over with fiery tinsel. I watched, all a daze. I wanted a bath. I thought of hot water, filled to the brim. Steam too and soap and bubbles and towels and not the scabby ones either, the shop-window ones, the ones in the ads, the length of a carpet and thick as a sponge.

I sat on a bench on the second floor eating the ginger nuts. 'Santa Baby', for the third time. The biscuits, dry and sweet and, without a cuppa, stuck to the roof of my mouth. I used my finger to peck the build-up, that same way I had when we were given wafers to practise with, by Sister, before our First Communion. I'd had my knuckles reddened by a ruler and was told never to put my hands on Holy God again.

2

'Oi. Hop it,' he says. 'That's my spot.' I was sat on the arch of the Ha'penny Bridge; elegantly it dovetailed north and south. It was the best spot, as long as I could stand the wind, cutting through its delicate ironwork.

'It's mine now, so fuck off,' I say. 'Move it, cunt, or I'll fucking drown you.' I say it quickly, without hesitation. A junkie: young, nasty.

He watched, he measured really, then spat at me and ran off over the bridge, shouting, 'You'd better not be here tomorrow.'

I pulled my sleeping bag up over my knees and a while later removed it and then, putting it back, couldn't decide which was colder. The moisture in the bag had begun to freeze and it wrinkled like crisp packets. My body had begun to shake then and I had no way to stop it. I settled in and performed my magic trick, putting one upturned hand out and I was invisible.

A pair of the shiniest ox-blood Docs I'd ever seen planted down in front of me, followed by yellow socks, washed dungarees and a long woollen coat. A man: his head was shaved, but not a skinhead, something else I didn't have a word for. He was all cheekbones and lips and eyes. I held my hand out then, open, waiting for that warm coin to fall into my palm. No money came.

'Can you spare ten pence, please?' I say.

He crouched down slowly, as if not to spook me. I looked away from his face towards his joined hands and saw how both palms carried heavy scars. He was eye level then, and he says a word that I hadn't heard in a long time. He says a name, my name. He says, 'Juno.' He brought his hand towards my face and he says it again, 'Juno.' I blinked and stared vacantly and felt nothing but a sharp intake of breath. I turned from him, clutching the dark ironwork and looking up the quays. I wanted to run.

'I've been looking for you,' he says. And I felt his hand on my shoulder. He took hold of my rucksack and I turned and pulled it back from his hands.

'That's mine.'

'OK,' he says and let it go. 'Come on,' he says. 'Come with me.'

'I can't give up my spot. It'll be taken, I've things to do.'

'I know, you can come back, it won't take long. Come on.'

I was so confused. I rested my bag against my shin so I could feel where it was and I began to carefully roll my sleeping bag. I set about checking in my empty pockets and checking the ground for anything I may have dropped. He waited; I could feel him there.

'Can I help you with that?'

'No, I know the way I like it. I know.'

He walked over the arch of the bridge and I followed. Looking down I caught the lank of his gait, and remembered how I knew that much. He stopped now and then and turned to make sure I was coming.

'Stop looking at me,' I say. 'I fucking mean it.'

He paused outside a cafe and opened the door, standing

aside for me to go in. I couldn't go in. Something had quietly and very suddenly moved inside and I couldn't breathe and I shook and shook and my eyes burned.

'Oh fuck, I can't,' I say. 'I can't, I can't. Please, I don't want you to look at me, please.' Legs folded his arms around me.

'You're alright, I'm here now, I've got you.' I could feel heat from his pressed body, and a smell like tobacco and something fresh at the side of his face where our cheeks had met. My face folded inside the nook of his shoulder and I was being held, held up, and I thought how tired I was holding myself up and I had no strength for it any more and wanted to stay that way and just rest. He held me for some time. My eyes stayed open, watching the faces of passers-by, before I felt his arms loosen and I could only look at the brass buttons of his dungarees.

'Come on, will we eat something?'

'I'm not going in there.'

'You're with me now, come on.' He took hold of my hand, and I felt how his fingers clung to my fingers and I allowed myself be led inside. Tables were filled with lunchtime diners. My pack was suddenly huge as I held it in front of me, defence-less against anyone who could just look and know. Legs found a small table and I was navigated into a seat. A roly-poly wait-ress came to us.

'Now, love,' she says, and stopped and looked at me.

'Three days in a tent, in the rain, what a festival.' That's what Legs says, he says it loud, so that not only the waitress could hear, but the people to our left and to our right. It settled something for the waitress and she warmed to me.

'Tea and toast, gaggles of butter and jam – that good for you, Juno?'

'Yeah.' I found myself picking at my fingernails, some were

broken, embedded with hallways and builders' yards and parks. I hated them and kept them hidden on my lap. I watched him, I tried to remember what he was and see what he had become. His pale eyes, and circles painted with watercolour, blue mauve beneath. Tired, I thought. A vertical white scar stamped on his left eyebrow; the hairs parted both sides of it and left its white line exposed. He had a small amount of uneven stubble, but barely a spring growth. He was in there alright – I could see it then, my own boy.

The waitress put our plates in front of us with her thumb pressed into the butter.

'There you are now, my loves,' she says, and without thinking, sucked the butter from her thumb as she walked away. I could feel my body was still shaking, pushing back against the warmth.

'Going to the loo,' I say, looking around trying to locate it.

'It's downstairs, just there.'

I stood, and as I began to make my way, I felt Legs' hand gather at my arm and I paused. It was a careful touch, not a grip, not forbidding.

'Juno, you can leave your bag here – I'll watch it for you. Promise.'

I saw how it swung between my hands, rubbing past the tops of my feet. I placed it down, like it was a casual act.

I went slowly down the winding stairs, finding there was lashings of hot water, and a real bar of soap – it was filled to the brim with lavender oil and rose, maybe, and I remembered reading how in Lebanon roses were harvested at dawn, while their scent was in full bloom, before the sun scorched the petals and the scent was taken. I scrubbed and scrubbed and scrubbed, but still. I wrapped the soap in toilet roll, but without my bag to hide it in, was forced to keep it in my front pocket where it bulged and made my thigh wet.

Legs had waited for me to return before starting to eat. We sat silently. I waited for questions; they never came and I was never so grateful. He focused on his food. The waitress hadn't given us a knife so Legs used his spoon to carefully cut the crusts from his bread and left them in rows next to his plate. I reached over and ate them. He chewed and sipped and his mouth waxed scarlet and a few blackened crumbs clung between the gaps in his teeth and as he drank he slurped his tea loud enough to draw attention from the next table.

'Sorry, missus.' He leaned his head towards a table of older women. 'But Juno here doesn't get out much.' He smiled at the one closest then, and she was charmed.

'She's a holy disgrace,' the woman says.

'Oh, she is,' says Legs, delighted. 'A holy disgrace.' And his eyes flicked up to me for the first time and he winked.

'Are you not going to apologise to the nice woman, wrecking her lunch?'

'Sorry, missus,' I say.

'I can't bring her anywhere,' he told her, and even after, when I waited outside, the woman wouldn't let go of his arm. He looked out through the glass and found me and made a face.

After, he says, 'What does she mean, she wants me to touch her Holy Mary?'

We went back across the bridge as it started to rain. Junkie boy was in my spot. He didn't see me and I wondered if I'd been transformed, so quickly fortified by tea and heat. I took fifty pence and dropped it into his empty cup.

'Thanks, missus,' he says. The poor frozen bastard.

We walked along the Quays together. I think it was a struggle for him to slow down to my pace, and still I wouldn't surrender my bag or let him help. We turned up Bedford Row towards Fleet Street as the sky started to darken. We'd hardly spoken since the cafe, there was so much to say that it had bottlenecked and we were quiet and I wondered if he was already starting to regret finding me.

'Are we going somewhere?' I say.

'Yeah, I told you, we're going to me granny's.' And he turned and smiled, a big smile, chuffed with himself.

'Are we really?'

'Yeah.'

It made me think of a fairy tale, going to Granny's. It made me wonder if, like the little matchstick girl, I was still on the bridge and frozen dead.

'Your granny's still alive?'

'God, I hope not. We buried her a month ago.'

Granny's flat was hidden at the back of a first-floor red-brick terrace. We went up a flight of metal stairs, past children playing in a doorway. A TV was on, and I could hear a ball being kicked, steadily beating against a wall and echoing sharply from the courtyard below. A mattress slumped to the side of his door.

'Look at the stain on that mattress,' he says. 'Look, can you see it?'

'The stain?'

'Me granny, she died on it – look, they didn't find her for days, you can see her outline.'

'You can?'

'Well, yeah, it's vague. I was going to cut around it and display it at my show, call it Granny of Turin,' he laughed.

'What show?'

'My show.'

He turned the key and the door opened into a tiny living room, still filled with old-fashioned granny furniture: dark cabinets too big for the room, an upright piano and hand-stitched doilies, stained now. There was a Madonna and Child print that Legs had covered in glitter and strands of gold Christmas tresses and fashioned into the shape of a heart.

I remembered the last time I'd been inside a house, some bloke had taken me off the street with the promise of a meal and a bath. I knew what he was saying really, and still how easily I went.

Legs dropped his single key in a bowl, saying, 'The neighbours can be a bit hostile. I'm kinda squatting – Granny wanted me to stay here, but they keep calling the council and complaining. I'll probably be a goner once the paperwork goes through and they figure out she's dead. Me mam died, did you hear? Do you want a cup of tea?' He left me alone there and I watched him in the little kitchen: he sparked a match and held it until the blue jets flared and slowly reddened under the boiling kettle.

The room smelled, not in a bad way, stale, like smoke and something else, something I didn't know, maybe it was his smell. The carpet had worn down in a single track leading from the front door through to the kitchen. Its brown-and-orange swirl faded at my feet. Fresh tobacco cut out of its cigarette skins littered a coffee table alongside filters and rolling papers. Books on the arm of the couch, folded open and laid face up. There were sketch pads too, dropped and let rest where they landed. Pencil drawings, vague outlines, disjointed bodies. A male torso, a hand. More pads stacked on top of each other, different sizes, hoisted up the end of the couch where the leg was missing.

There was a house plant on the mantel. I suspected under Granny's reign, it had flourished. It was dead now, but leaves clung on, petrified golden and, I thought, beautiful.

Legs came back into the room holding a tray. He looked at me and stopped, tilted his head some and smiled.

'You're impossibly gorgeous, Juno. Do you know that? You've grown up perfect.' He folded himself onto the couch and took a lump of hash from a tin and started burning it with a flaming Bic. It smelled like leather and wood and an unknown exotic and his hand trembled a bit and I wondered if he was nervous too. I put my bag down and sat at the far end of the couch and felt the springs slump under me.

'Is that her piano, the one you told me about?'

'Yeah, it's a bit banjaxed now, but yeah.'

He slowly rolled a smoke, his white fingers scattering loose tobacco inside the paper cone. Rich brown tar stains under his nails, and between his forefinger and thumb lay tiny dots of blue-black ink, tattooed into his skin. He lit it and took a few drags and the room filled with smoke.

Outside the world drifted past and we were stoned. He played some records, music I didn't know, and he sketched with a soft pencil, and I watched him and forgot to ask to see the drawings.

'Is that what you did in there? Draw?'

'Yeah. I did. I drew a lot.'

I watched how his mind seemed to rush to something past, and he flooded with memory and then his head twisted a little to one side and they were gone.

'You might say some day . . . tell me, if you want, what happened. I'd like that.'

'Yeah, and you.'

'Yeah.'

More tea was made and he showed me the rest of the flat. Not much really, a small dim bedroom in the back, off the kitchen. It was dark and cold there, away from the electric heater.

'Would you let me have a bath?' I asked and he said I could and put ten pence in the geyser and in the pink-tiled room he ran the water. He apologised, once for the miserly inch of hot water and again for the small used blue towel. It's the only one, he says. I lay in the bath, and splashed the water on my chest; it dribbled down my arms already cooling. I went mad with the bar of lavender soap, making the water turn milky and then lay back and closed my eyes and listened to the drifts of music coming off the record player and suddenly found I was giggling to myself. I must have been in for ages – he spoke through the door checking on me. 'I'm grand,' I say, already on my knees by then, wiping the line of dead skin clean with a handful of toilet paper. Later, hours past dark, he gave me a pillow and some blankets, laid them on the couch and asked if I'd be alright there.

'Yes,' I say. He paused by the door frame, looked at me and I, fool, thought maybe he wanted and say, 'Are you not going to tuck me in?' He looked at the floor and one hand found the other and they rubbed together in front of him. He slowly crossed the room, came towards me in silhouette, as if leaving the colourful part of himself curiously watching behind. I felt as his hand folded under the blankets at my feet and calves and thighs, creating a small cocoon, a mermaid shape. He skipped my bum and went up to my shoulders, gently pinning me back. And I looked at him; I wasn't trying to be all seductive or that – I'm not a complete tit. But I did hold on to his eye in a level stare and raise my chin up to his face.

'Goodnight, Juno,' he says, and stood after kissing my forehead.

'Night,' I say. He went to bed and I lay there; my hands fumbled blindly for a smoke. I made figure eights and circles in the dark with the lit end of the ciggy and listened to the sounds of him through the thin wall, settling into a silence, and I wondered if that feeling was me missing something as the electric heater hummed and swivelled, sending a short glow of orange into the room.

3

I could hear Legs making noise in the kitchen as I was waking up and I felt all of a sudden at home. This feeling inside flared and I longed for nothing and let my eyes drift back down, my body head to toe warm and the blankets dry.

He walked through, wearing Granny's nightgown and matching robe, pink quilted and shimmering satin.

'Where's your hairnet, dolly?' I say.

'I don't go to the salon till Tuesday.'

'Blue rinse?'

'Is there any other colour?' He had two chipped mugs in his hand, held on to one, handed me the other, and sat. I could feel the heat of his skinny arse at my feet and didn't move. He sipped and stared almost aimlessly towards the window. There were voices out in the courtyard drifting up; somebody was calling a name, over and over.

'Any plans?' he says.

'No.'

He lit two cigarettes and the smoke pushed against early light.

'Wanna stroll about with me?'

'Yes, I do,' I say. He passed the lit cigarette and I touched his arm. 'Sorry about your mam. Were you able to see her?'

He didn't bristle or move. I'd made him uncomfortable.

'No . . . Today's Tuesday?'

'I don't know.'

'I've to sign on. Thursday.'

'Thank you,' I say.

'For what?'

'. . . Looking for me.'

'Stop,' he says and patted the blanket near my knees.

He went to the record player and turned it on. Then he picked up the needle and his hand trembled slightly as he carefully placed it into the dark groove of an old album. It pulled across, making that static scratching sound I loved. And Vera Lynn came droning on, the white cliffs of bloody Dover: '*There'll be bluebirds over, the white cliffs of Dover, tomorrow just you wait and see.*'

'Very punk,' I say.

'So punk, she's post-punk.'

'She's punk-modern.' And he took to singing word for word.

'*I may not be near, but I have no fear . . .*'

He sang and he danced and after, he says, 'You can do almost anything in prison, but you can't leave and you can never dance.' Then we were quiet and more than once he caught me watching him and when I looked away, shy, he says, 'It's alright, I understand – it's hard not to look.'

'Am I alright here, for a bit?' I say.

'To stay here?'

'Yeah, just for a bit. Just till I sort something or that, just till I get fixed up.' I panicked and rushed on. 'I can clean, or cook you your dinner. Or anything, I mean, if you want it, you can,

I don't mind – I just need somewhere to stay still for a bit . . .
Me head, it's wrecked.'

'You live here now, you big eejit, of course.' He walked off
towards the kitchen and in the doorway, he stopped and turned.

'Were you just offering a ride to stay in this kip?'

'Did I fuck. Ride you for a stay in this dump?'

'Whore,' he says, and gave himself a good chuckle.

'Not if it was the Taj Mahal.'

'Cheap whore.' He disappeared into the kitchen.

Still in his granny's robe, Legs added a woolly hat and slippers
to his get-up, and holding a mug in one hand and a stack of
ten-pence pieces in the other, said he'd be back, he just had to
go to his office for a bit and went outside. I leapt from the settee
to watch, pulling the window lace aside in time to catch him walk
down the metal stairs and cross the courtyard to the phone box,
where he set up shop. He rested his mug on a torn phone
book and lit a smoke, before feeding the phone and dialling and
becoming suddenly animated with whomever he was speaking,
his long pink shimmering robe swishing across his bare legs.

I emptied out my bag and washed my clothes in the sink.
The ones that were beyond, I binned. I went through his granny's closet and pulled out a long-sleeved green dress and tried it
on. It had an embroidered collar, shiny big black buttons and a
thick belt that pulled in my waist and I decided I looked chic
with my work boots and an overcoat that belonged to Legs.

Before lifting the piano seat to put Mam's tin box safely
away, I opened it for the first in a long time. I didn't read her
horoscopes, but saw how the newsprint had begun to yellow at
the edges and in the corners particularly. I took out one of
Legs' drawings of the poppies.

When he came back, frozen cold and the puff knocked out of him from the stairs, he stopped in the doorway and looked at me. He really looked. He told me I was never more beautiful. Imagine!

'C'mere,' I say and lead him to the mantel, where I had placed his drawing.

'I kept it. I've all of them, but that's the first one you did, I think I like it best.' He picked it up and ran his fingers across the little watercolour. 'There's a poem Sylvia Plath wrote about poppies,' I say, 'it's lovely, I'll dig it out of the library when I'm there.'

He looked at it for a long time and a quiet settled over the room. He saw something in it that I didn't see, even though I'd looked for ages.

'I think we'll leave it on the mantel,' he says and I nodded.

'Granny would definitely approve,' I say, then, '... Sister interviewed me in the classroom the day after you were taken in.' I hadn't planned on saying it, not a bit, and if I was asked a moment before, I could have denied it without a lie. I was standing behind him and hearing her name he looked at me quickly, in a serious way, not a reprimand. His body stiffened and if it weren't for his breathing and the swell of his chest, he would have been a statue. 'I have to tell you,' I say. He picked up the picture again and was looking down as if some new curiosity, unseen before, presented itself.

'You don't have to tell me anything.' And he returned it to the mantel, and when he looked up, his face had become weary and reluctant.

'Do you already know?'

'I know nothing, I see nothing, I say nothing.' He smiled falsely and crossed as if there was something on the other side of the small room he had to attend to suddenly. Stopping at the old piano, he lifted the lid and pressed the keys closest to hand. The notes vibrated, causing a delicate stir in spite of their age.

'I don't know if that's the right word, interviewed? Talked to me? I kept telling her it was an accident, how you'd tried to put out the flames and all. That she was there, she saw the same as I did. But then she asks if maybe I had given the suggestion, if it had been my idea ... And I lied, Legs, I lied and I said no and I signed this bit of paper. I did that, Legs. I signed it and saved myself.'

'They got us good, didn't they?' he says with a smile, without a drop of regret, and held me there under the paper hoods of his unblinking eyes.

'I'm sorry,' I say. 'You're disappointed.'

'Not with you, never.' He came closer and I felt his finger slide across my cheek and throughout my body a quiver. I felt I wanted to cry suddenly to someone not there. That 'us', years before, when we were still young.

'You don't have to forgive me,' I say. 'I wouldn't.'

'It made no difference. None.'

'Still, I signed.'

'You're a peach.'

'A plum.'

'The whole fruit salad.'

'I'm sorry.'

'I'm going to dress,' he says, 'try and catch up with your fabulous look.'

'Good luck with that.'

He went into his room, and although I listened through the wall, I heard nothing, and when he came out of the bedroom, he'd shed every word I'd spoken.

'Let's go sell Granny's kit,' he says. 'And I want to show you something.'

We filled a laundry bag with the rest of his granny's clothes, and as dusk fell, we went out.

Legs knew a place: it wasn't called a pawn because it sold vintage clothes, which are the same as second-hand clothes that they call vintage so there's less chance of getting crabs and they can charge more.

The group of boys and young men that had been laughing and smoking in the courtyard went quiet and sullen as we passed, gawking at us. When they laughed again, it seemed as though something cruel had been said. I checked over my shoulder that they didn't follow. Legs seemed unfazed. We turned out of the courtyard and went away from the river to Fleet Street, turning west towards Temple Bar, over the slippery black-oiled cobblestones, passing the small shops and boarded-up buildings.

'They're going to turn all this into artist spaces,' he says.

'Who?'

'Who?'

'Yeah, who's going to?'

'They! They are going to do it.'

We stopped outside a red-brick warehouse. It looked abandoned, except for a large plate glass that was being carefully set into the walls at the ground floor by several men wearing colourful hard hats. Legs took me by the arm and led me to the other side of the narrow street, planting himself there, fixed and watching. The men shouted back and forth with increasing intensity.

'Have you taken a shine to the building trade, Legs?'

'No.'

'Is this what you wanted to show me?'

'Yes.'

'OK, that's great. Can you stop showing it to me now, please?'

'Do you know what this is?'

'It's literally a hole in the wall.'

'It's a gallery space. It's going to open soon and guess who's having the first show?'

'Fuck off!'

'Yep.'

'Are you joking? Legs?'

'It's good, isn't it?'

'It's fucking amazing!' I cried and flung my arms around him. 'I'm so so so proud.'

'You're the one I wanted to see it, you're the only one that knows everything.'

He slung the black bag over his shoulder and I tucked myself tightly into his side as we slowly walked up to Dame Street.

'You're an artist, I can't believe it. An actual real working artist.'

The vendors under George's Arcade looked like pop stars, hair dyed and cut into styles I'd never seen. Legs knew them all and joked and laughed and says, 'This is Juno.' I was pushed in front of them and that was alright because I was Juno, because I was with him. Records and costume jewellery and old fox-fur shawls lined up under the towering red-brick ceiling in postbox-green stalls.

He directed us up the tiniest set of creaking wood stairs and into a thrift shop on the first floor. I was struck by the smell, of old clothes I suppose, scent embedded as they journeyed, stories clung to thread – watching out a window in minor regalia, before a doorbell rang or didn't, sitting in a darkened cinema alone, or a finger nervously undoing a first clasp – I smelt that smell and flooded with affection.

The shop was divided into small rooms and all along the walls clothes hung on rails packed to bursting, bowed in the centre. Behind the counter was a girl, a very beautiful one.

'Legs!' she says, her arms reached out and she went to him. I could feel a jealous burning under my ribs. 'Legs.' I'd given him that – it was mine – I'd given it to him and he'd taken it and shared it with strangers, diluted it. She kissed him in the familiar way a lover might. She had dyed hair and bright lipstick that smudged across his mouth. She says, 'Hold on,' and held his face between her hands and with her wet thumb wiped away the mark. Legs stood still for her. Beside their ease and charm and beauty, I became very small. They talked about what they had done together and what they had done since and it was all so foreign to my ear, this talk. But then Legs took up my hand and held it tight, and lifted it to his mouth and kissed it as if it were lovely, saying, 'This is Juno, she's with me.'

I'm Juno, I'm with him. I'm with him. I'm with him. And I could feel I was about to burst and I rushed closer to his side, desperate for a new era.

'Are you blushing?' says the girl behind the counter and she hugged us both. 'Bless you, angel. Never trust anyone who doesn't blush, my dad said that. Where did you find her?'

'Juno found me,' he says.

'Hello, Juno. Agnes.'

'You're so gorgeous,' I say, because it was true, and she laughed and it wasn't coy, her laughter, and she hugged me again. 'Oh, she can stay, I like her,' she says. 'Juno, look at your beautiful hair, it's on fire,' and she reached and touched it and I was delighted I'd had a bath the day before.

Legs looked at me then, he says, 'Juno here had an aunt who was married to an earl, very very posh, and now that she is resting peacefully, we have the best of her swag. Juno?' I tipped the bag up on the counter and we assessed the cascade of bric-a-brac and I wondered if Legs had oversold as we all stepped back, away from the reek of mothballs.

'This is more of your granny's shit?'

'An earl's wife, I'm sure.'

Before we left the shop, Legs, holding six pounds, triumphant, turned to Agnes. 'Juno's looking for a job – she'd be brilliant here.'

'Are you, Juno?' she says. She hadn't dismissed the idea out of hand and it made me shy again, so unsure I could only nod at first.

'Yeah, yeah, I am.'

'Have you ever worked retail before?'

'No.' Agnes' head tilted looking at me. She had that very pale and unblemished skin that people call porcelain, but it's not porcelain, it's warmer than that, softer.

'At least you've no bad habits.'

'She'd be better than that last one you had – what was her name, Bitchy McCunt?' says Legs.

'Shut up, you,' says Agnes. 'I'm not in tomorrow. Why don't you come in the day after, around eleven? – we'll have a chat.'

'Yes, I will. At eleven.'

Legs trailed me around town and happily I held on to him. We sat outside the Coffee Inn, on a small and cobbled street, and people passed all around us in gangs of twos and threes and in this Dublin I didn't know, people were bright and they were fearless. The damp road shined and we were sat on small steel chairs and plastic tablecloths fell on our knees, red-and-white check like it was Paris but waterproof, just in case.

Legs ordered coffee and a young girl smiled and brought him a ludicrously small cup.

'For fuck's sake, she could have at least filled it,' I say. I had hot chocolate and whipped cream and some sprinkled yokes and went mad at it with a spoon.

'I don't understand,' I say, 'how you got from there to here.'

'From where to where?'

'You're a bit dapper, bit hooked up, for a fellow just out of the clink.'

'I've been out a while, and it's a small town.'

'Compared to where?'

'Anywhere.'

'But how do you know that? I wouldn't know.'

'Me neither.' And his head tilted. 'Not really, not yet. It's all pretend, Juno, you know that – you're the only one who knows.'

'Don't worry, I'll tell no one.'

'My da's brother had money, knew people. My ma kept hounding him till he canvassed to get me out early. So after four years, I was sixteen then, he worked it out and I was transferred off to a boarding school that he paid for.' Legs had said these words before, I thought. He finished his coffee in a single sip, watching me carefully as he set his cup back onto its saucer.

'A boarding school? Are you joking?'

'No.'

'So are you posh now – is that how that works?'

'You're adorable.'

'Fuck off. You probably spoke Latin and had a bum boy and everything.' I laughed, but he looked at me suddenly, and I saw how he didn't think much of me at all then.

'Sorry,' I say, 'I'm sure after prison, going there was horrible and all. I can't even imagine.'

'Better food.'

'Can I be adorable again? I liked that.'

He sat back, looking over the far end of the street, past the flower sellers, as far as the brightly lit Bloomsbury. 'Prison and boarding school require the same attention.' He lit a smoke and inhaled deeply, plucking a string of tobacco from his lip, and smiled.

'One guy, Rico, complete nutter, he was in for GBH. Every morning I meet Rico: "Good morning, Rico," I say. I see him in the afternoon: "How are you, Rico?" Dinner time: "Alright, Rico?" Now this goes on for weeks and months and years and then one day you're fucked off cos of your food or post or books or whatever and you pass Rico and forget to say, "How are you, Rico?" Now, Rico goes to his cell, he has nothing else to think about, nothing, and all he can think is, that cunt Legs didn't say hello. And the next time you see Rico, he has a knife and he's looking for you.'

'Jaysus. And what about in boarding school?'

'In boarding school, you are Rico.'

Outside the off-licence, we gathered our coppers like loose shrapnel, bought a naggin of whiskey and swooped into the mini-market. I could hear Legs and the cashier laugh while I filled my knickers with frozen chicken nuggets. We paid for a batch loaf and left. Outside I howled on about my poor frozen fanny and at a small children's park near the flat we stopped by a rusting carousel. Legs gave a good push and stepped on. I sipped the whiskey and the brown grain burned down my throat and filled my chest with heat; my head tilted back watching the dark branches overhead. The carousel squeaked with every rotation. Legs rolled a smoke and said, 'Give us a whack of that, doll.' The road in the distance was quiet and even the brass pendulums of the church bells were tightly wrapped.

Squeak squeak, says the church mouse. Squeak, says the carousel.

'You're a gorgeous man, Legs McLeggies,' I say, just because I felt the drink and the night air suddenly sway like a Charleston. I didn't want to push anything away.

'You're something of a plum yourself, the full fruit cocktail.'

'You've already used that one!'

I wanted him to kiss me, just then. I wanted to take on the weight of his body, let it bear down. I could take it, I could happily be blown through the trees, divided by their dark limbs. He must have known that and so his smile was tepid. I did know, I really did, that same way when you roll a cigarette, hands frozen and free of all sensitivity, still you know it's tobacco under your fingers.

We made our way back to the little flat. Legs was telling me a story and working his way to the punchline, our voices echoed through the narrow alley and up the stairs to the top row. Each door was a different colour, pink and blue decay, red too, and the bubble and blister of age, paint skins that chipped and fell and danced with sweets wrappers and Players please.

Our door was the last one along. Our door. It had been spray-painted in tall ugly lines, still wet, and from the courtyard came the cruellest laughter.

QUEER
FUCK
HERE

We paused outside.

We say:

Nothing.

I watched Legs for understanding. There was only the escape of cold air from his mouth. He opened the door silently and went inside, shaking off the cold and rubbing his hands in a fit. I went to the kitchen, put on the grill; the metal rattled and grated.

'They're all soggy,' I shouted through to the next room. 'The nuggets ... Must be me roaster of a minge.' I watched him carefully from the door. He did not laugh, Legs. He sat and flicked through a paper pad.

'Cos me fanny's on fire ... cos it's so hot,' I say. 'Legs ... Legs?' And I could feel the charm of the day drift and sully like fool's gold.

'Legs?' I say again. The near-soundless room, save a gentle scratching of his HB pencil marking the stiff page.

He laid the pad down at his side and stood. 'I'm going out,' he says to the room. He hadn't taken his coat off, but just then he buttoned up for the night air, his head low, and I saw the boy that was still him and flinched when the front door closed with a gentle click.

I was all of a sudden displaced. I turned the grill back on, thinking I should eat, then turned it off, opting instead for a smoke and more drink. I stood in the open doorway, looking out and drinking. Dark streets lay quietly under a thousand amber polka dots. In the unlit alley around the back, I watched a couple as they crept excited, running to the shelter of the dark. It was silent then, their footsteps halted and the woman laughed. I put my finger carefully on the spray paint to see if it was dry and then thought about how in the morning I could paint over it, and how heroic. But I'm not heroic, I'm just not.

I went back inside, cold suddenly, and turned on the little heater. Legs had left the drawing pad lying on the couch, his perfect sketch of his own graffitied front door, except he'd added a perpendicular 'I' to the words. I felt a fool for being there still, that there was nowhere else for me to go. I went to his room and stood, looking into his bedroom like a wish.

I slowly began to undress, peeled myself away, layer by layer, until even in the dark of his room I could see myself, naked. I lay there, on his bed, drinking, and eked a sort of pleasure from the squalid and cold sheets.

I think I was asleep when he came home: the sound of the grinding metal lock brought me back into that lit haze that exposed my skin in small flecks. The uneven blanket lay in folds at my feet. I felt a chill, maybe from the swing of the closing door, but still I wouldn't cover myself. I wondered if Legs saw the couch empty and felt. Anything. His feet were a gentle sweep across the floor as he went and pissed and washed. I imagined the cold water in streaks down his neck as he chased them with the feeble towel. It went so silent then, was he sitting? On the side of the bath, the floor? A long time and no sound. My head hurt and I felt in my mouth a dry metal ache.

He found me then, on his bed; my closed eyes hid what that was for him. Did he pause, even out of curiosity, or look at me pleased in any way? I don't know. The mattress springs pressed down as he perched at its edge and shoes, one after the other, tapped the floor. I opened my eyes to see him pull off his shirt and sit forward to remove his trousers. His back was narrow and between his shoulder blades a deep crevasse. I shut my eyes again as he stood and I felt the drape of a blanket close like a curtain across my body. And ever so easily, he rolled himself into bed, barely disrupting an old spring.

He faced the wall away from me, most of him under cover but a small part of his shoulder protruding and polished by the dim light. I wondered if I was to tell him everything would he be appalled? He was the same, I knew that, inside, his secret life, the same dark unwound knots. I put my hand on his back and it felt warm under my fingers.

'You're awake?' he says.

'Yes.' I waited to see if he'd say more.

I could see the knuckles of his ribs drawing little breaths. He turned then, around in the bed, and watched me and touched my cheeks, ran his finger the length of my nose and I made a face and he smiled.

'I think you've been through the wars,' he says.

'Me? What about you?'

He pressed a finger to my nose again.

'Get away from me bleedin' nose. Who touches a person's nose, Jaysus.'

'Has it been broken?'

'How would I know?'

'Cos it's your nose.'

'So?'

'So, has it?'

'I don't know ... it might have been banged a few times alright.'

'Juno, they're supposed to be straight.'

'Are they?'

'You're my girl, you're lovely,' he says. 'I've always thought so, you know that, don't you?'

'But not lovely, not like that?'

'Not to me. No.' I felt the blanket drift down to my elbows, my breasts were exposed and I saw how I'd been holding in my stomach. I lay on my back and covered myself.

'My breath stinks,' I say.

'Mine too, I'm sure.'

'You're a fucking poof,' I say and it shocked me. I knew it hurt him; maybe I wanted him hurt.

'Don't,' he says, 'not you, I couldn't take it from you.'

'Does anyone else know?'

'Everyone, but everyone knows.'

'Well, I fucking didn't . . .' I turned away from him then.

'I think you did.'

'Shut up . . . Did your mam know?'

'Course she did, she thought she could scrub it away.'

'And Father?' I looked back at him and saw how even the mention of Father affected him still.

'Yeah,' he says, after a while.

'Ah, Legs.'

'Will you still be my girl?'

'It's a bit ruined, isn't it? I always thought – I thought something else. I never get what I want.' I watched his sharp face, his eyes flickered over me, how open and how watchful.

'Turn over on your side, I can't look at you any more,' I say, and he went to kiss me, and I swatted him off. 'Away, you, like being kissed by Judas fucking Iscariot, 'cept he has the horn for Peter.'

He turned and settled.

'I love you, Juno,' he says, and it came as a shock when he

said it, though I knew it to be true. I'd never been told before so it was sudden and shocking, and I wanted to say it back without caution. I did want that.

'Fuck off,' I say and I stroked the ends of his hair, his swan's neck, and I'd taken to cry.

'You've secrets,' he says.

'You've secrets,' I say.

He didn't move, there was something. He says, 'You sure you're OK?' But that was not what he was thinking.

'Of course,' I say.

Outside the sky was blueing and the air was cold, and as I could smell how it was with his sleeping body, I closed my eyes.

4

Legs stood near the sink. He had two slices of bread laid out on the counter, and as he spread the hard butter, the bread pulled under the knife and ripped and he was trying to patch the holes with his fingers. He had gotten out of bed saying he was going to send me off to work with a packed lunch.

'I haven't gotten the job yet,' I say.

The previous night, I'd started to sleep on the couch again, but when the lights were off and he'd tucked me in, I decided I didn't want to be on the couch, and rather the same way a dog decides he wants to be close to the fire. I nosed my way into his room and crept soundlessly under the blankets, holding my breath and waiting to be sent back to my bed, but he didn't send me back, he just says, 'Juno . . . ?' like it was a question, and I started to giggle. I almost didn't recognise the sound as it came out of my mouth, but it was a giggle, I'm sure. And then he started and the two of us were in fits. When we finally settled and I'd turned into the shape of him with my hands resting over his chest, I say, 'Legs, you're too thin, Jesus God,' because his ribs were raised like the ebony keys of a piano.

He says:

'Looks good in a suit.'

I say:

'Looks good in a coffin.'

In the middle of the night, he'd gotten out of bed, bringing the heater into the room and plugging it into the wall closest to him and shivered in the bed beside me. Later, he was up again, in the bathroom. I heard the noise of him shuffling about for what seemed like an age and I couldn't remember him coming back to bed.

He put one mangled slice of bread over the other mangled slice of bread and pressed them together. He wore dark suit trousers, his feet bare and a blanket draped around his shoulders, cloak-like. It trailed in places along the floor. He peeled the bread off the counter and held it up, confused then.

'You haven't really thought that one through, have you, dolly?' I say.

'I've nothing to put inside it.'

'No.'

'I've nothing to wrap it in.'

'You're very pretty,' I say, taking a big bite of the bread. 'It's perfect.'

We sat on the couch and drank tea. Legs kept pulling the blanket tighter around himself, saying, 'It's Baltic, puffin-arsed fucking Baltic.' And before I left the flat, I settled him back to bed and told him to sleep and to drink tea only and his head must have popped up out of the covers as I was closing the door and looked grimly at the ugly graffiti.

He shouted:

'Keep an eye out for a green or chocolate-brown velvet blazer.'

'A what?'

'Two-button with a double vent.'

'Dear God.'

'Wide lapel . . . And tell Agnes to double your wages and tell her I said her arse is fat.'

The walk to the shop was quick and this sense of purpose swirled about me in delight and panic. I was forced into the same green dress – there was nothing else – and without Legs at my side I just felt shabby and that Agnes would take one look at me and know she'd made a terrible mistake. The old arcade was damp and quiet and water fell in long drips from the cracked roof, dampening the red bricks, turning their pretty colour to a rusted raw umber. There were a few merchants in overcoats and hats, rearranging their wares. They looked up without any real curiosity. Most of the stalls were closed, their shapes sculpted under heavy tarpaulin pulled tight with rope.

I stood at the base of the wooden stairs and watched the hands on a large clock, high in the distance. I wanted to be on time, not early, not late. I lit a smoke and pulled at the hem of my skirt but it was no use and I wondered if I'd ever wear a dress that a single generation had not perished in. I fretted up the stairs, announced by a hollow knocking on every tread, and my hand visibly shook as I twisted the door handle. There was no one behind the counter and across the floor there were small piles of clothes strewn in an unknown order. I could hear movement from one of the smaller rooms and there was that comforting smell of the shop.

'Agnes,' I called. Silence first and then quick footsteps and then she appeared, breathless, holding an enormous bouquet of colourful dresses. When she saw me, she beamed.

'You came. I'm so glad. Finally someone to save me from

this madness,' she says, and flung the dresses, creating a new pile on the floor.

'Let's have a coffee before we do anything.'

She led me into a cramped room, not a kitchen exactly, a sink and a kettle on a shelf. When she moved, she was effortlessly elegant, her faded jeans rolled up her ankles, and this shocking-red jacket with gold stitching that would have looked at home on horseback in a military parade. She set the kettle to boil and looked at me for the first time and in a way I didn't mind at all. Still, I was aware how the tips of my fingers scurried about inside the deep pockets of Legs' overcoat, scraped through tobacco dust and lint and finally settled on an old bus stub and folded it about over and over again. My palms felt hot and disgusting. She had a coffee jar open and was spooning granules into two mugs, then she threw open a tiny fridge and stuck her nose in the milk, announced that she thought it was safe. Posh people drank coffee – it was the first lesson I learned and Agnes was posh. Posh in the way I think Legs wanted to be posh, where it seemed not to matter, that it was not the most important thing.

'Did you have far to come?'

'No,' I say. 'I walked. It was nice.'

'Where are you living?'

'With Legs.'

Her eyebrows shot up in amazement. And I wondered then if that was a secret and if I'd broken a trust.

'That must be lively. You must be completely mad.'

I decided I didn't want to talk about the way it was lively, that that belonged to me and I desperately wanted to keep what I could of it to myself.

'How do youse know each other?'

'We were in school together,' I say cautiously.

'Oh, I thought he went to a boarding school; an all-boys one.'

'The school before that one.'

'I can't even imagine, you two must have been cute as buttons.'

'Yeah,' I say. 'How long have you been here, had this shop?'

'Over a year? Yeah, it is, it's over a year now,' she says, and clicked her finger to show how fast time had passed and handed me a mug and walked me back through the shop. 'It's all changing so quickly around here, the rents are going mad and all the little shops I'd started with are having to close. It's a bit shit, really.'

'I thought they were giving it to the artists?'

She looked at me and her nose scrunched up in a mock-confused way.

'Who told you that? Santa?'

'Legs,' I say, and she laughed. 'No, I saw his gallery, it looks brilliant ... Legs' gallery, over the road.'

'Do you mean the property development Francis is involved in?'

'I don't know who that is,' I say dimly.

'Don't worry, pet, none of us do. Here's what I say about that: see everything, believe nothing, and definitely don't ever lend money. And I have to include Legs in that, I'm afraid.'

'I don't have any money.'

'Good, you're a third of the way there. Oh, I suppose I should be professional and ask you interview questions, hard ones to trick you, mmm? Are you on drugs? I mean, right now?'

'No,' I laughed.

'What's your favourite colour?'

'All of them.'

'Good answer. Eh? Have you ever stolen or been arrested?'
She was joking of course and I knew that, but she stopped
smiling when my face did something I didn't want it to do.

'Well,' she says, 'maybe we'll come back to that one.' And she
laughed, unfazed, and says, 'You're hired! Can you start now?'

'Yes. Thank you,' I say as she sipped her drink, with both
hands around the cup, watching me.

Agnes sat down on what looked like an old bar stool and I
across from her. I saw, pushed against the wall and tucked under
stacks of fabric, a sewing machine. It wasn't steel or curved into
the limbed shape of the Singer. It looked boxy and precise and
wonderful.

'Does the sewing machine work?'

'Yes, it should. I have one at home. I haven't used that one
since college.'

'Why would you need a sewing machine in college?'

'I studied textiles,' she says, and I could only imagine a class
filled with students holding magnifying glasses over swathes of
linen and cotton.

'There's a college for textiles?'

'Of course.'

And here was proof then of what I think I'd always
suspected – the world was another, a vast other, in which I'd
occupied a narrow and separate part. Agnes was the first person I'd ever met who had been to college. I decided then that
I wanted to know everything she knew.

We sat quietly for a bit, and in secret, I watched her. She was
older than I'd first thought and crow's feet had lightly pressed
both sides of her eyes. She was lovely to watch, lovely company
to keep, but a part of me knew she'd never call me friend, her
friend, not really. She'd tell a story of me, not unkind: I'd be

funny in her story, she'd be wise. But that friend role was taken and locked away safe. She was secure in what she knew and so her curiosity was halted and reserved.

'Can you sew?'

'A little, but not on anything like that. Me mam had an old Singer.'

'I started on a Singer,' she says. 'Do you still have it?'

'No.'

I felt a flutter in my belly and Agnes maybe did too and she didn't ask any more about Mam's Singer. She passed me a straight and lit it and lit her own and it dangled from her mouth when she says, 'Right.' As if that was a full stop she placed in the air and went on to explain the value of the piles on the floor. 'These dresses can be altered,' she says, 'but only so much before you lose the original and the dress is gone. Really, you can only pull in or take out so much.' I knew that, Mam had told me. Someone had brought in a dress from when she was several stone lighter and asked Mam to let it out and after the woman had left, Mam, adding a swatch of fabric, says, 'A parachute couldn't be let out that much.'

Agnes walked me through the rooms, and as she spoke about the clothes on each rail, her fingers leafed through them like the pages of a book. She did not exactly talk about them as if they were objects, but instead of their personality and their history; they were neither living nor dead, but an entity that waited for the right person to fit and be brought from that place to life.

I spent the day moving stacks of clothes off rails and setting them on different rails. Folding and refolding until I got the lines right. And when a customer came in I kept my head down, so as not to be asked a question, in case I'd look a fool in front of Agnes. But I watched how she was, what she said. That easy way she had with people without giving up an inch of who she was to it. At six o'clock, she locked the door. The sky had darkened and the amber floodlight beamed along one side of the domed ceiling outside leaving the mannequins closest to the window in silhouette. It was quiet on the arcade floor. There hadn't been much in the way of sales, but she was not bothered and said it was the weekend the sales happened. I continued to work until she looked at me and laughed, saying, 'We're done, stop.'

'I can keep working.'

'I can't.' And she poured wine into two glasses and we drank and sat together on the floor.

'Can I try that sewing machine sometime?'

'Yeah, there's a box of scraps around you can practise on.'

And before I left she gave me ten pounds, and says to keep note of my hours and she'd settle me up on Sunday. She tapped the metal cap of a small paint tin I had fetched instead of lunch, along with a small cheap brush.

'Decorating?'

'Legs' kitchen,' I say.

'Can't imagine, don't want to. But very glad to see he's on the mend.'

'How do you mean?'

'Oh, about a month ago he was in ribbons. I just happened to run into him. And he was all, I'm fine, I'm fine, but he was really in a bad way.'

'Yeah, he's good now alright.'

I bundled down the steps and out into the night air. I passed the Quays, the long line of idling buses, their bright windows vibrating and opaque with condensation. The slick oiled streets, black smoke and shadowed faces beneath umbrellas. And beyond, the impenetrable weight of the slow-moving, argent Liffey. I searched along O'Connell Street until I found what I was after. To my delight, under its modest red-and-white awning, it was still there. I bought a half-dozen jam doughnuts and then, at the local shop, a pan of bread and two cans of soup, tobacco and a whiskey. The playground was deserted and a team of lights spread orange evenly over the tarmac, and beyond, a first twinkle of fairy lights shone through windows, making me think of Christmas without dread.

There was no one on our first-floor landing, so I set down my messages and shook the paint tin and cracked it open with a two-pence piece. I'd discovered it in a bargain bin, at the back of the shop, and the old man working there told me he'd no idea what colour it was. I'd thought about him after, his glasses on his head as he peered at the tin. A little wine-coloured cardigan. He'd worn a tie over an old blue shirt, frayed at the cuffs and collar. And this heavy denim apron, with cracked leather piping. He thought it was incredible to not know the colour. 'Dear God, imagine that,' he says. 'I mean, imagine, not knowing something like that. I can't fathom it.'

And when I told him, 'Mister, I'll take it – it'll be some colour, won't it?'

'Well, it will,' he says, 'some colour alright. It's more an act of faith than a tin of paint, what? Give me fifty pence. Is that alright?' And on the way out the door, he touched my shoulder. 'You'll let me know – I'm dying to know.'

I was right, it was a colour, but only a white one, and I was a little disappointed at that. But I spread it out with the stiff brush over the graffitied letters and I should have covered the entire door but as soon as the letters disappeared it began to feel like a chore, so I gave up. Still, I opened the door chuffed with my endeavours. The living room was quiet and dark and my cup untouched where I'd left it on the coffee table that morning. I found Legs cocooned in bed, his breath light and steady and his two feet poking out at one end. I closed the door over and went to the kitchen and warmed the soup and buttered the bread, and before I started into the whiskey, I put the six doughnuts on a plate. And I suppose I must have gotten carried away, with the scrubbing of pots and washing dishes, because I heard Legs' voice through the thin walls.

'What in God's name are you doing in there?'

There was no tray in sight so I found the biggest plate and sliced the bread into fingers and spread them in the circle around the bowl of soup and brought them in to him. He'd turned on the side lamp and was half sitting up then, in a big green jumper and a yellow woolly hat.

'Why are you using a jackhammer in the kitchen?'

'Shut up, you.' I rested the plate across his narrow lap.

'You made me soup with fingers.'

'Well, almost – I heated soup, with fingers.'

He looked deathly pale and at his forehead beads of sweat emerged.

'Have you been in bed all day?'

'No, if you must know, I've been up a number of times to puke. And other unmentionables.'

I sat on the side of the bed and put my hand on his forehead. But I didn't know what I was feeling for, like some fool gawking under a car bonnet and pretending.

'Eat your soup,' I say. 'Agnes said she saw you last month, said you were sick?'

'She's mad as kittens that one. Is that whiskey?'

'None for you. But look it,' I say, and I presented the plate of doughnuts. 'You can have some of these if you finish your soup. Do you remember?'

'Course I remember. You're so good,' says Legs.

'I'm not really, but thank you.'

I unlaced my shoes, freed my feet and rolled into the bed beside him. The bed creaked; he stared down at the food and we were silent for a long time. He lay back after a while and exhaled and closed his eyes. He says, 'Thank you, Juno.' The soup he'd stirred about, but it remained uneaten and cooled at his side.

'You should go to a doctor in the morning.'

'Mmm, yeah. I'm feeling a lot better after that,' he says, and I knew he wouldn't. 'Tell me everything about today, first day at work – I want to know everything.'

And so I did, and he asked all the right questions and listened and I could see he was tired and how it was a strain for him and I said so, but he insisted and asked what dresses did I like the best and what colour and were they embroidered and reaching beyond the knee.

'Did you know there's a school for textiles? Agnes went to it.'

'Yeah, I did know that.' And he took my hand in his and turned into his pillow. 'You should go.'

There's really nothing to prepare a person for having their hand taken in just the right way.

'Go wan outta that,' I say, after a gulp of my drink.

'You should, you'd be brilliant.'

'Yeah, they'd be queuing up to have me.'

'I'll put it together.'

And I laughed at that.

'Will you, Legs? Just put that together, will you? Just pop that one in the oven. Cheers. I'll give my notice tomorrow so.'

I put the whiskey to my mouth again and Legs watched and smiled and says, 'Slow down.'

'She has this sewing machine she doesn't use, a modern-looking one, says I can have a go, you know, practise and that . . . I didn't think I'd ever use a sewing machine again.'

'Why?'

'Just Mam and all. I don't know who she was, me mam. I love her and everything, but . . .'

We were quiet a long time before his head had found its way into my lap, heavy and warm. I scratched and stroked under his woolly hat where his shorn hair met his neck until his eyes closed.

'I went with people, sometimes. Men, you know, for money.' I say it softly, so as not to wake him. You have to tell someone, even in a whisper it has to be said, out loud. If you don't, you'd go mad and start screaming and not stop.

He slept for hours, too hot, too cold, and I'd wrapped him up tight and went to the couch with a book and read and smoked and drank. Outside it was quiet and I sealed off that crack in the curtain where the street lights poured in. At midnight, he came through wrapped in his blanket, his woollen hat sitting high off his head, and I told him he looked like a condom. He sat down, bleary-eyed, and rubbed his face.

'Do you think Father is still alive?' he says quietly into the room. He didn't look at me; his worried face pretended to be interested in the collected lint he picked from his blanket.

'I don't know. I hope not,' I say.

'I wonder was he all that bad.'

'I don't.'

'Yeah,' he says, uncommitted, blowing a big billow of smoke into the room. 'They're not all bad though, are they?'

'If I ever meet one that's not, I'll let you know.'

'I met one. Inside.'

'A priest?'

'Well, chaplain I suppose ...'

'What about him?'

'Nothing, except that he wasn't a bastard. He was ... something else.'

'What else, what was he?'

Legs was lost to me then, drifted into cloud cover, so I couldn't see or follow him.

'Kind. I think he was kind.' His mouth carefully opened around the word – it was tender, this kindness, delicious in his mouth, and I felt suddenly plain and jealous beside it and wished for once to be spoken of or remembered that way.

'Kind how?'

'Just kind, in the way anyone can be kind.'

I wondered if he thought I was a fool, a lump, an unseeing, unfeeling lump.

'Fuck off,' I say.

'What?'

'No really, fuck off. Kind, me hole. What? Did you fancy him? Did he fiddle with you inside, made you a queer, and you like an eejit, you fell in love with him?'

Legs took a breath. I could see how he steeled himself not to be cross with me, not to fight the way some part of me knew only how to fight.

'No, he never did that.' He looked away as he spoke and a quick tear shot down his cheek. 'I prayed, Juno, I prayed and prayed that he would.' I moved over beside Legs. And I fixed his hat around his ears and wiped at his cheeks with the back of my hand.

He told me then, how he had been set upon within hours of arrival. He'd gotten himself put into solitary as soon as he'd figured out the how of it. Twenty-three hours a day alone in the small cell, fifteen minutes to travel to and from the yard, past screams and shouts, pausing at steel locking and unlocking of doors. His silent steps through the yard, when even the guard had to look away, out beyond the chain-link fence to the hills and beyond.

When he was let out they were waiting – what else was there for them to do? The assaults would intensify as punishment for trying to escape them. Later, the chaplain had found him – not like that, not like the rest. He'd talk to him, sometimes for hours, and never about God. He was older, this chaplain; his voice would reach in and was a comfort. I watched as Legs talked about him, words spun from a bright and tumultuous place, a secret gully filled with love. Actual love, imagine.

The chaplain had gotten him work in the library where he drew and he read and he drew. And he said that between the chaplain's influence and him being a bit of an oddity, he was saved. I think it more likely that Legs possessed his own violence, and a bloody stand was made, flesh ripped and bones maybe smashed. And still each evening the chaplain would come to him; they'd talk softly and the chaplain believed that burning Father was an accident and Legs felt free to tell almost all of himself. Season by dense season, they talked, until Legs, upset one night, embraced the chaplain, and felt safe and encouraged enough to hold that embrace, and hold and hold and hold, until the older man understood something of Legs' love. He disentangled himself and he stood and said goodnight in the normal way and he never returned. In the corridors or yard, he would greet Legs in a friendly way, but it had broken.

In truth, that was not his word, not love. He never said that word. But I saw his face and the way he didn't say love. The way his body sank into that unrequited place. That was what Legs showed in the game where he showed me his and I showed him mine and we told each other our stories.

5

'I'm sorry,' she says, 'but does this look ridiculous? Please be honest.' I was on my knees at a low rail; I'd been trying to arrange woollen jumpers by colour and was as far as brown. In my arms a scrumptious Donegal cable, thick as a baby, with a roll neck. I looked up at the girl, a teenager, her frame large. She was pulling the ends of a dark and ill-fitted dinner jacket together. Her face was round and flushed, and she may have at any moment begun to cry.

I was about to tell her to see Agnes, that she would know best, but Agnes' voice could be heard in the next room, laughing with a customer, and I had noticed how Agnes was careful with her attention, fixing it more heavily on some than on others. I stood up and looked at the girl.

'Stand straight, pet,' I say, and the poor yoke stood rigid, tortured at being watched. 'No, it's not ridiculous, it just doesn't fit you. C'mere.' I manoeuvred her into the next room and took down two similar jackets. I forgot to be frightened of how I seemed either to the girl or to Agnes, and quite suddenly I knew what was to be done.

'Take that one off you.' I held her sleeve. 'Pull.' When she was relieved of the garment, I give her another to try. 'It's better,' I say. 'Nearly – here, try that one.'

She looked at herself in the mirror: she was horrified. At first I thought it was the jacket I'd chosen, but saw then the horror she felt was the horror she always felt at her own reflection.

'I look like a circus tent,' she says.

'You don't, it's too big for you is all.' I buttoned the jacket and walked behind her; while looking over her shoulder into the mirror, I pulled and shifted the fabric. I gathered up some safety pins and began to fasten along the vertebrae of the seam.

'Stand still, straight, let your arms drop. Now lift them up and drop them again. OK, just relax there.' I had several pins in my mouth when I caught sight of myself, and I was shocked to find so much of my mam there, watching.

'Thanks,' she says, after I'd finished pinning and rolled up the sleeves. 'I was about to have a conniption.' And she laughed.

'You looked a bit on the edge alright.'

I stood back and looked at her. 'It suits you; you look great. So just bring it to a seamstress or that, tell 'em it's pinned already, they'll know what to do.'

'Oh …' She was unsure again. 'Can you not do it?'

'Mmm, I suppose I could, yeah, alright.' And a part of me delighted and I felt how I smiled, and when I looked up I saw Legs standing there, at the doorway smiling too, with a look on his face that I was sure was pride.

'What are you doing outta bed?' I say. 'Jaysus, you've brightened up. Give us a twirl, dolly.' Legs came in wearing a bright pink jumpsuit, gold rings and a paperboy hat, tilted low over his eyes. He looked magnificent. He stood before the girl with a raised hand, he says, 'Shall we?' She took his hand without thinking, and he waltzed her around the room. When they stopped, with a flourish, he was breathless. I saw, under his light make-up and lined eyes, how he was flushed and, I thought, high.

'Darling, you look as though you fell out of a Christmas tree,' says Agnes, drawn in by the commotion, her arms already reaching for him. And soon there was music and we were sat among the Christmas decorations we'd hung that morning, drinking wine, and when the girl tried to slink off, Legs drew her back, insistent that she stay and drink with us and so she did, still in her pinned jacket.

By six o'clock, the doors were locked and an ever-growing party of us paraded down the stairs and through the emptying arcade, cries of laughter reflecting off the high walls. Each of us had had a hand in the clothes rails and sequinned gowns and furs and costume jewels shone across our bodies as we crowded into a chip shop, starving, and deciding where next.

We'd picked up more strays on Drury Street and, aware of our own spectacle, crowded together as shiny as tinfoil and piled inside the William Tell. I saw us from the outside in: I was separate. I felt old, not pretty, worn by that unwatched feeling and passed over. I could feel the scrape of nearby flutters, approached only by those who wanted to feel Legs close. They bought me drink and so I drank. They said words like 'authentic'. I'd remind them my glass was empty and they would howl and say that that was exactly what they were talking about. Some of them spoke about their poverty as a badge of honour. They were artists and had chosen their life and so had something to look forward to – it was not their birthright; it was not a sad or oppressive poverty.

Legs came to the bar, to save me, I think, and he ignored my glum face.

'Leave in five?' he whispered in my ear. 'Just you and me.' He winked at me and I winked at him and he took hold of my arm and pulled me to the centre of the room, pressed tightly between hot and damp moving bodies. In the crush of dancing torsos and spinning lights, Legs held the end of a small bottle to my nose and told me to inhale as hard as I could: I did and suddenly my chest beat wildly and I was overwhelmed with sensation.

'Now snog someone.'

'What?'

'Snog someone.'

'Who?'

'Anyone!'

I pressed my hands around a nearby head, turned it to me and felt across the high bone of its cheek, allowing my fingers to drape along the neck as far as a collarbone. I pulled it to me, confidently, as if I knew how to kiss, that way, as if I'd done that before. Its mouth opened, its slow lively lips. My eyes never left Legs' eyes. My body moved and I burned on the inside.

Outside, Legs curled his coat around me, walked me from the lounge along South Anne Street. The night clear and cold. We drifted past the fights and shouts and kisses – invisible and untouched, we were separate.

Legs guided me down steps into a basement and still beyond that into a deeper cavern. A small wine bar he knew and in which he was known. The bartender greeted him, French style, a smack on each cheek and a third where they mocked their own theatrics. I stood off to the side, watching. He ordered, and two flutes were filled with champagne. Legs walked them to a corner table, away from the scatter of nightbirds.

'It fills up here, later,' he says. He'd never reached to pay for the drinks. I don't think he had two pence in his pocket, but it never seemed to matter. The barman says, 'On Francis?' and Legs nodded and there was an agreement. Saint Francis.

'Is this really champagne?' I say and I sipped. I didn't like it, not at first: it was too gentle, too sweet, but slowly from somewhere inside, it began to work. 'It's no wild Irish rose.'

'None of these people know what we know, only what we tell them. Remember that,' says Legs, leaning forward in his chair.

'And what do you tell them?'

'I tap their little elbows just so' – he reached forward and I could feel the gentlest way his fingers pressed – 'and I smile and I watch and I tell them maybe. Just maybe.'

I could see the patrons, mostly men, standing alone or in small couplings; some were watching, dark-eyed, coloured by the low red light.

'You have a fan club,' I tell him, but he didn't look over. 'I think they're becoming restless.'

'I've been thinking of trying to get a new place, for us. After the show, maybe go abroad.'

'Abroad? Where?'

'Anywhere.'

'I like the flat,' I say.

'It's a cell.'

'Well, you would know.' I felt suddenly sullen and ungrateful. I didn't like myself much; I didn't like being watched as we spoke. I wished to be back in the flat, near the glow of the heater, surrounded by his granny's knick-knacks, and for the first time I felt crushed under the weight of his enthusiasm.

'Sorry,' I say.

'It's OK, it's funny.' He lit two smokes and passed me one.

'Are you alright, dolly?' I say.

'Yeah, course.'

'Yeah? Well, good, we're both fine. It's fine, you're fine, I'm fine.' We drank and the music's volume was nudged up by tiny degrees and the room started to fill, a well-heeled crowd in which we were an oddity. Legs' eyeliner had begun to run a little, not in that tired and tearful way, but in the pop star I've-been-on-stage-for-hours way. He sat, polished by looks and glances, he shone.

The bartender was at our table then; he slowly refilled our glasses and set down a tray of six oysters on a bed of ice. His tattooed forearm showed a long-legged lady – she watched, lifting her own short skirt just past her thigh, enamoured with her own boldness. I could feel the tongue of my shoe, under the white tablecloth, crack with age, and my dress jagged where I'd cut the label in a hurry.

'You're going to love these,' says Legs, excited.

'Are you having a laugh?'

'Have you had oysters?'

'I'm not going to answer that.'

'You're in for a treat.'

'Why has that man given us a half-dozen wet minge?'

'Don't be a philistine.'

'You put one of those near your mouth and I'm going to boke.'

He pulled the cig from his mouth, took hold of the mollusc's shallow vessel and set about loosening it with a small silver fork, rested it to his lower lip then, mouth wide, it slipped down past his tongue, disappearing without a bite. He then exhaled the smoke he was holding as a kind of finale. And really it was beautiful to watch: Legs, still holding the empty shell, silken grey and blue, smiling wildly.

'How is it,' I say, 'with this lot?'

'The same, when it gets down to it.'

'The same as what?'

'I think I used to think if their wallets were full, it made them different.'

'Doesn't it?'

'Only worse. The first time they are greedy and rough and it usually hurts, but at least they're quick. A few times after, they think they know you. They're bored. They're still greedy and rough and it definitely hurts. It just takes a long time.' He says this without regret. 'Know what I mean?'

'I do, I think you know I do.'

'Have one,' he says. 'Do you know what this is?' He pointed to the condiments.

'No.'

'Horseradish, you'll like it. It has some heat.' He spooned a small amount onto the oyster. There was a thick slice of lemon wrapped in a blanket of raw linen gauze; he squeezed its juice evenly across the tray.

'Why do you ask?' he says.

'I was just checking costs.'

'That's for people who have a choice,' he says.

'And we don't?'

He didn't answer, so I put the oyster to my mouth and tasted the freshest salt water. I held back my head and allowed the slow slide, and found some part of me engaged.

'Peggy wasn't serving them up on a Friday night, wha?'

'Fuck, that's good,' I say. And we both fell sideways laughing, knocking the low table and erupting again. The plonk had worked its charms and we were utterly seduced.

'Legs, why is my flute empty, you cunt?'

'You're flute-less.'

'A flute-zzy.' And because these were the funniest words ever spoken, we howled, actual tears streamed. I looked about the room, from charmed face to charmed face, their low voices, sipping drinks, and I saw that this was all against us, this was the world and it didn't give a rat's. I knew and understood and didn't care.

'Let's see if the fuckers bleed,' I say. And I lifted my glass in the air, ready to fling it, for the sake of pure ruination, into the most crowded centre of the room, but before I could swing, the glass was swiftly removed, and my empty hand was held by the hands of an older man. I swear they were the softest hands ever to touch me: they gave me a chill, those hands, as if holding the skin of another animal altogether. I pulled back from him at once.

'Well, look at these festivities. Look what the elves have brought. My dear, your glass is empty. Legs! Who is this wonder and why have you been hiding her?'

'Juno, I'm Juno. I'm with him,' I say, like I was picking a fight.

He took my hand again and I thought for moment he was going to raise it to his mouth and kiss it. But he surrendered it after only mock-kissing it twice.

'Let me replenish you both.' He lifted our glasses and went to the bar.

'Legs, what the fuck was that?'

'Saint Francis,' he says with a smile. I looked across at Francis: he was short and wide, stood beside others at the bar, dressed in the soft furnishings of a posh hotel. His sense of self grander than that self, but people stepped quickly aside to allow him easy access to the bar.

'Juno, goddess, Regina herself, tell me everything.' He had hold of my hand again, sitting close enough that the edge of his spread knee kept pressing off mine. I twisted away from him and my back started to ache.

'Do I call you Francis, Saint Francis or Mr Saint Francis?'

'I like all of those options very much. Dear Juno, you can call me what you like. But only behind my back.' At this he laughed and lit one of those small brown cigars with a silver Dunhill lighter. He showed us all his props, all the while checking across to see the rise or fall of Legs' attention. Does he like this word, this gesture, this look? I could do it this way, that way, the other. And suddenly what I found grotesque in him fell away, and in the rubble what remained was a desperate schoolboy crush. He was giddy; he was in love, I suppose. A kind of love that I had no doubt could be vengeful and petty – he wanted Legs, his youth and beauty, and it made me pity him.

I looked at Legs as he sat back, a cigarette burning between his long fingers, sharp attentive eyes in a veil of smoke.

'Tell me, how do you know Legs?' he says.

'Yeah, Legs, how do I know you?'

'Like the back of your hand,' he says.

'He tells me nothing,' says Francis. 'He just gives me the bill and happily I pay it, but only because I adore this man. I think he is a very great talent, and that talent must be encouraged and nurtured and then we will see. A very, very bright star.' He patted the end of Legs' knee, and let his hand rest a moment, before moving his small cigar and letting the long ash tip to the floor.

'And what is it you do?' he says.

'Don't know,' I say, because he was the first to ever ask and because it was true. I say, 'Nothing, really.'

'I don't believe you, not for a moment. You just haven't found your place. Tell me what is your passion, what do you love?'

I thought for a while, and the two men watched me. I was going to feel uncomfortable but then didn't.

'Don't think,' he says. 'What is it you love?'

'Him,' I say. 'I love Legs.' I'd made Francis stumble, drop a line in his play, like a performer dazed in the beam of stage light. He went to smile and then didn't and then he did, like I'd played a trick on him and he'd just caught on, his face pulled back in reflex.

'Ahhhhhh,' he says, and stood and hugged me tightly to him. 'You wonderful, wonderful girl.' His thick body leaner and more powerful than I had imagined. I smelled vetiver and something else, citrus maybe? I thought how Legs had felt this embrace; I was sure he knew its entry and exit points the impassive way doctors follow the trajectory of wounds.

'Please, Legs, you must bring this girl back – I want to introduce her to all my friends. If you young people will excuse me, I have to attend to an extremely dull matter, dull as a very dull day ... An absolute pleasure, my dear.'

We regarded each other briefly, and I thought of hungry dogs across the remains of a carcass. I suddenly stood and flung my arms around Francis. He was taken aback, flustered.

'Well, my dear, well well. A pleasure indeed.'

Legs and I watched him go; a cluster receded as he fell into the fold. And then, like poker players, Legs and I, we watched each other and gave nothing and said nothing for some time except small knowing smiles that secretly delighted us, and made us feel so much more clever than we ever were.

'I think you've given Saint Francis the willies,' he says finally.

'No, baby. That's you.'

'Baby?'

'Baby.'

'That's my word.'

'You must learn to share, the way Francis has.'

'Francis is going to give me a show.'

'Is he?'

'Yep.'

'Even horrible people can have their hearts broken, you know.'

'Come on,' he says. 'There's a party.'

I stood and my knees knocked the little table, nudged the last shards of gleaming cut ice into its own warming puddle. The twisted lemon and trapped seeds spread over the silver tray. I took one of the shells, careful not to be seen, and all evening I passed my thumb across its perfect mother-of-pearl.

It was an impromptu party, in a house that used to be grand. There was the smell of hash and everyone's teeth were stained wine red, and Legs was surrounded. My conversation was small and cautious. A girl called Rags smiled at me; she was all bone, and when she spoke, she held my wrist between her red-glossed nails, stroking my fingers as though draped from a hospital bed.

She says, 'Daddy and I have fallen out, we haven't spoken in weeks.' But just then Legs' head appeared between us, grinning.

'Juno and her da fell out – took three days to wash the blood off the walls.'

I freed myself from her grip and we danced, Legs and I. He was soon distracted. A boy over my shoulder had caught his eye. Legs knew I was watching: he swung me around and didn't hide what he wanted. He trusted my stamina.

I was squeezed onto a couch, facing into the room. I watched as Legs kissed this boy; it was the first time I'd seen a boy kiss another boy. It thrilled me, that kiss. My own boy, I thought suddenly, without a lick of that human instinct that cuts fresh flowers in bloom and takes them home to wilt and die. His fingers fell over the boy's face as their mouths joined, and one finger gently scratched along his cheek. Their lips would part and they were held suspended, locked. Legs danced some more and the boy sat back and watched. Legs' body lost inside his oversized jumpsuit, in full charge of his limbs, as the music from the boom box echoed from the other room and through the empty space. Legs moved forward again, his lips finding the boy's neck this time. Then he whispered something bold and the boy smiled and took his hand.

Beside me, a boy with a small cleft in his upper lip – this I rather liked, the feline upward curl. He leaned in to me and told me a random fact about the music.

'Wha?' I say. By then I was so drunk, I let this boy take me to an empty room. He was gentle and tentative and I felt myself become bored by it.

Later, when he was asleep and I'd stolen his cheap Casio watch, I lay on the sheets and felt dull. I no longer cared to be alone and it was Legs I needed. I went to their room. Legs and the boy slept, naked: a little light cut in from the street, drew a fixed line across their torsos, shined over their skin – statues released from their pedestals and fallen. I lay beside Legs, and pulled him to me. He half woke, called me baby and reached his hand behind and draped it across my thigh. His skin was warm and I fell in step with his long breaths and ran a nail up along his neck into his hairline and he let out a little sigh. I kissed his back and it tasted cool, breeze-dried sweat. Coal charred from the night's long burn hung in the room and I slept.

6

Agnes had handed me a key to the shop. 'Oh,' she says, an after-thought, reaching inside her pocket, 'I got this cut for you.' And she began to unclip a silver, freshly cut key from a rattling metal ring. 'Here.' She put it into my hand. 'In case you're in before me or that.' And when she went, I held it like a prize and thought about getting a ring like that myself, now that, in only a few weeks, I had a second key to keep with the first.

I locked the door after Agnes had said goodnight, pausing to ask if I was sure I wanted to stay late on Christmas Eve. I said that I did and set up the sewing machine on my own. Outside the arcade floor was empty, the floodlight spilling out, creating long oily shadows, and a church-like quiet transformed the room. I smoked a cigarette and heard a satisfying clip from the worn floorboards as I walked through the rooms, tidying up and turning out lights as I went.

Agnes had asked after Legs more than once that day. 'Where's that great big queen you live with? I've not seen him around.' And then later: 'Is he alright, Juno? It's not like him.' She was annoyed at me for being vague, but didn't say.

I sat at the table and switched on the task light. The sharp needle shone. I had that jacket to take in and a hem to fix. Agnes had shown me how to set up the sewing machine and how to operate it. She had confidently bound scraps of fabric in a perfect zigzag stitch I had never seen done before.

'It's like magic,' I say, sitting close as she conducted the demonstration, aware of this gentle scent that drifted from her – like some perfume made of gold, it blended into the shop's smell and was heavenly. Her sewing machine was a different animal, quicker than a Singer, and I thought of it as a tireless teenager, bright and eager, and still some part of me ached for my Singer. Its weight and indestructibility.

'There was a tradition,' Agnes says, 'of stitching and embroidering into the hems of garments, in prisons and internment camps and when men went off to war. Sometimes to remember, sometimes to be remembered. A child's name, a lover, a flower from home.' She knew so much, and for a quick moment I felt I'd been brought into the fold, bonded to the past. And I wondered if Mam knew she had been part of that too.

I had found an old suit, Legs' size, in dark navy and bought it. Agnes would only take half the money, though I slipped the rest into the till when she wasn't around. It was a heavy wool, with strong chalk pinstripes and the wide lapels that Legs wanted. I opened it up, at the back, the lining glistening as I removed it and let it drape across my table, carefully stitching into it large and blazing red felt cut to the shape of a heart. And then with gold-threaded swords, I pierced it twice and wrote his name, and my own there beside it.

I stopped the machine, and in the silence I carelessly lit a smoke and straight from the bottle finished the last of the red wine. I stared into space and began to cry.

I had wrapped the suit in shiny paper and as I walked it had become damp under my arm, its crispness lost, and, once home, I set the package underneath the Virgin Mary portrait. It now had its own blinking Christmas lights, wrapped like a crown of thorns. Legs had added a dab of lipstick to her mouth, and in a particularly cruel mood, I'd written 'whore' across her chest. I found Legs on the bed, fully dressed, lying across the covers. He'd been reading that bloody Mary Oliver again; he tilted the book of poems away from his face and looked at me and says, 'My tender parts have never been loved.'

'I told you not to read that cow – we can't handle her.' I snatched the book from his hands and flung it. 'How are you feeling?'

'Unloved, Juno, I feel unloved.'

'Yes, besides that.'

'Terrible.'

'Have you eaten?'

'Yes.'

'Liar,' I say. 'What are you all dressed for?'

'I always dress on Christmas Eve.'

'Come through to the living room.'

'I can't.'

'What do you mean you can't?'

'I just wanted to look nice, Juno, you know? I was excited, and when I was dressing I had an accident and then I was worried about trying to get off the bed in case I'd have another accident and now I'm stuck.'

I saw then how he clutched his sheet, holding it across the middle of his body. It was all so sudden and I felt I was unprepared. I swallowed hard, locating the smell then. Illness, I saw, even the slow ones, could only be sudden.

'Is that the tie Francis gave you?'

'Yes.' He ran his finger across the mustard silk.

'It's beautiful.'

'Well, yes.'

'You look beautiful.'

'I don't, I know I don't.'

'A complete ride.'

'Go on, say more.'

'Wanna get locked, you gorgeous man?'

'Honestly, you and the drink.'

'I know, I know, but it's the only tradition the family kept and it's Christmas.' I sat beside him and rubbed my finger over his knuckles.

'You won't leave me, will you?' he says, looking away from me then.

'I won't leave you if you don't leave me.' And I think for the first time I was unable to hide my fear.

'Stop haggling.'

'Fine, I won't leave you if don't leave me, much.'

'Yes, let's get locked.'

'I'm going to run you a bath,' I say. 'Then I have a surprise for you, to change into . . .'

I went to stand, but didn't, instead I froze at the violent hammering sound at the front door. We looked at each other, Legs and I, like two children suddenly caught. The banging continued.

'It's OK,' I say, on my feet then, and closing the door to the bedroom over. I could hear cries and laughter outside. I crept slowly to the door, peering out the small window. There was a crowd on the landing. I could only make out the shadow and silhouette of dark figures.

'I can see her, look, she's there.' I clamped my foot against the door and unlocked it, allowing it to open only by inches.

'Darling, what on earth are you doing?' It was Francis, his face strangely close on the other side of the door. 'Silly girl. Open up.' His apparition had so dazed me. Silly girl, me? That part of me that believed him capitulated and moved from the door and Francis and his swarm of beautiful boys and beautiful girls invaded our home. I stepped back, unsure, as their footsteps crowded in, their bland curiosity and detached interest.

'Where on earth is Legs, my dear?' he says, looking impatiently past me towards the bedroom.

'I don't know,' I say. 'He left, to meet you, that's what he said.'

Francis's face remained neutral: he pursed his lips a little, unconvinced. His party had quickly tired of watching me, and then began to drift further into the room. One of them reached over and took up a sketch pad and was about to start leafing through it.

'Put that fucking down,' I say. He dropped it instantly and looked at me with fear and sulking indignation. Francis came closer. 'Juno, darling, I have a car waiting, don't embarrass me. Please. Go and tell Legs to come along. You can come too, of course – it's Christmas, my dear. All I want is to give everybody a night they will remember, always.' He turned to his party: 'Isn't that right?' They were bored already, keen to move on. Another one began to flick through the records; she picked up an album cover and the vinyl fell from the sleeve and crashed to the floor.

'Ah fuck's sake. Get out the fuck. You too, Francis, I've had enough. Out.' As I bent down to collect the record from the floor, Francis slipped past and on to the bedroom. He had the door open before I could get to him.

'Legs, darling, what on earth are you doing?' When I got to Francis's side and peered into the dark room, I could see Legs, perched on the side of the bed. He'd taken up the sheet and covered himself in a hurry.

'Are you alright, Legs? My dear boy, what's the matter?' Legs watched Francis, his sheet pulled to his chin and two huge, unblinking eyes. I tried to bar Francis' way as he stepped into the room. He brushed me aside and his party crowded the doorway, finally enlivened.

'Francis, baby, I've had a little accident. Ropey curry. I'll catch you up.'

'You look dreadful, what has happened?' Francis looked frightened; he clutched his nose as the smell caught up to him. 'You're sick, darling, you're really sick.' And then he started to back away from Legs, towards the door.

'No,' says Legs, 'it's food poisoning, Francis. Honestly, I'll catch you up, we'll have the best time.' Legs' voice was desperate, it was pleading – it appalled Francis, who had become pale himself. Still holding his nose, he says, 'I'm not a fool, I know what this is.' He turned from the door and ran quickly through the living room and outside with his crowd trailing behind. The front door was left open and in the cold street I heard an engine start and the slamming of doors and then silence.

I watched Legs and he watched me, and we were left with that thick unnameable loss that gripped the room. To stem the flow of tears, Legs tightly pinched his eyes closed and allowed himself to fall on the bed and roll over with his back to me. His narrow shoulders shook then, though there was no sound, as if it had been turned down, the way you could with the news.

7

No child's delighted cries had come streaking up from the yard. Not yet; they would still be in their pyjamas, waiting to be led to the blinking trees. This Christmas quiet, an anticipation I'd only read about.

My eyes were closed. Opening them would bring about the start of what I didn't want to begin. I was on the couch; he'd asked me to sleep there.

'It would be better,' he says.

'Of course, whatever is best.' We were polite, the first graceless brick in a wall between us. After Francis left, Legs stayed on the bed for a long time. I offered to run him a bath; I said I had enough coppers for a decent one: 'An extra few inches, doll face, just the way you like it.' But he didn't want that, he'd take care of himself.

'I'll leave the money by the geyser. Door open or closed?' I say, but he didn't answer. 'I'll leave it open a tick, case you need me, you can just shout through.' And I stood watching from the small opening in the door. When he went through to the bathroom, I stripped his sheets and left them tied in a black bag by the door. I replaced them with the sheet from the couch. I was unable to calm myself. The look of terror from Francis made everything real: his poor face that had been so greedily hopeful a moment before, wilted. I tried to read but found the same senseless line repeating over and over. I drank, of course; it made me listless without the accompanying numb I was after. When I heard movement from the bathroom, I made myself not look when the door opened. And after, when he came out, when I'd hoped he'd come sit with me, I heard the click of the door closing shut.

Under the weak morning light, I finally slid off the couch and the blankets tumbled rope-like with me as I sat on the floor in front of the red bar of the heater. I lit a smoke I didn't want and tried to see through the gap in the curtain, far beyond the browning net lace to the balloons of cloud that would litter the Dublin mountains and hills in a patchwork of soft calico grey. A blue sky poked shyly from behind and I tried to be happy for the children that would play on the rainless streets with shining bicycles.

Legs' door was still closed when I passed it. I made tea and took a first swig of whiskey. My white knuckles made the tiniest drumming sound on the wood of his door and I went inside and saw how his head was set gently into the pillow and his pale face looked carved and free from all tensions. 'Morning, mutton chops,' he says, eyes flickering to life and a slight move pulled his mouth into a small smile. 'Happy Christmas.'

'Happy Christmas.' I leaned down and kissed his forehead and his skin was hot, tacky at my lips.

'Did Santa come?'

'Dirty bastard, probably. How do you feel?'

'Good, better.'

'Good. Drink some tea. I'm going to make breakfast so we can pretend to eat before the drinking begins.' I stood up, resting my eyes on him still.

'I was on a funny one, last night,' he says. 'Bit dramatic. I'll go and see Francis later, work it out – it'll be fine I'm sure.'

'Yeah, of course it'll be fine.'

'I just got a bit carried away – Francis will understand that, won't he?'

'Yeah, definitely.'

'I feel great, all better.'

In the kitchen, I set about scrubbing oily dust off the pocked frying pan. I could hear his coughing fit, barking at me through the wall. I waited.

'You want an egg?' I called through.

'No.'

'One or two?'

'Neither.' I rested the pan on the heat and cracked an egg on its raised rim, but misjudged, splitting the yoke, and watched helpless as it bled into the whitening gel. The second egg didn't go my way either, but one stayed intact and I cooked it and carried aloft buttered toast like a crown. Legs had not heard me come through and was knelt at the side of his bed, head lowered, prostrate. His hands lay across the mattress; they were clasped so tightly together that his fingers reddened at their tips. I stood, breathless, watching.

'Are you praying?' I say, and felt how my voice was a disturbance in the quiet room. He didn't move at first, like he was finishing a band of a rosary. His head lifted a little and he watched his own fingers slowly unbraid.

'No.'

'Are you sure? You look awfully like a fellow that's praying.'

255

'I was looking for a shoe, under the bed.' He smiled at me then and was suddenly shy and after he'd perched on the side of the bed, he says, 'I pray sometimes.'

'Here, this is for you.' I put the plate on the bed beside him and passed him a knife and fork, before sitting off to his side on the hard chair.

'Did you eat?' he says.

'I will, in a bit.'

I lit another cigarette and felt heavy and although the smoke made me light-headed and ill, I continued with it. I wished I'd added some drink to my tea.

'What are you praying about?' I say. Legs went through the motions of deconstructing his food without ever bringing it past his mouth.

'Don't know, just a habit.'

'Like picking your nose?'

'You're disappointed in me.'

'No. Not that.'

'Then what?'

'Surprised, I think that's it. I'm surprised. What do you get out of it?'

'Nothing.'

'So why do it?'

'Comfort, I suppose I find it comforting.'

'They hate you.'

'I know.'

'But really, hate.'

'I know,' he says, and I felt jealousy rising like damp, a dark and spiteful jealousy, shining from that place in me that could never be shared.

'It's a bit like being caught having a wank,' he says, and when he laughed it was a watching laugh, and hollow.

'I wish you were having a wank, I could understand that. Is it from your chaplain that you learned it?'

'No ... yeah ... I don't know.'

'Let's go to mass,' I say, like it was a dare.

'Mass?'

'Yeah, Christ is born. New Testament stuff, the bonnie wee bastard, let's go and celebrate.'

I watched him carefully. He was interested then, I could see.

'Only if you feel up for it, if you feel well enough.'

'I do. I'm better, I said I was. I wouldn't go except that I was looking at a picture of Holbein's *Christ* and maybe just for research, for the show and all.'

'Yeah.'

'Yeah.'

'I got you a prezzie.' I stood and went to the living room, where I had left the wrapped gift underneath the modest virgin.

'You're gorgeous,' I say, as he stood dressed before me, the sharp line of his body covered by the sharp line of the suit. He posed and strutted a bit, not like before but I think his spirits were lifted. When he'd opened the parcel, he had done so slowly and with great care. 'Just rip it,' I said but he wouldn't; he undid knots and slipped his fingers between the uneven tape and the suit was revealed perfectly pressed and folded. I showed him my embroidery where his name sat next to mine. I'd gotten carried away with the story I was telling, the blazing heart laid out, a declaration, and I could feel my cheeks redden. Legs smiled, a big smile – one of those good ones I'd almost forgotten.

'I love it.'

'It's to remind you who you really belong to,' I say, feeling bold then. 'Me, not some cunt God.'

'It's sort of your version of a dog pissing.'

'Exactly,' I say and I kissed his cheek.

I was unprepared for the flocking droves at mass. The polished congregation stepping out of vehicles and calling names across the car park. The poorly turned bright ties men wore and the too-thick make-up of their partners. Young girls, with their hair pulled painfully back and folded into tight plaits, were held at their mothers' sides and commanded to be still.

I had blocked this world, but now it came pouring back and I was a child again. I took Legs' hand and held it so tight he shuddered with pain and told me off.

We were seen, though glances seemed to go around us, across our shoulders and even through us, but we were seen. A priest stood at the top of the stairs surrounded by a small procession of altar boys. He was a younger priest, and as we came along the steps I saw that from cheek to ear he was covered by a red mark, a birthmark, coronation red, and I thought how he must have hated that, how as a child it was all anyone could see in him. Probably as a priest too. Our way was blocked by a bottleneck of worshippers and the boy priest was keenly struggling to shake every hand as it passed. I tried to go around but could not, my hand was clasped then, and we looked at each other and he smiled.

'Welcome,' he says, and I could feel how his hand was warm and soft, warmed by all the other hands that touched his hand

and now that hand was warming my own hand and that's the way it goes. I looked away from him quickly, down at the tangle of paused and slowly moving feet. I knew when Father looked at me, even in his young way, he saw past everything: he saw through to my bones, broken as a pink stick of Blackpool rock, he saw the word 'sin'.

Inside, the church remained cold, despite its full capacity; voices echoed high into its dark, pitched roof, babies cried and were rushed out the door by attendant mothers. At the second-to-last row, Legs and I excused ourselves, silencing quiet conversations as we moved knee by knobbly knee to a space on the varnished pew. And as we sat and settled ourselves, I wondered at my own shaking hands and regretted ever bringing us to this place. Legs was unreadable: he sat rigid, fixed ahead, facing the altar and cross.

'You alright?' I whisper, but he wouldn't answer or look. 'Legs, Legs, you alright?' He shushed me then and I looked away. My breath rushed out of me in a long sigh.

'Let us pray.' The priest had found his way to the altar. I couldn't see him, but his amplified voice came across the tannoy, a small charge of static clinging in the space between his words. We all rose. My body remembered – I stood, I sat, I knelt without having to be told. I tried to laugh at it as if it were nothing, as if it hadn't clung to me at all, but I could not. I had not become that kind of adult. That voice inside was still the same, hardly grown at all.

I felt cold and miles from Legs, sitting there at the back of the church. His face was mostly turned from me, but I could see the damp catch on his cheek.

'Come on, dolly,' I say, 'there's nothing here.' He looked down for a moment, his jaw set and tightening. Slowly he reached for his cap and popped it back on his head, then stood high over the congregation and led us outside.

The air was fresh and the wind had picked up. I could feel it at my face, gently lapping, setting my hair to a waltz. Legs' usual quick gait had slowed, but still, he seemed strong, pushing against the breeze.

'I feel greatly restored after that,' he says.

'No, you don't.'

'I do, a religious balm.'

'Put your arm around me,' I say, and he did, pulling me close, and we walked that way home in silence, our thoughts, the new ones and the old, pulling at our hems.

We'd been home for some time, Legs was on the couch and I sat on the floor close by and together we'd watched the last pink ribbons fade from the darkening sky. When we had returned from mass, we had promised ourselves we would eat, but had started drinking and never did. I had stood up and turned the record over and just sat back when Legs, seemingly uninterested, says, 'That priest today, with the yoke on his face, did you see it?'

'Yeah, couldn't miss it.'

'It looked like something on a map, didn't it? I wonder if he believes he has it because of his sins?

'Why would anyone believe that?'

'Well, it's in the Bible, isn't it. "God disciplines sins through illness and death."'

'I don't read the Bible.'

'It's in there, never stops banging on about it. "Because of their iniquities they were afflicted." All that stuff, and he's a priest, so he believes all that.'

'Do you?'

'I don't know. I just wondered what kind of sin would do that to his face, if it was true?'

'Sister believed all that.'

'She did, didn't she . . . Father too.' He held the arm of the chair, rocked slightly back and forth, and looked at me, squarely. 'It wasn't an accident, I did it,' he says. 'I think it's why I'm sick. I did it on purpose.'

'What? Did what?'

'With Father, it wasn't an accident. I went to burn him.'

'What are you talking about? I was there – you saved him. I saw you save him.'

'The school he was going to send me to, with the special programme? It was a conversion therapy up at Queen's University. He said it could help sick boys like me. "It'll shock the girl out of him" – that's what he said to Mam, and she was so quick to go along with it. She was disgusted by me. He did that, he took her away.'

'Legs . . . I'm sorry.'

'I remember when I saw you that morning, in the classroom, you'd been through so much and still . . . You were brave, Juno. I wasn't, I just wasn't.'

He lit a smoke then; it made him cough a few times, a barking, sick-person's cough.

'I thought, you wouldn't let them do that to you, you wouldn't. So I ran to his office and I sat there, waiting. "You have something to say, McGuire?" he says when he came in. He had this face on him, he was enjoying it, the sport. "I know what you are," he says. "There are names for boys like you." I had the lighter fluid and a lighter ready. I looked up at him, leaning against his desk. He was a big man, do you remember?'

'Yes,' I say.

He ran the end of his smoke round and round the ashtray, gently raking the ash before inhaling again.

'He picked up his Bible, the big blue one. He came behind me, calling me names. "Fairy." He started with that. And I felt this dreadful pain in my head and it took a second, but I knew he'd hit me with the book and he did it again, "Faggot," and again, "Bender," "Bum boy," "Queer," and I didn't make a sound, none. I knew he'd run out of words. He went over to his desk and sat watching me. I was crying. "I'll make it my duty to see you leave this school in accordance with God's law." I took the bottle out of my pocket – there was this little blue finickity top, and I was trying to get my nail under it so it would open.' Legs made this gesture with his thumb as if the bottle was still in his hand.

'When I got it open I just started spraying him with the lighter fluid. He was confused: he hadn't joined the dots, like I was spraying him with a water pistol. He was worried about his garb, I think. I fetched out the lighter, flicked it a few times till it took. He was up then, trying to get out the door. I jumped on his back and we struggled. I kept trying to get the lighter going again at his chest. I think I wanted to go up with him. But then this huge flame shot up his body, and when I felt the pain of it on my arm, I leapt back away. He was screaming, trying to get to the door. His face was covered and then his hair went whoosh. The whole place was full of black smoke and the smell and then he was out the door running. It was the screams I couldn't stand, those screams. I only ran after him to make them stop.' Legs' toes had been digging against the swirling-carpeted floor; when he finished speaking, they lay flat and inert, and he looked into the centre of the room, wrung out and lost.

'Jesus, Legs. I'm so sorry.'

'I'll never be forgiven for it.'

'He was a sadist and a bastard.'

'Was he, Juno? I don't know any more.' When Legs had saved me on the bridge, when he'd taken me in his arms and said I was alright, because he was there, with me, I believed and surrendered to him. I sat on the floor looking up at my own boy crumpled into the couch and I was unable to comfort him in the same confident way.

8

After Christmas, Dublin shuddered back to life; its convalescence took more than a week. Eventually, shop by shop, lights came flickering back and buses could be heard, tumbling up Aungier Street. A notice of eviction had come through the post and sat unopened under the Virgin Mary. The council had announced their intention in bold red letters on the front of the envelope. Neither of us spoke about it. When the cinemas reopened, I was able to manoeuvre Legs out of bed and out the door. We'd been quiet around each other and that dreaded politeness continued. I'd tried to be crude and rough with him, but that easy way never returned. I was too watchful, and he was making plans that couldn't include me, I knew that.

'You have stubble,' I say to him in the afternoon. 'You never have stubble.' He was propped up on pillows and I'd already switched on the light. Although it was hardly three, grey winter dusk crowded in. I got off the bed and gathered up Legs' very beautiful shaving kit. It was vintage. 'A gift from an admirer,' he says coyly.

'I can't stand it.'

'What? What can't you stand?'

'Your face in disarray. It doesn't suit you at all.'

'I've been avoiding mirrors,' he says.

I filled a bowl of warm water and set it down, dipping his thick badger-hair brush with its heavy silver handle into the water and working a lather into the shaving soap. His stubble was light, a boy's stubble really.

'We should go out,' I say. 'The cinema is open and I've to go back to work tomorrow.' I ran the brush over his cheeks, his skin pulled tight as a drum.

'What's on?'

'There's some Jane Fonda revival.'

'The space bunny one?'

'I'm not sure,' I say. 'Jaysus, that's sharp, it's like running a squiggly over glass. It might be the proz one, you know, where your man is trying to kill her.'

Legs had closed his eyes so I slowed down and tried to make it last. Afterwards, I dried his face and thought how I should have warmed the towel.

'You scrub up nice, dolly.' He ran his fingertips across his chin and looked at me, says, 'C'mere,' and I folded into his arms. And he thanked me then.

We sat in the darkened cinema, light flickering overhead. Legs had taken something and was pepped up, and I think it was a struggle for him to sit still. It was the one about the murderer and I got the fear and he was useless. We left early without knowing who done it. Outside, we stood rolling smokes under the bright marquee. Dublin was a quiet place; I felt this lonely part of me growing and biting at my belly. A young couple stood waiting for a bus along Eden Quay: she was elegant, in that effortless way tall people are always elegant. Her eyes followed the flow of the dark river, over to Butt Bridge and out towards the sea. Her partner looked down in front of him, silently, at the path around his feet.

'You ever think what it would be like to come out of the cinema and not feel disappointed at what city you're in?' says Legs.

'You disappointed?'

'I'm not thrilled.'

'I love Dublin,' I say. I surprised myself a little when I said it.

'Do you really?'

'Yeah. I think I do.'

'What in God's earth do you love?'

I felt my shoulders shrug and I'm sure I had a blank look on my face.

'Don't know, it's a complete kip, isn't it? Grubby as fuck; I hope they never clean it.' Legs reached and fixed the collar of my overcoat.

'I think my love affair with Dublin is coming to an end.'

'Let's get a drink,' I say.

And we walked south over the bridge, an aimless stroll, where the quiet between us was soft and pleasant, and I felt almost at ease. Dame Street was empty from the college to the castle, save for some workers in hi-vis digging a hole or filling it in.

'You want to go to the George?' I say.

'Certainly fucking not, not the way I look.'

'The William Tell?'

'No.'

'Barkly Dunnes?'

'No.'

'How bad do you think you look?'

'Grogan's,' he says.

'Jesus, Legs.'

We went the long way, past the Trinity gates, turning into Grafton Street. A woman's voice could be heard up at the Green, her voice carried through the empty street, singing a song I didn't recognise. In a doorway, a man covered in black plastic slept. He'd broken down a cardboard box and it lay like a sheet beneath him. Grogan's Lounge was dark and warm and, through the cloud of cigarette smoke, Christmas decorations blinked. There were a few around – in groups large and small, their voices and laughter occasionally flared. We sat at the bar. Legs ordered a whiskey, a double, and drank it quickly, playing with a coaster on the bar, his nail picking apart the sodden paper.

'Look,' he says. 'It's my painting.' And he pointed: the wall was filled with paintings.

'Which one?'

'That one.' His index finger shook towards the wall.

'Oh, I see it,' I say. 'I'd have recognised it anywhere. Look at you,' I say, and I slapped his shoulder. He smiled and waved for the barman.

'He's good, your man that owns the place, he'd always throw you a few bob for a picture, if you're stuck or that.' He finished his drink and called again. 'It's a wall of artists' credit . . . You know, I tried to find him one time, my chaplain.'

'The one you fancied?'

'I'm not sure if that's the right word.'

'The one that gave you the horn?'

'Well, yeah, he did a bit. He'd been transferred out of the prison to Maynooth, you know, the big college there for priests. I suppose he was looking to get himself ordained.'

'Right, move up the spiritual ladder.'

'Have you ever been?'

'What, to that Maynooth? Yeah, I'm always saying how I should go more often.'

'Have you really?'

'Have I fuck.'

'It's huge. Wall-to-wall garbs, otherwise it looks like any university – young pimple-faced yokes up from the country on a calling.'

'Did you find him?'

'That's the thing. I decided, "This is ridiculous, I'm never finding him and even if I did, then what?" So I'm sitting outside, this big open courtyard, and I'm having a smoke and I look up and I'm not joking, he walked out the door, like I'd conjured him. He was with two others – mid-sentence, he looked up and saw me. And the face on him, Juno, he nearly shit himself. He kinda faltered and the two men looked at him and then over to me. But he caught himself then, gave me this look, like he could fucking murder me.'

A crowd came into the pub just then, one of them dressed like Santa, except his white beard had been removed and was being worn by the woman at his side. Legs, looking down into his drink, rolled the liquid around in his glass a few times before emptying it.

He looked again for the barman. 'Actually, I think I wanted to thank him. In spite of everything, he was good to me, you know.'

'Maybe we should go away somewhere. Just the two of us, just for a while,' I say. I knew he'd heard me. He had raised his hand and was waving to the barman. When he had his attention he turned to me and says, 'I have my show, I can't. Do you want another one?'

Outside, we smashed into the damp night air, drunk. I felt

how the rain peppered my face, and I could see it falling, lit by the great blobs of orange street light, and landing at our feet before collecting in pools.

'Let's get you home,' I say. He pirouetted like a spinning top and lost his balance, staggering a few times.

'No, it's still early – I know where we'll go.' And he stomped off, splashing through puddles, calling for me to follow. I did. I followed, back across Exchequer Street, past the bright rain-soaked windows of Brown Thomas. Grafton Street had fully emptied save the well-heeled crowd waiting under umbrellas, in line for Lillie's. Legs screamed, 'Wankers!' His hoarse voice echoed down the street towards them. They shouted a reply, but it was muffled and lost.

South Anne Street, and I saw where we were going. I took to fret; I stopped him halfway down the stairs and pressed him against the wall.

'Legs,' I say, 'let's go somewhere else.' He pushed past, his arm slid along the wall keeping him upright. He sank into the tiny room, crowded and dark, into the plumes of dim red light, faces huddled tightly around tables and, at the bar, the lazy exhale of smoke.

I recognised the barman from before; I remembered his tattoo, his small grouping of gold loop earrings. Legs had man-ouevred through the crowd and stood before him – he leaned his face over the bar, expecting the same kisses. None came. The barman's head tilted away from Legs. I think Legs was still smiling, perhaps bitterly now. I crowded in, roughly pushing someone aside.

'Champagne, darling, and of course, Merry Christmas,' says Legs. The barman silently set about pouring the drinks as Legs, unfazed, looked across the little horseshoe shape of the bar.

'John ... John ...?' he called across the bar. 'John ...?' he says again, and a man not much older than Legs turned and looked with only the slightest recognition towards him. He'd been intently speaking to a younger man, a pretty one, with curls that tumbled past his ear. He half nodded at Legs, but without any warmth.

'John, John,' Legs called again. But John didn't turn this time.

'He's an old friend,' Legs says to me. 'Terrible whore, but a complete Mensch, a darling.' Then his mouth found my ear and in a tickling whisper, he says, 'Sucked him off in the toilet in Dáil Éireann.'

The barman set down the drinks. Two long and sparkling flutes. Then he reached under the counter and produced a perfect set of pink rubber gloves – the kind that mothers wear to wash dishes. He slowly put them on, pulling each up like sleeves and allowing a loud snap as he let them go.

'Sixteen pounds,' he says.

'What?' says Legs. His mouth was wet and a tooth gathered around his lower lip, pulling it for a second before releasing.

'Sixteen pounds,' he says again, with more force, and then his gloved hand moved towards Legs and he held it there. A sound came out of Legs' body – it was laughter, I suppose, but it came from an awful place inside him and brought all of the awfulness out into the room.

'No. No. Sixteen pounds? It's on Francis, Saint Francis, you know that, baby.' And Legs picked up the glass and handed it to me.

'I've no idea what you're talking about. It's sixteen pounds for those drinks.'

'What? No. Francis, it goes on his tab. Why are you being like this?' The barman never cracked, and for a moment I started to second-guess myself. If it was the same barman, the same Legs. I put my drink on the bar and began rooting through my pockets, then I felt how Legs had put his hand up, stopping me.

'That's alright, Juno. Joe here is mistaken.' He lifted his own drink and turned his back to the bar, tilting the glass to his mouth.

'It's a bit flat,' he says after and looked around the room. 'Let's find a seat.' Legs' pallor was beyond pale. A greyish shade had taken hold and his mouth hung loosely and the hollow of his cheeks darkened in the red light. He was mortified, I could see that. More people took notice of Legs at the bar: their eyes discreetly flickering at first, then with greater hunger. The barman seemed to take flight, around the bar, pushing, drawing the room's attention towards us.

'Legs,' I say, and I touched his arm, warning him. The barman roughly bundled Legs' shirt into his fist. He leaned in to Legs and quietly says, 'Sixteen fucking pounds, you plagued cunt.' Legs had frozen, not with fear – it was something else, an animal's confusion at the loss of its geography, the destruction of its landscape. I thought about how slight Legs' body had become, how his hollow chest seemed to be made of powder, how a strong wind could dispose of him. I tried to step between them, pushing my body across Legs.

'Take your fucking hand off him,' I say. Gripping the flute tightly, I felt a chill of liquid splash across my wrist and run up my arm. Legs gave out a relieved, childish cry; he'd seen Francis come down the steps into the room. And he called his name over the watching faces.

'It's OK, Juno. Francis will straighten everything out. Francis, Francis,' he called.

Francis showed no sign that the room was not exactly as he had expected to find it. On his way across to the bar, he took several moments to stop and speak in a cheerful way, his hand resting carefree across the shoulders of friends. Legs watched so intently his eyes seemed to glaze, expectant in a way I could hardly bear. Francis looked impeccable: a pale brown suit stretched across his wide body, and a chocolate square of silk paisley in his top pocket. When Legs went to embrace him, he hadn't allowed for the barman in his path and so lurched forward and was held back at the same time. 'The little street urchins are in for their chestnuts,' Francis says.

'Francis, baby,' says Legs, trying to raise his crumpled body into a straight and dignified line. 'What's happened, Francis?' says Legs, softly, pleading. His voice was this gentle scratching sound and a hot little tear had fallen down his face. Francis smiled, and tapped the barman's arm. 'Thank you, Joe, I'll have my usual.' The barman released Legs then, and trailed slowly back behind the bar.

'You dear boy,' says Francis, 'I'm afraid you and your little friend are going to have to go. You're upsetting people, you see, and we can't have that, now can we?'

'No, Francis, I haven't, I promise. It was just Joe – Joe thought that you'd cut me off.'

'You've been very naughty, Legs, haven't you? And what's worse is you've gone and gotten yourself caught. Silly boy, you've caught a bug and now you have to go away.'

'No, no, I haven't. I had food poisoning, a ropey tummy. I swear.'

'Please, Legs, you're embarrassing yourself now.' Francis looked at me. 'My dear, do him a favour and take him away. This is very tedious.'

'But the show – what about my show?'

'Darling, there was never a show. Who are you kidding? That would be like bringing a pony to a horserace. You don't have the schooling, the breeding, the intellect. Know who you are, you'll be so much happier.'

'Who am I?' says Legs. 'Who am I?'

'You know, my dear, you're a rent boy. A Quay queen. But only rough trade from now on, I think.'

Legs stood, his mouth pulled to the side, set and ugly. Francis tilted his head a little, as if curiously searching for the man he had known. I gripped Legs' arm and pulled him as hard as I could. He let me, his will eroded, and what remained was light: I think he'd have let anyone pull him in any direction. I got him past Francis, and the space around us cleared. People moved quickly. Legs stumbled on the first step, catching himself and then mounting the stairs, past the heavy red curtain, outside.

'I have to sit down. Just for a second.' And he rested on a half-wall, where the iron railing stopped. I saw that I was still holding the champagne glass, empty now, and the juice sticking to my fingers. A short man in an expensive tan overcoat, several sizes too big, emerged from the bar and came up the stairs behind us. He looked at Legs with great tenderness.

'Legs, I'm so sorry,' he says. 'I should have said something, in there.' Legs slowly raised his head as if struggling to locate the voice; he squinted towards him.

A taxi drove slowly past, wet tyres and old tapping diesel engine, and Legs watched the car until it turned at Mansion House towards the green and a hush returned to the street. When he looked back at me, his face had flushed with a wild sorrow.

'Fuck off,' I yelled at the man. 'Just fuck off.' I threw the champagne glass and it smashed and he stepped quickly away from the flying shards. I howled, no longer drunk or sober, I howled. I slumped down beside Legs and pressed my arms around the rung of his knees and, holding tight, I told him that he was not dying.

It was still dark when we got home and into bed, although I had opened the curtains in hope of seeing a brightening sky. I turned on the little heater but it seemed the sheets would never warm, so I wrapped Legs in blankets and towels and overcoats.

'I think tonight was a roaring success,' I say, and when Legs smiled I saw the glint of a tooth and how his sharp cheekbone caught in the light coming from the open door. All the way home I'd been filled with the questions I was afraid to ask out loud, and so nothing was said.

'Maybe a little holiday would be a good idea,' says Legs lightly, as if it had just come to him.

'It *is* a good idea, it was my idea and it's fucking great.' I sat on the edge of the bed and felt the old mattress springs push against my weight before collapsing underneath. 'What about your uncle? The rich one?'

'What about him?'

'Maybe he could help, with money or that?'

'There's no rich uncle, baby,' he says in a voice so low I strained to hear him.

'That was Francis' idea. After he'd picked me up on the Quays and thought it would be fun to bring me along to some opening. He dressed me, told me what to say, how to be.'

I lit a smoke and after a few draws held it to his mouth. He

exhaled slowly and I imagined him, so willing to discard everything of his own, how even his name was made up.

'You could have said ...?'

'I wanted you to think I was wonderful.'

'I do.'

'I wanted to take care of you.'

'Can take care of myself.'

'I know, but wouldn't it, for once, be lovely?'

The room filled with smoke and I could feel the rise of his
chest at my side and he pressed my arm and his eyes shone a
little in the dark room.

'I can get us money, I think. Where would we go?'

'Paris maybe?' says Legs.

'Or Marseille?'

'The Riviera.'

'We could become card sharks in a casino.'

He says nothing for a long time and I wondered if he was
already there, reposing in that clean light.

'Juno, I think I might just go it alone for now, suss it out a
bit, and if I decide to stay longer, I could send for you.' I
remained very still and felt at my back the cold wall, a chill
biting at both shoulder blades.

'Oh,' I say. 'Oh.' He lay across me, inert, his head nestled into
the soft round of my belly.

'I think it would be best,' he says.

I searched out the window for the first pale glints and rolled
his head off me to the side, swinging my legs over the bed and
bracing my feet against the floor.

'Do you want some water?' I say and left the room, running
the tap in the kitchen.

'Juno?' he called. I put my hands on both sides of the draining board and, head low, I closed my eyes. He called my name again. I walked back and stood in the doorway, watching.

'Is that alright?'

'Yes, yes of course.' I was laughing, 'Thank God,' I say. 'Thank God, I won't have to stay in this kip. I'll be fine, I have my job and my sister is always at me to stay with her, help with the kids and that.'

'No, she is not. She's a geebag, you told me.'

'She wasn't always a geebag. She'll come round.' Legs stretched across the bed, kicked free from the mess of tumbled blankets. My hands had begun to tremble, and from the frozen cruor of that old pain, my want and want and want.

I say:

'I think I should come with you, I will, I'll come.'

He says:

'No, Juno.'

Imagine. The kindness of that.

I looked to the dissolving corners of the room, at the crap desk light, the broken chair, the bookshelf, all dragged like me in off the street, our books and the pictures loosely littering the walls, held by single thumbtacks. Legs, in a fit of enthusiasm, had started to paint the wall but after a few strokes of the roller was distracted and left the wet square, announcing later it was his homage to Rothko. This was our room, it was home, and even there in the thick silence that would last till morning, like the silence of reading or reading about people who love and must part, I thought it perfect.

9

'Do you want a sandwich? Or an egg? The blueberries are in season, bursting now, they get on your fingers, mucky ...' He looked away without any focus, Dad. 'There's going to be rain, I think. I might have to look in on the garden later, the weeds ... Maybe the allotment too.'

'What allotment?' I say.

'Allotment? There's no allotment, you know that. It's been gone for years. The grandkids will be here soon – they love their grandpa. I better get my nap, they're a bag of beans.'

'Are they?'

'Yeah.'

'Like them coming, do you?'

'Of course I do, they're what I look forward to most.'

'Mmm?'

'Don't wrinkle your face like that. It makes you look like a thick, as if you didn't already ... Cherry-picking is a great skill, you know?'

'Is it?'

'Cherry trees are big. Up a ladder, basket strapped to your waist. Imagine, wind blows. Apples are better.'

'They keep the doctor away.'

'... I always wanted to sail. I know a fella intends to sail. He doesn't have children, three daughters to burn up his money.'

'Neither do you.'

'Juno will be here soon. She's a good job. Doesn't stop her visiting.'

'I am Juno. It's me.'

'Job for life.'

'Dad?'

'Great job, brains to burn.'

'I have to go,' I say.

'She was always trouble that one ...'

I stood up and pushed the small chair back towards the wall. Dad stayed watching the spot where I wasn't, even after I walked past him and paused at the window. Grey identical buildings across the road and the small green between us.

'Juno will be here, best girl, the best girl so she is.'

I could feel how I was crying – it was a surprise because I swear I felt nothing.

'Likes me all to herself ...'

Dad was sitting in his pyjamas and his slippers, the leather heels downtrodden, and the powder dry of his foot made me look away. His mouth tirelessly moving as if there was something he was grinding between his molars. His hair was completely white now and his face unshaved. He began to say my name, without calling it, a meaningless sound, over and over. I walked past him and opened the door, and could hear the chant of my name along the hall.

Derry had made the house unexpectedly pretty in a way that Mam, despite all her efforts, could not. The old carpet had been removed from the stairs and the floorboards painted white. When I came slowly down, there was nothing to absorb my steps and I no longer recognised the sound of myself moving. The year had made me cautious, heavier. Derry had paperbacks in small piles, stacked on the steps, thumb-worn and frayed, the sort found in bins in front of second-hand shops. It shouldn't have surprised me at all, but it did, and for that I felt a sort of shame. Even reading, which had always been mine, had come from her.

'Something smells good,' I say, stood at the table, my hand wiping across its pocked blond wood. Derry was in the little kitchen, steam piping between the pots and their ill-fitted lids. She came out and stood at the other side of the room, careful not to come too close as if some scales would tip and the world would be set off-kilter. She looked at me in quick bursts and then her glare was redistributed throughout the room, resting finally towards the midriff of my body.

'How's the Ogre up there?'

'The Ogre?'

'That's what the kids call him.'

'He's gone, eh?'

'Yeah,' she says, 'head's away, fucked.'

'The place looks nice,' I say, but she thought that was an ask and it wasn't and I was sorry I'd said it.

'It's alright, lot of work.'

'Yeah, I'm sure.' We were quiet then.

'You been drinking?' she says finally.

'Yeah, a little.'

'I can smell it. Want to watch that, turn into that yoke upstairs.'

'Yeah . . . I need money,' I say, and when she looked at me I thought about crying again, and I was fed up crying. I even felt that heat in my chest and a first stinging at my eyes, and then it simply went away, like a trapdoor had been opened and it poured under that polished floor and disappeared.

'What do you need money for – drink?'

'Jesus, are you joking?'

'How am I supposed to know?'

'You could ask.'

'I don't have any money, Juno,' she says.

I still had Mam's biscuit box tucked under my arm. She'd seen it when I first came in, when I pretended it was Dad I'd wanted to see. She'd seen it and it had affected her, but she didn't say, so I didn't say. I had thought we'd open it together and understand something.

'Right, it's OK, it was stupid to ask.'

'Do you want a cup of tea?'

'Nah, you know what, I'm alright . . . I'm going to take off.'

'You're sure?'

'Yeah . . . I'm sorry, about what I said, last time.'

'I don't remember.'

'Yes you do. It's not true, you weren't always a shite big sister. Just sometimes.'

'Yeah, well. I probably wasn't great.'

'You did your best, wasn't your job anyway. I just wanted us to be . . . I don't know, I liked it when you played with me and that . . . Sorry . . . I'm sorry.'

I quickly buttoned my coat and started towards the door, feeling myself slowing as I got closer. She stayed quiet, even as I stood with the front door open and my shoulder resting against its edge. Out on the green, her children were wildly playing, their cries flung towards the sky.

'I could spot you a tenner,' she says.

I turned to Derry. Her face had leapt by years.

'It's OK, it's fine. Thank you,' I say. 'And I'm sorry.'

'I don't mind you asking, I just don't have it.'

'I'm sorry about Mam, treating you that way.'

She looked quickly away.

'I shouldn't have said it, just remember her in your own way.'

'It wouldn't be true, though, would it?'

'I wouldn't worry about it, true doesn't care if you believe in it or not.'

'I care.'

I saw how it was, how I might never see Derry again, how I should have held on, forced myself into her life. I didn't. I watched the ground around my feet, there by the floor, where the threshold was stained and worn. That I'd remember, that part was Mam and couldn't be so easily scrubbed.

Outside, Dad's cars were gone, along with the breeze blocks they had rested on. Missus G would be delighted. As I walked out to the green, the two small children crowded close.

'You want to see something burn?' I say, lighting a smoke and crouching on the wet grass by the tree, Mam's tin box at my feet.

'You're smoking,' says the boy, tut-tutting.

'Yeah, I am.'

'It's bad for you, that.'

'Yeah, I do it all the time. Does your mam talk about your granny at all?'

'Our granny?'

'Yeah.'

'Granny lives with us.'

'Your other granny, your mam's ma.'

'Mam doesn't have one.'

'I know that, pet, but she used to, she was hit by a bus.'

'A bus?' says the girl.

'Yeah, them buses can get you if you're not careful,' I say.

'Wheeee, bang.'

'Youse are well dressed, clean, aren't you? Your mammy takes good care of youse, doesn't she?'

'She'd smack your bottom,' says the boy and he laughed. The girl watched.

'Do you say your prayers?'

'Yes,' says the boy.

'Yes,' says the girl. 'Glory be to the Father, the holy motherland . . .' She was confused then; it bothered her.

'Do you?'

'Nah. Stopped saying my prayers, long time ago. Do youse want to see something?'

'Yeah.'

'This box belonged to your granny, wait till you see what's inside.'

I opened the box; some part of me was expectant of Mam's smell, a dull tobacco-and-toffee smell that might emerge from the box. Scraps of tar-coloured newspaper pressed inside, their edges roughly torn and frayed. I took up the first horoscope and read, 'Mercury is in retrograde. Watch out for an old friend on Thursday. The weekend will go your way.' The two children were silent, watching. 'That wasn't much good, was it?' I say.

'Don't know.' He made a face and raised his shoulders high before quickly dropping them.

'Do you want another one?'

'Yeah.'

'OK. You pick one.' The little boy's grubby hand rummaged about inside. He drew a scrap of paper and handed it to me.

'I think this will be a good one,' I say. 'You are going to meet an old friend, by the weekend, sparks will fly . . . Jaysus H. What was your granny thinking? Do you want to pick one?' She moved forward slowly and for the first time her thumb and forefinger left her mouth, red and wet. She dug about inside the tin and pulled out a large piece of paper.

'Oh, that's not a horoscope, sweetheart. That's something else.'

'What? A biscuit?'

'No, not a biscuit, you big dafty. It's a picture, it's not sup-posed to be in there,' I say. 'Do you know what that is?'

'A flower.'

'It's a poppy. An old one.' It was drawn on the ruled page of a school jotter, the ink faded and the biro lines ghosted in places.

'Do you know what poppies are for? Remembering, isn't that lovely? I think we should all do lots of that when we are older. But not yet, youse are too young. I'm going to light a fire in this box and you can say a prayer for the granny you never had, if you want.'

'Have you matches?'

'I do, yeah.'

'Not allowed matches.'

We stepped back and I let a lit match drop into the papers, and like a tinderbox, there was a quick lick of flames. We were mesmerised. I took the children by the arm and we danced around it until they heard Derry call their names. I looked: she was stood at her gate, her arms tightly folded, and from that distance she seemed stout, Mam's shape. I waved and she waved, but she didn't move out from the other side of the railings.

'Go wan, your mam wants you.'

I sat back at the tree and watched the children run across the green. The grass deadened their steps and as they fell against each other they roared with laughter. They were beautiful, beautiful children and I thought, surely we were beautiful children too – why didn't anyone say? We should have been told of it, our beauty.

10

I was late to work, and when I put the kettle on, my hands shook. Agnes half smiled; I think some part of her imagined my life different than it was and it impressed her. 'I know what a night out with Legs is like – nearly killed me last time. I don't know how he keeps going,' she says, and she asked how my Christmas was and I asked about hers and she didn't lie.

'Oh, Juno, there was something I wanted to talk to you about,' she says, as I unpacked several boxes. She hovered close, watching and pretending she wasn't. 'I've had an idea. Well, actually, I can't take all the credit. It was Legs who came up with it.'

'You spoke to Legs?'

'Yeah, he called this morning.'

'Here at the shop?'

'Yes, here at the shop. Is that strange?'

'It's not, of course it's not, sorry.'

'Anyway, he was saying, wouldn't it be brilliant if, and only if, you wanted to study textiles or fashion or something like that?'

'He did?'

'Yeah, and I'm friendly with the woman who runs the academy over on Herbert Place, and if you wanted to meet her, I could introduce you. Do you want to study?'

'Yes,' I say, 'very much.'

And it was true, very much. And as Agnes described that life, for a moment I allowed myself to be that person she spoke about. I saw it, coming along Herbert Place, a bag over my shoulder filled with my drawings and pencils and a lunch, moving up the steps and onto the soft carpet and closing the heavy door, the world outside.

'Juno, what's happened?' she says.

My head dipped down low and I'd pressed my hands on the cardboard box to remain standing. I wasn't crying or anything, I was past all that.

'Thank you,' I say. 'Thank you, Agnes.'

This was Legs' influence, cajoling Agnes to speak on my behalf; from his sickbed he had done this, he'd gone shivering to the phone box, in his granny's robe and silly hat, a small pile of shining ten pences.

'You know, you don't have to do it,' she says, 'if it feels like it's too much.'

'It would be a dream,' I say. 'A dream.' I knew what I had to do and so I couldn't look at her then. 'I need the jacks,' I say, and walked quickly away.

We spoke only through necessity for the rest of the day: the fat of our conversation had been coarsely trimmed. She had expected something from me and I was dim and unwilling and she was disappointed, I was sure.

Near closing time, after the last customers had left, I told her that I'd be glad to finish up and she should go on home. She looked relieved. She stood at the counter putting on her long coat and scarf and gloves and says, 'Are you sure you're alright, petal?'

'Yeah, of course,' I say and I went into the next room. I heard her call goodnight as I was crouched down, sliding hangers along the rail. When the shop was silent, I went behind the counter. There was no safe, just a metal box screwed to the floor. I opened it and found a white envelope with cash. The float was fifty pounds and then there were some tens and twenties taken during the day. I took the money out and counted it. I put the cash back into the envelope and the envelope into my pocket. I heard movement then at my side and turned quickly. Agnes stood a few feet from me, watching.

'I held on. I was going to see if you wanted to come and have a drink, so we could talk.'

'Oh,' I say.

'Are you stealing from me, Juno?' She wasn't angry, she was confused. She had begun to believe I wasn't that sort of person, and that was my fault, I had tricked her.

'Yes,' I say. 'It's a hundred and forty-eight pounds and I am taking it. I can't tell you why, but I am.'

'You know I'll call the police?'

'Yes,' I say.

'They'll come for you and you'll be in trouble, you know that?'

Agnes didn't try to stop me – she wasn't built for it. When I came around the counter, I had to pass closely by her and then I stood in the silent shop for a moment as she searched my face. I thought to thank her, I did think of it, but then couldn't quite. I felt my fingers move across the crisp folds of the envelope, and then reached further inside my pocket and produced the key she had given me. I didn't hand it directly to her – I just left it on the counter. I think I lowered my head, or maybe I closed my eyes; either way, I have no recollection of the moment I turned and left. I remember my heels on the wooden steps.

11

The sailing would be seventeen hours, from Rosslare to Le Havre. I packed him a suitcase and tried to keep it light. He'd insisted on more shoes and shirts and jackets and the open case piled higher and higher. He was telling me he'd need these hats and these silk scarfs, that he would be alright. I packed my own bag, a small one. I was telling him that I'd be alright too. When I handed him the money he looked at it and was silent.

'Derry gave it. I'll pay her back. She made up a room for me and all. Delighted with herself, so she is – I'll end up having to raise them bloody kids myself.'

He went into the living room and took down his picture that I'd hung and turned to me saying, 'I'd like to keep this.'

'It's yours.'

'I'll trade you.' And he took off the jacket I'd embroidered and says, 'Will you keep this very safe for me. It's my favourite thing in the whole world.' I turned and he helped me put my arms through it and I felt the almost weightless material touch at my neck and shoulder. He looked at me then and with a delicious smile says how I'm perfect now.

'You're perfect,' I say.

'It's just a quick trip,' he says.

I don't think either of us slept and when I came through from the bedroom at five he was sat upright on the couch smoking. Below his haunted stare, I saw real terror.

We walked to the station and were quiet. Legs' suitcase pulled at him like a leash. On the platform, we stood shoulder to shoulder as the horizon paled on the other side of the awning. A trickle of people started to file in past the turnstile and stand in a straight line up and down the platform, checking their watches against the station's clock with growing impatience.

The train slowly tumbled into the platform with a sharp hissing of hydraulics and its enormous diesel engine halted violently against our silent aubade.

'You'll never guess the name of your ship,' I say, 'the bleedin' *Oscar Wilde*. You couldn't make it up.' I felt his hand at my side, how it gathered up my own, his fingers stiff and cold, wrapped tight until they weren't.

I felt my seams unravel, string pulled from our embrace, set to the waiting train's timetable. I stood at the platform and did not wave and he did not wave, and when the train departed I stood, vacant and in shock.

'I won't forgive them,' I thought. 'I won't.'

12

That evening, I walked the old way, through the grasses and the ferns, the broken bottles and cigarette butts gathered like men around a fight. Past the tall church steeple, the silent yard. I stood and put my face to the window of my old classroom, holding my hands against the glass to see. Small chairs neatly pushed under tables, wooden pegs void of coats or hats, and the black-board wiped clean. I walked on, as though I was saying goodbye. But I wasn't saying goodbye. I was remembering, all of it.

One light went out as I approached the library, but Missus H could still be seen inside, winding down like an old clock. The books had unburdened themselves for the day and been set back in neat rows by letter. She'd gone for blue satin, Missus H, a bit muted for her. I pushed against the glass door but it was locked and made a rattling sound. Missus H looked up and seemed nervous coming towards the door. She said something, I saw her mouth move and I knew she was telling me they were closed. I think I was ready to give up. I remember turning back to the empty street, darkening behind me. Then I knocked again.

'It's Juno,' I say, and the worry fell from her face and I saw how she said my name with a sort of delight and she unlocked the door.

'How are you, Missus H?' I say.

'Ahh, Juno,' she says. She'd looked me up and down and says my name again, 'Juno, come in, come in out of that night.' And she ushered me inside. 'How are you? Sit, sit,' as she pulled a chair out from under a desk. 'You've grown up, Juno. Isn't that something marvellous?'

'Yeah, suppose I have.'

'You'll tell me all your news.'

'No news, Missus H. Same as always, me.' I think I said that.

'Molly.'

'Wha?'

'Molly is my name, Juno. Or did you think I hadn't one of my own?'

'Well ... Molly. To be honest, I'd never given it a second thought.' We laughed at that, me and Molly.

'It's not something I tell the young ones, the power goes to their heads.'

'You're a dark horse, Molly.'

'I am.' She pulled a chair out for herself, and sat close.

'And how is it here?'

'Same, books are taken out, most of them are brought back. I've a young girl comes in, reminds me a bit of you, years ago.'

'I'm sure she's a delight.'

'A delight.' And she thought a moment before speaking, running her hand across the smooth of the table as if there was something there that needed wiped.

'And are you working?'

'Yeah, doing a bit, here and there, you know.'

'Aren't you the best girl, I knew you'd turn out great.'

'Yeah, great,' I say.

'And tell me, have you someone special?'

'Special?'

'A fella.'

'Oh,' I say. 'A fella, yeah, yeah, I do.'

'I hope he's good to you.'

'The best.'

'Good, good,' she says. We sat silently for a while. I looked down at her worn, flat navy shoes, tied by a single band, held with a single button. I felt her eyes searching. 'The last time I saw you, Juno, I think you were in a bad way. I went looking for you, to be honest. I was worried.'

'Did you really look for me?'

'I did.'

Blue and black ink stained between her fingertips, small dots of it, where she held a pen all day. I wondered if she scrubbed like hell every night, only to begin again the next morning. I wanted to ask, once located, what she'd have done with me?

'You don't have to worry,' I say. 'Tough as old boots, me.'

'Well, if you say so,' she says, and I tried to laugh. She tapped the table then, saying, 'Well, that's great, I'll let you get on, I'm sure you've lots to do,' and began to rise, so I rose too. I knew I'd treated Missus H like a fool and she was not a fool.

'It's good to see you,' I say, making my way to the door. I could see my reflection in it, and the nothing beyond frightened me. 'You reading anything good, Missus H – Molly – sorry, I'll get used to it.'

'Few bits, I always try have something on the go.'

'Right.'

'You?'

'Few bits.' I put my hand on the door – the steel of the

handle made me shiver. 'You were good to me, when I was young. Weren't you?'

'When you were young and I was Missus H.'

'Yeah.'

'Could be a song.'

'Yeah, or a T-shirt.'

'Juno? Where is it you're off to?' I turned. Molly's face had hollowed a little, her back was no longer board-straight and she had developed a small stoop.

'I'm just going . . . I'm going to visit . . .'

Her hands were set lightly inside the pockets of her pleated skirt. She watched me without moving.

'Juno, where are you off to?' she says again, and I could feel the first sting of a bastard tear. I saw how I was holding my breath, my head was lowered.

'I don't know, Missus H. I don't know where I'm going.'

'You don't have to go.'

'I am just so, I don't know, I just . . . I don't know anything any more.'

'Tell you what, why don't you come and have a cup of tea at my house, before you set off, if it suits?'

I looked at Missus H and thought some day I would go shopping and buy her the brightest blouse ever made and present it to her with flowers.

I say, 'That would suit me very well, Missus H.'

She came forward and I felt her touch my shoulder, that way I'd seen her touch a particular book, one that she was fond of, that she had read and liked. She led me back inside the quiet of the library, setting me down like good china, and went off in search of her overcoat.

Acknowledgements

To everyone at Harvill Secker: Aidan O'Neill, Louise Farrell, Kate Gunn, Leah Boulton, Suzanne Dean, Lily Richards and especially the brilliant Kate Harvey, thank you for your incredible care and precision.

Thank you, Anna Stein and Sophie Lambert, dream agents.

My early readers, Marsha Swan, Michael Almereyda and Laura Fraser, thank you for your endless patience, advice and support.

My sincere thanks to everyone at Centre Culturel Irlandais, for laying out a welcome mat and offering me a place to catch my breath, in particular Nora Hickey M'Sichili.

Thank you: Phillip McMahon, Maeve-Ann Austen, Ciara Mackle, Steve Kingston, Sean Byrne, Gerry Conlon, Lisa Hayden, Sue Elliott, Jonathan Lee, Ursula Burke. Catherine Conroy, Joby Hickey, Celine Leroy, Dermot Burke. Angie Harms.

Thank you, Ella Murtha, for generously entrusting Tish Murtha's remarkable photograph here.

Thank you, Billy, and thank you, Lila.

My sincere thanks to everyone who has offered me guidance, instruction and inspiration. Far too many to list here.